SUCH PERSUASIONS AS THESE

A PRIDE AND PREJUDICE VARIATION

EMILIA STRATFORD

Quills & Quartos
PUBLISHING

Edited by Debra Anne Watson and Jan Ashton

Cover by Susan Adriani, CloudCat Design

The cover image shows a young man and young woman in regency era attire sitting on a couch together.

ISBN 978-1-967030-27-9 (ebook) and 978-1-967030-28-6 (paperback)

To my sweet husband—your love teaches me how to love, your faith strengthens my faith, and your generous spirit moves me to give. I am so glad I chose you.

PROLOGUE

Fitzwilliam Darcy kept his eyes directly ahead as he neared the field atop Ramsgate's famed chalk cliffs, his cousin Alec Fitzwilliam keeping pace at his side. Dawn was breaking over the distant blue horizon, casting the sky in muted hues of pink and lavender. Beneath his boots, the crunch of gravel gave way to a faint slapping noise as he turned into the tall blades of dewy grass. Darcy cared not for the delicate, low-growing flowers being trampled in his course, nor the majesty of the waves as they crashed against the jagged white walls below him.

He was here for one purpose.

A lone figure appeared far in the distance, standing near the only scrub tall enough to call itself a tree on these barren cliffs. Darcy halted, and Fitzwilliam followed suit, turning to face him with a puzzled expression on his brow.

"Is it not your office to deter me from this course?"

"Strictly speaking, yes," Fitzwilliam answered, looking to

the far-off sunrise. "But, as I would be doing the same had I the opportunity, I cannot bring myself to do so."

They exchanged a resolute nod and continued towards the gnarled yew—and the blackguard standing beside it. Darcy was almost shocked to see his old friend; it was not George Wickham's habit to answer for his transgressions. He was much more likely to steal away in the middle of the night, leaving a trail of debts and feminine tears behind him.

"I am surprised he presented himself," Darcy confessed.

"I am not," his cousin said with half a grin. "I have had two men stationed outside his quarters from the night you called him out until this morning. He has not had a moment of privacy these three days."

"Where did you find such men amongst a society of strangers?"

"Truly, Cuz. It wounds me that you continue to question the extent of my resourcefulness."

Darcy grunted a mirthless laugh.

A rogue wind rushed past, causing the tails of his great-coat to flail behind him and a chill to cut through his riding breeches. The ominous mist that clung to the open field before them lumbered about in a slow swirl.

"Did you engage the surgeon?" Darcy asked, determined to ensure that his second had performed his duties. He would not be accused of behaving dishonourably in this contest of honour.

"Two of them."

"Two?"

"If you are both shot, it would not be proper to leave Wickham to his wounds while the only surgeon tends to you. And I would not allow that rotter to be saved while you lie grievously injured. So, yes, two."

They were close enough now that Darcy could make out the features on Wickham's despicable face. Darcy's blood raced hot through his veins. A picture of Georgiana appeared before him, her tear-stained cheeks, her inability to meet his eye in the humiliation she felt at having been taken in by Wickham's claims, promises, and lies.

And the hurt.

She might never recover from the horrific things that had spewed from the dastard's mouth about her that evening. Wickham had not attempted to spare her tender feelings, not even after having spent the previous weeks making love to her. Instead, he had made it clear to Darcy—within Georgiana's hearing—that he was only interested in her dowry, that he 'never intended to play house with the chit', that as soon as he secured her fortune, he planned to deposit her on the doorstep of Pemberley and never look back. His undying devotion, it seemed, had perished with the prospect of gaining her thirty thousand pounds, and Wickham had taken pains to make that clear.

The tension was becoming a knot in Darcy's gut as they drew nearer to the traitor. Wickham was watching them as they approached, his coat unbuttoned and his stance lazy, as if this was nothing more than a morning's diversion. The corner of Wickham's mouth twitched upward, and Darcy wished nothing more than to remove the smirk from Wickham's face permanently. He would aim for the heart, but perhaps if he missed and fate was kind, his bullet would tear through that pretty visage. One could only hope.

The pair stopped several yards from their opponent. Wickham swept them a mocking bow.

"Ah, Darcy, you came. I was beginning to think you had changed your mind."

"You hoped I would, I dare say. But not this time, Wickham. You have gone too far. Where is your second?"

Wickham shifted on his feet. "I know nobody here, Darcy. Unlike you, I do not have the coin to summon my minions from town at the drop of a hat," he said with a sneer towards Fitzwilliam.

"What he means is that, though he requested the presence of several of his cronies, none of them felt the least inclination to stand with him. One of them even professed that he was looking forward to reading his death notice."

"He shall have to get used to disappointment," spat Wickham, his pretence of nonchalance slipping.

"Enough," the colonel interrupted in a firm, quiet tone. "We all know why we are here." He went on to set the number of paces and remind the men that no shots were to be fired until they had turned fully, that they were each permitted only one shot, and that regardless of the outcome, honour was considered satisfied after this morning's affair was concluded. The pistol case was opened, and Fitzwilliam carefully loaded each weapon before their eyes. Wickham chose first. Darcy took the other. "At my signal, both parties shall confirm their readiness, and you shall begin taking your ten paces."

Darcy nodded with a steely glare at his opponent. Wickham's acknowledgment was less assured, his Adam's apple bobbing in his throat. Fitzwilliam held up his handkerchief, paused for two breaths, then dropped his arm in signal.

Darcy turned, his boots sinking into the damp earth with each deliberate step.

One. Two. Three.

This was for Georgiana. She had been put upon, devastated, dishonoured.

Four. Five.

Darcy had to believe that Wickham deserved to die for these transgressions. He had no doubt he himself would walk away from this field in his own strength; he only hoped Wickham would not.

Six. Seven.

What if Wickham's bullet finds its mark?

His breath faltered. If Darcy died this day, would his sister not be doubly heartbroken? Who would care for her? Who would protect her from the Wickhams of this world? Could he trust his cousin to carry that mantle? Georgiana might be left alone.

Eight.

No. He could not let that happen. He would not. The panic that threatened to seize him melted away, leaving only an iron resolve in its place.

Nine.

He tightened his grip around his pistol, the weight of the weapon grounding him as he prepared to shoot. There was only one acceptable outcome to this duel.

Ten.

Darcy turned on his heel, raised his arm, steadied his aim, and pulled the trigger.

The force of his bullet sent Wickham's body toppling to the grass.

Darcy sensed more than saw two figures running towards them, leather satchels in hand, but he could not hear their footfalls. The shouts of Fitzwilliam as he hurried to meet him did not penetrate the thrum of blood rushing in his ears. The roaring thinned to a high-pitched whine, and his every movement seemed protracted.

Time itself slowed. Darcy's limbs released all strength as an inky void gathered in his periphery. The sky above him tilted. The horizon went askew.

Then everything was dark.

CHAPTER ONE

"For a single man in possession of a large fortune must be in want of a wife," Elizabeth Bennet exclaimed, laughing with her elder sister, Jane, as they listened to their mother rave about the incoming tenant of Netherfield Park. The woman, it seemed, had no doubt that whoever this man was, he would soon be upon her doorstep begging for the hand of one of her five daughters.

"Yes, he must," Mrs Bennet proclaimed, turning her attention to Mr Bennet, "which is why you must visit him directly when he comes." Haranguing her husband had scarcely moved the man to action before, but his lady never failed to try the tactic. It seemed her nagging was commensurate with her nerves, and in the matter of her daughters finding husbands, Mrs Bennet suffered no little anxiety.

Elizabeth had put forth much effort to understand this constant state of preoccupation. As a girl, she had not been able to puzzle out why her dear mama was so worried about her daughters' marriage prospects; were there not many years before they would even be out in society?

As time went by and no heir appeared, however, the answer became clear to the perceptive second daughter of Thomas and Frances Bennet. As the family's estate, Longbourn, was entailed upon Mr Bennet's nearest male relative, having no son meant her home would pass from Mrs Bennet and her daughters upon her husband's demise. Elizabeth's keen understanding of the cause of her mother's relentless concern had allowed her to endure it with grace these last several years. It only made sense that a mother of so many unmarried females would be industrious in arranging how she was going to dispose of each of them as they came of age.

As to her hopes of immediate action on Mr Bennet's part, however, she was to be disappointed. They had heard reports of their new neighbours from family and friends, but Mr Bennet was keen on tormenting his wife and thus chose to put his visit off till another day. By the time he was ready to importune Mr Bingley and his sisters, however, an unceasing rain had descended upon their shire, preventing him from meeting the gentleman at all. Thus, the entire Bennet family would have to wait until the upcoming public assembly to be introduced, which was an interminable three days hence.

As the Meryton Assembly approached, the five Bennet daughters could do naught but newly trim old gowns and entertain themselves the best they knew how. Soon enough, as each pastime lost its lustre, Jane, Elizabeth, Mary, Kitty, and Lydia began taking turns watching the great drops of water race down the windows, sighing and wishing for a break in the weather.

At length, Papa announced that he had just received the latest Navy List. He knew his daughters adored dreaming up stories about the officers and ships found therein. As there were two cousins on her father's side and one dear friend of the family who were now seeking to make names for themselves in His Majesty's fleet, it was incumbent upon them to always keep a current Navy List at hand. Elizabeth smiled at the thought of that *particular* friend, his constancy in kind attentions to herself and her family, and how well he was doing in his profession.

Lately, however, instead of seeing the list of gallant men and imagining the battles in which they procured their frigates or sloops, the youngest Bennets had turned this game into one focused on romance and fantasy. After having dismissed a great many names of officers as sounding stodgy or cruel, or indeed far too French, Kitty settled on an entry of which she approved.

"Ooh, the honourable A. Maitland of the captured French frigate, the *Pique*. How fine that sounds—Catherine Bennet Maitland, wife of Captain Alastair Maitland, late of Sussex, now residing at Burbank Hall in Somersetshire after having brought home twenty thousand pounds in prize money."

"Well, I have been receiving letters from..." the youngest, Lydia, eagerly read over the names, "Lieutenant..." she had to imagine a first name, for only an initial was supplied, "Jefferson Harvey of the *HMS Haughty*. He has already brought in thirty thousand pounds in prize money and intends to double that by the time he makes admiral." Lydia beamed triumphantly.

"*Pique*? *Haughty*? I much prefer Mr Clay and his command of the *Raisonnable*," Mary added in an ineffectual effort to teach her younger sisters some prudence. "But I suppose you could have chosen the *Insolence*, or the *Nimrod*..." She relented as she let the booklet slip carelessly from her hand. Jane and Elizabeth exchanged a glance, though neither of them noted aloud how Mary, as censorious as she was of her younger sisters, had joined in the diversion. Evidently, there was a romantic fancy smouldering beneath her pragmatic exterior.

Lydia eagerly retrieved the booklet and began perusing it again. A gasp from her direction claimed their attention.

"Lizzy, look here—Freddie has finally got his own ship!"

CHAPTER TWO

E lizabeth was in her best looks for tonight's assembly. She had taken special care with her appearance, as had each of her sisters. She would never, as her mother often reminded her, be as beautiful as her sister Jane, but even Mrs Bennet had to admit she was quite pretty this evening.

She was looking forward to making the acquaintance of the Netherfield party. Mr Bingley's sisters, Miss Bingley and Mrs Hurst, as Elizabeth had heard, were everything fashionable and elegant, and she looked forward to much intelligent conversation with them.

Upon arriving, she noted that, once again, there was a dearth of eligible dancing partners. Many of Hertfordshire's young men were off fighting Napoleon on the battlefields of France and Spain, so this was not unexpected. Elizabeth was well-respected in the area, however, so she chose not to be discouraged. She was convinced she would dance this evening, whether her partner be a young banker or a greying squire. Or perhaps even a gentleman of five thousand a year.

Upon spying her closest friend, Charlotte Lucas, she waved, and Charlotte made her way towards the gaggle of Bennet ladies. Their greetings were interrupted by an abrupt suspension of the music. Silence spread throughout the crowd, and dancers seemed to instinctively part down the middle, all eyes turning towards the two handsomely dressed gentlemen and one clearly unimpressed young lady. She wondered which of Mr Bingley's two sisters she was and hoped the absent sister was not unwell.

The two gentlemen must be none other than Mr Bingley and his brother, Mr Hurst. A niggling disappointment arose in her chest, for they were both fine-looking men; it would be far better for the married gentleman to be plain and podgy. Instead, standing framed in the entranceway, was a fair-haired young man with smiling eyes and an easy bearing, well-favoured by any standards, and a taller, striking gentleman with dark curls and a severe expression upon his fiercely handsome mien. As she had heard of Mr Bingley's affable nature, Elizabeth deduced that the more attractive man was his married brother.

A shame, she mused, for there was something in his countenance that caused her stomach to tighten when his gaze alighted upon her. It may have been the brooding brow, the square jaw, or the smoky green of his eyes—all features that could not but please—but Elizabeth thought she saw something deeper in his visage. Along with his forbidding glare and arrogant stance, she recognised a certain careworn air.

And a definite wish to be anywhere but here.

Elizabeth shifted her attention to Mr Bingley's sister and not only perceived the sneer on the fine lady's face, but accidentally overheard her snide aside to the taller of the men.

"How miserable you look, Mr Darcy. And understandably

so. To be forced to spend an evening in such tedious company, hunted by every country maiden and money-hungry mama."

"Nothing of the sort," the man replied. "I am happy to render whatever service I can to your brother, and if this is what is required of me..."

Mr Darcy? So, this was not Mr Bingley's brother at all. None of the local gentlemen had mentioned Mr Bingley having invited a friend to Netherfield. *Who can he be?*

As the trio walked further into the room, their voices grew too faint for Elizabeth to comprehend, though the character of at least one of them she understood readily. She would certainly not be sharing much intelligent conversation with this young lady.

She watched them as they made their way to an effusive Sir William Lucas, whose position as a knight and magistrate made him the master of ceremonies by default for assemblies such as this. No doubt Mr Bingley was requesting that he introduce them about, as otherwise they could not dance with those outside their own party. While the two genial gentlemen spoke, Elizabeth noticed that the silent Mr Darcy was walking stiffly. His jaw was clenched, and a slight wince betrayed a measure of torment when the older man addressed him.

Was their presence so vexatious to him that he could only endure it with such rigid tension? Was he so above his company? Or might there be another reason for his evident agitation?

Elizabeth did not get to ponder long over this, for her large group was approached directly by Sir William, who presented all six Bennet ladies and two of his own daughters to the Netherfield party as if reading off a washing bill. "Mrs Bennet," *shirts*, "Miss Bennet," *cravats*, "Miss Elizabeth Bennet," *stockings*, and so on.

To Sir William, it appears, we are so much laundry. Elizabeth laughed inwardly at the absurdity, confident that their family's oldest friend regarded them with no such indifference.

Mr Darcy's gaze swept over the ladies as Sir William gestured to each without seeming to take notice of any one of them. Mr Bingley, however, paid rapt attention and, as might be expected, requested Jane's hand for his first set. As Jane was being spirited away, Elizabeth felt keenly the scarcity of partners. Young Philip Lucas, barely eighteen, had the audacity to request the hand of Miss Bingley, and she had the good breeding not to refuse. One by one, their little crowd dispersed.

Which leaves Mr Darcy...

The handsome, taciturn man was standing an arm's length from Elizabeth, and she wondered if he fancied himself a spectator in some badly costumed carnival. Mothers and fathers were prancing their families before him, some introducing their offspring, some simply parading them. Reluctantly, she admitted to herself that Miss Bingley's earlier accusations held some truth. As she regarded the tableau before her, she began to see him, not as a spectator, but as the strong man in this circus, forced to fend off the fawning felines and their flirting fillies. She could envision him spitting fire at them all. Indeed, he looked as if he wished he had a sword to swallow. Or fall upon.

Poor man.

Mr Darcy truly was miserable, as his companion had surmised. But not just because of the fluttering of eyelashes and swishing of gowns passing before him.

His grimace seemed to be one of *pain*.

Moments passed, and when conversation between herself

and the gentleman did not materialise, Elizabeth asked, "Are you not inclined to dance, Mr Darcy?" If he truly was so sore, he could not be expected to do so, but Elizabeth hoped her gambit might induce him into some semblance of conversation. To be sure, even standing seemed almost too much to bear. She wondered if she ought to point out to him a comfortable seat.

To do so, of course, would require further discourse.

"I rather detest dancing," he growled. "Unless I am particularly acquainted with my partner," he added more gently, evidently realising she had not said anything out of the ordinary; they were at a ball after all.

"I see. I am sorry to hear it," she offered, conceding the field. It was plain he did not wish to be disturbed. "Excuse me." She smiled sweetly and curtseyed her leave, taking her seat on a nearby bench. It was not long, however, before she heard Mr Bingley's voice behind her.

"Come now, she is an angel," he cried.

"She smiles too much," Mr Darcy groused. They were speaking of Jane, and Elizabeth laughed inwardly that Mr Darcy had to reach so far to find something negative to say of her saintly sister.

"I cannot have you standing about in this stupid manner. Why do you not get acquainted with some of the local ladies? Look, there is one of her sisters, and I dare say she is very pretty." Elizabeth's face immediately flushed as she darted her eyes to her lap, understanding that she herself was now the subject of their speech.

"She is tolerable, but not handsome enough to tempt me. Go. Go back to your partner and her smiles. You are wasting your time with me."

Elizabeth's first inclination was to be deeply offended.

'Tolerable?' How dare he! To say such a thing in a public assembly room where anyone, including herself, could hear him? Before she could become too ruffled, however, she heard a groan reverberating from Mr Darcy's direction. Glancing up at him, she noted that the gentleman was now wincing and bending his head in clear discomfort, his knuckles again tightening around the ivory knob of his walking stick as he made his way towards the card room. No wonder he had deflected his friend's enthusiastic entreaties; Mr Darcy was not simply 'sore', but in agony.

MR BENNET, BEING ALMOST AS EAGER AS HIS LADY TO see his daughters well-settled, had attended the assembly in hopes of making the acquaintance of his new neighbours. Young Bingley, he found to be cheerful and inviting, quick to smile and satisfied with everything about him. He and his friend, a great tall fellow, could not have been more dissimilar. This intrigued Bennet to the point that, when he noticed Mr Darcy slipping into the card room, he followed him, bringing himself to that man's side.

It soon became clear that the gentleman was not wont to engage in conversation. Naturally, Bennet felt it would be a shame not to force him.

"So, Mr Darcy, is it? You and Mr Bingley are friends of long standing, I gather."

The self-important man deigned to nod.

"And are you as satisfied with the neighbourhood as your companion?" Mr Bennet asked, seeing the answer plainly written on the younger man's face.

"I find it perfectly agreeable," said Mr Darcy, not bothering to move his gaze.

Bennet's compulsion to tease the man momentarily over-came his desire to see his daughters well-married, and he could not stop himself from replying, "Is that so? I could not tell it from your expression. You do not look particularly over-whelmed with excitement to be amidst our society." If there was such a term as *under*whelmed, he would dare say Mr Darcy would embody it.

Mr Darcy looked him directly in the eyes. "Excuse me?"

His disturbed response delighted Bennet to no end, compelling him to continue in the same vein.

"I have noted that Mr Bingley is everything affable and accommodating—a very gentlemanly man, I should say, collecting friends everywhere he turns. Perhaps you are just more reserved, observing his open manners and taking lessons, I am sure."

Bennet was sure Mr Darcy was decidedly *not* taking lessons from his friend. The insinuation seemed to irritate the fellow even further, thus hitting exactly the mark Bennet had intended. Before the gentleman could form an answer, or truly even digest the statement, it seemed, Mr Bennet bowed and, with a quick waggle of his eyebrows, said, "I shall leave you to your studies." He then moved on to speak to Sir William, suppressing the chuckle that threatened to escape at the fine young man's affronted and somewhat dumbfounded expression.

CHAPTER THREE

Darcy took umbrage at the older man's impertinence. He had come to Hertfordshire at Bingley's request, to help him settle into his new role as master of an estate. As Darcy had been overseeing his own extensive holdings for five years on his own (and several more with the guidance of his excellent father before his death), he was eminently qualified to guide his friend as he eased into his duties as landlord of this leased property.

Yes, Darcy was to guide Bingley, not the other way round.

What on earth can Bingley teach me? Darcy thought with a scoff.

In an opposite corner of the room, Mr Bennet, as the audacious man was called, began bantering with Sir William Lucas, in tones loud enough to be overheard by all.

"Capital, capital. Oh, Mr Bennet, you are a clever fellow. That must be where your delightful little Lizzy gets her sharp wit. I can see her saying the same thing; only she is much more pleasant to look at," Sir William said with something like avuncular pride. The hawk-nosed gentleman was almost roaring with laughter at the first man's drollery, while its source simply watched the effect of his words with wry gratification.

So, the insolent fellow has a daughter—a single daughter no doubt. Darcy pursed his lips as the pieces fell into place. Of course the father of an unmarried daughter would be impatient to procure the notice of the visitor rumoured to have ten thousand a year.

'Lizzy,' Sir William had called her?

Well, Darcy would be doubly sure to avoid *her*, especially if she shared the same 'sharp wit' as her father. He refused to be laughed at, particularly by a country miss whose sire was an impudent, brazen gentleman of inferior station.

As it was clear the card room would provide him no respite, Darcy returned to the ballroom, cursing his throbbing leg, this provincial village, and Bingley's refusal to allow him to remain at Netherfield with the Hursts.

Perhaps this whole sojourn into Hertfordshire had been a mistake.

He sensed keenly the dozens of eyes falling upon him as he made his way along the wall. There was no question. This had definitely been a mistake.

THOUGH ELIZABETH HAD NOT CHOSEN TO REGARD MR Darcy's dismissive words, they had been overheard by some of the village residents, and she could see the gossip mill beginning to churn.

"Conceit," she heard.

"Arrogance," another whispered.

"Why, did you ever?" from someone else.

She turned towards each voice as she heard it, sorry that the gentleman was rapidly gaining such a reputation based upon an unfair disadvantage. She knew these people—they would condemn him for eternity based on this moment, and his behaviour would mar the advancement in their society of both himself and his friend. Her mind was racing as to how this tide could be stemmed when, to her horror, she heard the voice of Mr Harper purring, "Ah, Mr Darcy, it is so pleasant to see you again. I am sorry that our humble gathering is not to your taste."

Clearly, Mr Darcy had left the card room, for there he was, not three yards from her bench, being accosted by the disingenuous squire. There was no time to lose. Mr Harper was a worse gossip than her mother, Aunt Philips, and Lady Lucas combined. If he were to experience the same coldness she had, Mr Darcy would be stained in the eyes of all of Hertfordshire, never to recover any footing in the neighbourhood, and his friend would be rejected right along with him.

She had to act.

"Mr Darcy, thank you so much for your patience," she said breathlessly, having shot from her seat to his side. "I am ready now. The stitching on my slipper is unharmed. It was very gentlemanly of you to step aside that I might ascertain the damage. I must say, though I promised you this set, all the excitement has made me quite warm. Would you be much put out if we walked to the refreshment table instead?" He lifted an inquisitive brow, then hesitantly nodded. She was relieved to see him raise his arm to offer his escort.

"Mr Harper," Elizabeth curtseyed to the old tattler as she set her hand upon Mr Darcy's sleeve.

SUCH PERSUASIONS AS THESE

"Miss Elizabeth," Mr Harper responded, bowing his head in return.

Mr Darcy bowed as well, and they were off. They walked a moment in silence and slowly, getting out of earshot of the dastardly gossipmonger, before Mr Darcy bit out through gritted teeth, "Though I appreciate you sparing me the inanity of another conversation with Mr Harper, I believe I made it clear that I have no intention of dancing this evening. Do not think you can, by your cunning, trick me into doing so."

What an unmitigated bore! Elizabeth thought, now unsure if the man deserved her gracious assistance. *No,* she reminded herself, *grace is never deserved. Grace does good to others despite being undeserved.* Still, she could not help but respond with some little archness.

"And here I was, looking *so* forward to spending half an hour in such agreeable company."

Mr Darcy was not amused.

She schooled her features to reflect the seriousness in his own, even if she did find doing so humorous. Not meeting his eye, she smiled to those she passed as they strolled— excruciatingly, she thought, on his part—towards the refreshments. "Sir, I do not mean to be impertinent," she claimed, pausing as he scoffed aloud, "but I can see you are in some amount of pain." He looked at her in shock. "Do not distress yourself; I do not believe it is noticeable to others, but as a student of human nature, I could not help but note the way your knuckles tense around the knob of your stick at intervals, and the crease in your brow. The problem is, Mr Darcy, your countenance...well...a scowl of pain can easily be mistaken for a scowl of disdain, and I fear some in the neighbourhood are getting that impression from you."

21

"How can they get any impression from me at all? I have said nary a word to anyone."

"That is just it, sir. Between your reticence and the glowering grimace you have worn since first appearing, I worry your friend's new neighbours may get the impression you think them beneath your notice. This I may have chosen to disregard, as Mr Bingley's friendly nature cannot but win him the favour of all," Elizabeth explained, undaunted by his fearsome frown. "However, when I espied Mr Harper making his way towards you, I felt I must intervene. That gentleman is not only the worst whisperer in Meryton, but he has a way of manoeuvring a conversation in just such a way as to wheedle the most damaging bits of information from his prey, coaxing them to admit to all manner of offences and catching them completely unawares."

"You believe this man would have...what? Finagled me into offending all and sundry?"

She wondered how he could form words whilst maintaining the set of his mouth in such a grim line.

"Frankly, yes," Elizabeth replied with a laugh. "And without much effort."

"And, as you are such a good judge of character, my being seen escorting you to the punch bowl will instead win me the goodwill of the masses?"

Elizabeth did not think she had ever heard one's eyes roll in the tone of their voice before.

"I do not suppose I would have put it just that way, but yes —being seen attending the very woman whom you so audibly slighted might do you some good in any case."

Evidently mortified at the realisation she had heard him, Mr Darcy attempted to vocalise some sort of apology, but she stopped him mid-splutter.

"No, no. I was not offended, though I am afraid others may have been on my behalf. I can see you remain unconvinced of the sincerity of my motives, so I shall tell you something." She leant closer, informing him in lowered tones, "You are in no danger from me, for I have long been spoken for."

CHAPTER FOUR

"And who is the fortunate man?" Darcy enquired, attempting to walk without leaning quite so heavily upon his cane, having refused her offer to sit. He did not much care to whom the presumptuous miss was attached, but he would do his duty by her, as troublesome as she was.

"He is a naval captain by the name of Wentworth. He is at sea at the moment, but I have his assurance he will soon be ashore again. And how wonderful that will be, for we all miss him so. He is open and friendly, always ready to dance, and he makes everyone he meets feel like they are worthy of his time and attention. He is much like your friend, I think."

"Yes, Bingley has always made friends easily. He is universally liked, quick to approve of everyone and everything he sees. His manner is far removed from my own, I must say," Darcy said, immediately irritated at his own boorishness. Perhaps if he was not, indeed, in so much pain, he could force himself to be more agreeable.

"Being reserved and of a more serious disposition is no

sin. In fact, Captain Wentworth is much like you as well—tall, handsome, and dignified—I think you two would get on. And while he is generally open and amiable, he is a thinking man, a man of discerning taste who does not feel the need to be great friends with everyone who comes before him."

Darcy was struck by her picture of himself—that she could compliment him without simpering or cooing or expecting the same in return was more than a little surprising.

And refreshing. Perhaps her company will not be so bad after all.

"I understand there is a great name to be made by industrious men in the Royal Navy. And a great fortune, as well."

"I believe you are correct, sir. Why, he has just been given command of his first vessel. It was recorded in the Navy List only this month—he has been made captain and given command of a ship called the *Asp*. How proud we all were to read of it."

"Indeed. I hope for your sake he continues to make progress in his profession. And remains safe—it is not unusual for these sea captains to meet with danger and adventure whilst performing their duties to King and Country."

"Yes, which is one reason our understanding has not come to fruition. My father insisted we could not marry until he had adequately advanced in his career. So here we are."

Darcy nodded, his mind wandering to another engagement, one that had been kept quiet to his injury. A silence ensued, which Miss Elizabeth finally broke by expressing her regret that he was in such discomfort and enquiring as to what occasioned his pain.

"I was shot," he answered before thinking better of it. His

companion's eyes widened. Perhaps he should have prevaricated, fabricated a fall or a fencing accident.

A moment passed before Miss Elizabeth's shock abated, and she laughed out loud—a light melodious laugh that put him into a daze and drew the attention of several bystanders. Darcy's face coloured under the weight of so many curious looks, but his impulsive anger at such impertinence melted as her mirth hypnotised him—so much so that he soon found himself smiling along with her, still in the dark as to what exactly was so funny. She took a moment to catch her breath, then complimented him on so expertly hiding such a sharp sense of humour.

"Oh, yes, it is obvious to all that you are an adventurer, a scoundrel of the lowest order. Called out by a duke over debts of honour in gaming dens full of opium, I am sure." Her eyes twinkled as she spoke.

He considered the picture she had painted of him—a prim and proper gentleman stumbling out of a gaming hell, losing so much money at cards that he would be challenged to duel over his obligations. It did seem rather implausible.

Her glee was catching and, before he knew it, he found himself playing along.

"Well, after hearing of the manifold allurements of your noble Captain Wentworth, I did not imagine that being the victim of Bingley's ill-shod horse during yesterday's ride would be very impressive."

"Oh no, Mr Darcy. Just think what would have happened had that shoe flown into the face of your mount. Or worse, kicked up in just such a way as to injure your friend. Your heroism in offering your knee to the errant horseshoe and therefore sacrificing your ability to dance even one set during the first assembly among your friend's new neighbours—

whilst allowing him to dance all of them—what kindness to dear Mr Bingley. Only a truly valiant man would throw himself before such danger and suffer such grievous consequences in the service of a friend."

"What can I say?" Darcy was laughing along with her as she teased.

Laughing.

Out loud.

In a room full of strangers.

THE ICE BETWEEN THEM NOW BROKEN, AFTER HAVING refused another offer to find a seat, Miss Elizabeth led him about the perimeter of the little ballroom. It seemed her aim was to introduce Darcy to the principal personages of the neighbourhood. Some, of course, he had met at Bingley's morning-in. Many, however, were new faces, and he let Miss Elizabeth take the lead with each.

To the dowager ladies, whose opinion on a single man refusing to dance he already knew, she noted how Darcy had graciously injured himself so as to allow his friend to appear to best advantage. One after another, they nodded in sympathy for the *poor, poor man*. "To be denied the opportunity to dance with the prettiest girls in England... Tsk tsk... You poor thing... Well, let us hope you recover soon." And one after another sent him away with their well-wishes.

To the farmers, she introduced Darcy as one of the same. "I understand you own some land in Derbyshire," she began for him.

"*Some* land, yes. And yes, I am very involved in its working. I wonder how differently things are done here compared to the Midlands, as our climate is far cooler. I cannot but wonder whether you have much trouble with flooding, as the landscape is so flat." This query led to many diverse and interesting answers, along with some solutions he could only describe as ingenious. He was so captivated by the discussion that he practically forgot how vexed he was to have been dragged to this unsavoury assembly—or how little interest he had intended to have in its attendees.

After several minutes of being ignored, Miss Elizabeth bent towards Darcy, who had unconsciously taken a seat with the others in eagerness to hear their stories, and told him sweetly, "My work here is done. I leave you in good hands. Good night, Mr Darcy."

He remembered himself long enough to stand—rather laboriously—and make her a bow of thanks. He even managed a small smile before sitting to resume his conversation.

A young lady Darcy assumed to be a relation approached her then, pressing her to see some bauble or other she admired on one of the dancers, urging her, "Come, Lizzy."

"*Lizzy?*" Darcy cried, at once realising that this beguiling woman before him was the very female he had vowed to avoid at all costs. Taking another look at her, he could now see the family resemblance between the lady and her impertinent father.

"Oy, mister, not so familiar if you please. That's Miss Lizzy to ye," cried one of the local boys, eager to defend the honour of the pretty daughter of Meryton's principal family.

"Oh, Henry, do not worry on my account." She alighted a quelling hand on the boy's shoulder and turned to face Darcy with laughing eyes. "Miss Elizabeth Bennet of Longbourn. I thought we had established that."

"Miss Elizabeth." Darcy again bowed solemnly, answering her repeated curtsey.

After she left, it took him several moments to fully attend the subjects being canvassed about him. He could not believe he had not connected the ladies he had been introduced to earlier with the Mr Bennet who must have been their father. Soon, however, he was speaking with animation about the methods he had used to improve drainage or increase germination. And sheep—someone mentioned lambing, and Darcy was fully engaged for the rest of the evening.

Any thoughts of the enchanting Miss Elizabeth being the very 'Lizzy' he had forsworn would have to wait.

CHAPTER FIVE

I t fell now upon the ladies of Longbourn to call upon the ladies of Netherfield Park. Darcy understood that Mrs Bennet had five daughters, but only the three eldest accompanied her this morning.

The intriguing Miss Elizabeth and her motives had crossed his mind several times in the days since they had met and laughed together, and he still could not decide whether to trust her fully. If she had heard his insult of her person, why would she not rejoice in his downfall at Mr Harper's hand? Could anyone truly be so good, so innately forgiving? He could not help but think of others he had known who had offered a convincing appearance of goodness while concealing rottenness to the bones.

Miss Bingley had been standing near his desk and observing him with a steady stream of compliments and interruptions as he had attempted to compose a letter to Georgiana. Darcy stood from his chair as the ladies entered the drawing room and took two long strides towards the visitors, relieved to be freed from Miss Bingley's unwelcome nearness. A bolt of pain shot through his thigh upon rising, but he reckoned it was worth it to gain some breathing room.

Before Miss Bingley could receive her guests, her brother bounded towards the ladies with voluble delight.

"Mrs Bennet, Miss Bennet, you are very welcome," said he, his eyes bright as they rested upon the handsome eldest Bennet daughter. Darcy cleared his throat. "And Miss Elizabeth, Miss Mary, you are welcome, too," Bingley added after himself with a bow.

Is that a smile playing upon Miss Elizabeth's face? He was reminded of her father, whose first object in life was a joke. Was she here only to observe their foibles and render them ridiculous?

"Might I introduce you to my sister, Mrs Louisa Hurst?" Bingley asked, indicating his eldest sister with a flourish of his hand. Mrs Hurst stepped forwards and nodded unsmilingly as acknowledgments were made. Her husband was introduced as well, bowing from his place in front of the settee on which he had nodded off after breakfast.

Mr Bingley did not appear to notice his sisters' aloofness. "How fortunate that Darcy and I had not yet begun our tour of the estate," Bingley said before turning to him. "Never again shall I reproach you for the excessive length of your correspondence."

Darcy, too, was glad they had not yet set out, for he did not believe the Longbourn party would have been so warmly received had he and Bingley been absent.

"He has much to say in letters, does he? It is a shame he is not so loquacious in person," Miss Elizabeth said, flashing him a sweet smile.

He met it only with a curt nod of his head. He would not

encourage her familiarity, for he was not sure he desired her to think them friends. He could feel his brow furrowing as she blinked at him, no doubt taken aback by his coolness. He could not remove the suspicion from his countenance, and part of him did not wish to.

Miss Bingley sighed as if resigning herself to their presence, shared a meaningful look with Mrs Hurst, then pasted on a smile that failed to disguise her irritation at being forced to entertain the locals, her sister following her lead. Gliding towards them with the utmost gentility, she dipped them the merest curtsey and invited them to sit.

While he had been and still was captivated by Miss Elizabeth, he could not help but wonder if she truly was different from the mincing women who often set themselves before him in hopes of winning his fortune. She had seemed sincere in her efforts to assist him, but did he dare allow himself to trust her?

He was not able to contemplate this for long, as his attention was commandeered by Mrs Bennet's shrill voice. "You have a sweet room here, sir. I imagine you are as delighted with Netherfield as you were with your new neighbours at the assembly."

Darcy was not surprised to watch this quarter-of-an-hour social call upon Miss Bingley and Mrs Hurst become a surreptitious attempt to gauge Bingley's impression of the neighbourhood.

"Indeed, I am, Mrs Bennet," Bingley answered. "My sisters and I have been quite warmly welcomed into Meryton society, and we could not be gladder of it. Why, in only four days, we have received invitations for suppers, card parties, and luncheons with all the principal families of the village. The Longs, the Lucases, even the militia regiment. I hope you will be attending some of them as well," he said, his eyes firmly fixed on Miss Bennet.

"We have received similar invitations, sir," she replied with a sanguine smile.

"Good, good. That shall only add to our enjoyment in them. After the reception we have been given, my sisters and I consider it an absolute obligation to acquaint ourselves with our neighbours, and we hope to form lasting connexions."

"Well then, allow me to add to your obligations by inviting you to Longbourn Monday next," Mrs Bennet said with almost a giggle, so enraptured was she with Bingley's enthusiasm. Miss Elizabeth raised her eyebrows at the invitation, as if unaware of such a scheme until this moment. He would wager her mother had been equally unaware of it—until having heard of other households full of unmarried ladies entertaining them.

"We would be happy to join you, Mrs Bennet. Would we not, Caroline, Louisa?" Bingley asked, completely oblivious to his sisters' blatant displeasure.

"Thrilled, I am sure," came Miss Bingley's dry reply.

"Better is a dinner of herbs where love is, than a stalled ox and hatred therewith," said Miss Mary pedantically.

"Indeed, Mary, as we all well know," replied Mrs Bennet, no doubt chagrined by her use of scripture with their new neighbours. They had not yet attended church, and Darcy wondered if Mrs Bennet was under the impression that they were a godless lot who would be offended by references to the holy book. "What a delightful tea service. How hospitable you are, Miss Bingley."

The tea tray was set before them, and Mrs Hurst was gracious enough to pour for all of them, no doubt eager to have Mrs Bennet's mouth stopped with Shrewsbury biscuits.

"HOW TEDIOUS THESE LOCAL LADIES ARE," MISS Bingley said not many minutes after the Longbourn party had taken its leave. "If one might deign to *call* them ladies. The insipidity, and yet the noise. Why, I could hardly keep my countenance when the plain one began speaking of preferring a supper of herbs and hating oxen."

"Who eats oxen?" asked Mrs Hurst in some horror.

"Obviously, these Hertfordshire rustics must, for Mary Bennet has certainly developed a distaste for the beast."

"I thought it was very kind of them to call," Bingley rejoined. "And I do not fault Miss Mary for preferring a dish of vegetables. Some people simply do not have the constitution to digest meat, you know."

Darcy closed his eyes against the urge to groan and inhaled deeply. Certainly, he had not been enthralled by the wit or conversation of any of the Bennet ladies this morning, but he had not been so insensible as to understand the younger sister to mean she had forgone meat in her diet. Turning back to his correspondence, he attempted to occlude the ladies' invectives from his consciousness, but the task proved to be positively Herculean, for Miss Bingley was determined to be heard.

"How very ill Miss Eliza Bennet looked this morning," she cried, turning an eye upon Darcy, clearly hoping to observe his response.

"Very ill," Mrs Hurst agreed.

He kept his expression neutral and his gaze fixed upon the paper before him, unwilling to snap at the lady's bitter bait.

"And how she sought to ingratiate herself to you, Mr Darcy, commenting on your character as if you two are such intimates," Miss Bingley pushed on. "The upstart pretensions!"

"Miss Elizabeth was of much assistance to me at the assembly," he finally said, unwilling to hear aspersions being cast upon her character. Even if he was unsure of her trustworthiness, she had done nothing to deserve their censure.

"Undoubtedly she was," Miss Bingley said, darting him a raised eyebrow. "I am sure she would like to make herself *very* useful to the most eligible gentleman in twenty miles. Why, I am surprised she did not divide her time between you and Charles to see which of you was more susceptible to her machinations."

"I find Miss Elizabeth quite pretty—though I know you do not agree, Darcy—but she is nothing compared to her elder sister," Bingley said, as if he had been holding in his expressions of admiration and searching for any opportunity to give them voice. Darcy could have mouthed along with his friend's next words. "Miss Bennet is an angel."

Bingley always was attracted to the heavenly, the ethereal, the celestial beauties in any crowd.

"Miss Jane Bennet seems a sweet girl," Mrs Hurst said in a rare show of generosity towards another of her sex.

"She does not put on airs like her younger sisters," Miss Bingley observed, "one of whom I would not trust for a kingdom. Be on your guard, Mr Darcy; I should hate to see such a harpy get her claws in you."

Miss Elizabeth a harpy? Darcy blinked at the lady speaking to him, amazed at her lack of self-awareness.

He found himself championing the young lady in response. "You have entirely mistaken the situation, Miss Bingley. Miss Elizabeth is engaged to be married."

"You mean someone has attached himself to her *voluntarily*? What could a man possibly see in a woman like that? And with such a mother? I pity the man who is shackled to her for life." She exhaled a twitter of laughter, her shoulders shaking at her own wit. Louisa Hurst laughed along with her.

Bingley proceeded to defend the Bennets, while Darcy contemplated Miss Bingley's accusations against Miss Elizabeth. It was true she was engaged; the farmers' having asked her for news about 'that rascal Wentworth' proved that. So, what *could* she mean by thrusting herself upon his notice? He had not forgotten whose daughter she was, and he wondered if she were only seeking his company to divert herself. Did she run home to her father and tell him of her triumph, how she had coaxed the proud stranger into conversation and forced him to interact with the local bumpkins? Was he just an object of amusement for her?

She certainly did not appear insincere.

In fact, Miss Elizabeth had stirred something in Darcy the night of the Meryton Assembly. He had enjoyed the company of strangers for the first time in his memory. And it was all because of this unusual woman who did not seem to want anything from him. He did not know if he dared trust her, but he did know one thing: he was fascinated by her and the effect she had on him.

As she was already spoken for, he risked nothing by furthering their acquaintance. He could not raise expectations in a woman whose heart belonged to another, after all.

CHAPTER SIX

Elizabeth did not know what to make of Mr Darcy's cold welcome the morning of their Netherfield visit. She could not but be taken aback by the heaviness of his brow and the intensity of his stare. He was observing her, that was certain, but not with the kindly reception of a friend, nor even with the curiosity of a new acquaintance. It was clear he was still in pain, given the way he had shifted his stance from time to time, but it was not a scowl of discomfort he had sent her way; that, she could have forgiven him.

No, his countenance bespoke what Elizabeth could only deem mistrust. She could not account for it; had she not put him at ease with regards to her intentions in seeking his company that evening? Had not her confession of a previous attachment negated any suspicions he might have had about her motives? Why had he looked at her so?

Perhaps he had not enjoyed her company at the assembly as she had presumed—though she was sure he did not laugh easily. It was perplexing, even for her, who prided herself on reading people so well. It was for the best, she supposed, for if he liked her, she would be forced to speak to him, and it was becoming all too clear what a proud, disagreeable sort of man he truly was.

And so, upon arriving at the Longs' dinner party, she did not expect him to even acknowledge her presence. She was, after all, a lowly squire's daughter with a fortune of all of forty pounds a year and no connexions of note.

But, lo, as soon as she walked through the door and divested herself of her outdoor accoutrements, Mr Darcy was standing beside her, bowing deeply, and offering his arm to escort her the rest of the way into the house.

He did not speak past a formal greeting, so she chose to respond in kind.

After standing near him amongst her neighbours in silence for many minutes, it became evident that none of them were willing to approach her if it meant braving Mr Darcy's glower. Elizabeth inhaled determinedly, turned to Mr Darcy, thanked him for his escort, and excused herself. She had put herself out for him enough, she decided. She certainly would not volunteer her services again, especially if she was to be met with only cold civility for her efforts.

No sooner had she greeted her friends Charlotte and Maria Lucas, relieved to be in the company of those whom she valued and who valued her, than she once again felt his looming presence. And looming he was, for he was easily a full head taller than she, though Elizabeth was no Lilliputian. Rather than asking whether the ladies had been introduced to Mr Darcy, as was the polite thing to do, she simply launched into conversation with her closest friend—ignoring him.

After exchanging greetings, Charlotte's eyes roved about the room, and Elizabeth found herself joining her in the exercise. In low tones, her friend pointed out the way Mr Bingley danced attendance upon Jane.

"I think they might do remarkably well together," Elizabeth replied, careful not to let Mr Darcy hear amongst the chattering all about them.

"It is clear he likes her very much, but does Jane return his regard? If only she could make her admiration more discernible. Especially to Mr Bingley."

Elizabeth looked over to her sister. She accepted the gentleman's attentions with sanguinity, but Charlotte's observation was sensible. If Jane's good friend could not perceive her regard, perhaps Mr Bingley might be unsure as well. Perhaps she should speak to Jane about this.

By and by, their discourse came to an end. Mr Darcy's presence, however, did not. Charlotte darted her eyes towards him then met Elizabeth's with a raised brow before departing. As the Lucas ladies walked away, Elizabeth gave him a thin-lipped smile and sighed. What was he about, hanging upon her elbow in such a manner? She did not have to wonder for long.

"Might we not make our way towards the gentlemen now?"

While the question was everything polite, it was now plain to Elizabeth why Mr Darcy had attached himself to her; he was expecting her to perform for him the same office she had at the assembly. He had magnanimously allowed her to converse with her friends, and now he wished to be accommodated.

Evidently, she was to be his societal cushion, a safe conduit between himself and the gentlemen of Meryton. Though she was at first taken aback by his high-handedness, her shock abated when she remembered just who he was.

This was a man who likely commanded scores of servants, who was doubtless never refused anything, who was accustomed to being waited upon. No wonder he fully expected Elizabeth to spend her entire evening catering to his unsociability.

She blinked up at him with an incredulous smile. *The nerve.*

It did not matter they had laughed together at their first meeting, nor that he had made himself agreeable to the farmers and their tenants. At his core, he was the disdainful, haughty fellow he showed to the world. Any display of something softer was an aberration, she was sure, and not a sign of some tender nexus hidden beneath the surface.

When he bent to meet her gaze, the fact of his continued presence reminded her of his discomfort. Mr Bingley had abandoned him at once in favour of a group of ladies at the far end of the drawing room, of which Jane was a part. Miss Bingley, whom she gathered looked upon Mr Darcy with rather more possessiveness than the gentleman would prefer, would not come near him as long as Elizabeth was upon his arm. He knew no one else. She supposed it was her own doing; had she not gone out of her way to make the gentleman at ease in her company? It was no wonder he had gravitated towards her.

While his presumption upon her time and exertions was irritating, she realised he must be reaching outside his realm of comfort to associate with these people at all. Had she not insisted he do so to help his friend become well-established in Hertfordshire? Clearly, he was willing to try.

She sighed, resigned herself to an evening of playing governess to a grown man she was not even sure she liked, and acquiesced. She would escort him to Mr Warner and enquire after his efforts to crossbreed a sheep whose wool was both soft and strong; Mr Darcy had expressed an interest in farming, had he not? Perhaps that would keep him occupied the rest of the night, and Elizabeth would be free.

Alas, Elizabeth had *not* been set free after introducing the subject of sheep-breeding between Mr Darcy and Mr Warner. She had gently led the men into conversation, as if laying down kindling and blowing upon it with small comments until their discourse ignited in full. Then, without formally excusing herself, she had left Mr Darcy to carry on under his own power.

Soon, however, she felt Mr Darcy's eyes piercing her from across the room. She caught his foreboding gaze as he stood amidst the other guests, a lone sentinel whose resting expression was unfortunately that of fierce disapprobation. Thus, she soon found herself once again at his side.

"Have you not met most of the gentlemen here, Mr Darcy? Certainly you do not need me to introduce you?"

"Indeed, I have, Miss Elizabeth," he answered. "But it does not follow that I know how to converse with them. I know nothing about them, nor they of me."

"True. But is that not what conversation is for—to become acquainted?"

"I am afraid I am ill-qualified to recommend myself to strangers," he explained. "I have not the talent which some possess of conversing easily, of appearing interested in their concerns, as I see some men do."

She stared up at him. Did he not realise how haughty he sounded?

"Perhaps you should *become* interested in their concerns, Mr Darcy. It is much more fruitful than merely appearing interested," she suggested. "And a more enjoyable way to spend an evening, I dare say."

Now it was Mr Darcy's turn to blink at her. He appeared truly baffled by her suggestion that he take any pains whatsoever to show genuine interest in those about him. She held his gaze with a challenging tilt to her head. He ended their deadlock with a smug huff.

"Very well, Miss Elizabeth. Tell me what is so interesting about these gentlemen, and I shall attempt to become interested in their concerns."

So, Elizabeth did.

Ignoring her exasperation at his conceit, she told him about Mr Long's having taken on the care of his three grown nieces, whose parents were of a reclusive and unsociable nature. She spoke of Colonel Ashe-Benning, the elderly widower in the corner whose utter attachment to his long-dead wife endeared him to all. Sir William Lucas, she informed him, had served as mayor of their town many years before and had the distinction of having been knighted during his tenure, the pinnacle of his life being his presentation at—

"The Court of St James's, I am aware," Mr Darcy said with a knowing smirk, eliciting the same from Elizabeth.

Next, she pointed out Mr Goulding and explained that he had recently inherited a small cotton plantation in the West Indies; he was eager to see it well-managed, but he knew nothing about the place, the people, or the crop for that matter.

"I have sold my cotton interests, as there is no profit in it without the enslaving of men," Mr Darcy stated matter-of-factly, as if profit were his only concern. Elizabeth could not help but discern that profits were nothing to him if it meant men were treated inhumanely.

"Indeed," was all she could reply, for this insight into his character touched her deeply. *Perhaps there is more to him than pomposity after all.*

Mr Darcy proved true to his word and attempted to make conversation with some of these gentlemen through the course of the evening. Each time he finished one exchange, however, he stood silently, plainly waiting for her to return to him. Elizabeth vacillated between exasperation at his high-handedness and pity for his unease. When he caught her eye, she would discreetly make her way towards him with a patient smile. He would offer her his arm, and she would walk him towards another party, fan the flames of genteel discourse, and leave him to converse. By the end of the evening, his cool expectation of her assistance was replaced with something warmer.

After having spoken to Sir William at length about that man's speech to the king during his mayoralty, Mr Darcy took the trouble of walking towards her and joining her as she conversed with Jane and Mr Bingley. She was surprised to see him approaching, as he had awaited her approach throughout the evening, and her astonishment was further increased when he met her eyes with an expression that almost resembled a smile.

"Miss Elizabeth, is there aught I might do for your comfort? Are you in need of a chair? Or some refreshment? May I not bring you a drink?"

She was so stupefied by his sincere solicitude, she thought she might indeed need a chair.

And a drink.

CHAPTER SEVEN

"What an excellent table you set, Mrs Bennet," Darcy said, having been coached on what his hostess would most like to hear.

The day before, as he had spoken with Miss Elizabeth after church, he had enquired as to whom he would encounter at Longbourn this night and how he might 'become interested' in them, as she had so boldly challenged him to do. His inability to feign curiosity in new acquaintances had long been his standard excuse for not speaking any more than absolutely necessary, but Miss Elizabeth had vanquished such reasoning with one arch eyebrow. Her logic was irrefutable. If he were to call himself a gentleman, he would need to depend on more than just his good breeding. He would have to *show* himself more genteel.

That was not to say he found the task an easy one. The inane drawing room chatter constantly pressed upon him would never fail to grate on his nerves. However, this was an entirely different thing—actually learning something of the persons surrounding him and choosing to find something interesting about them. He was glad that Mrs Bennet, in whose character, habits, or understanding, he could find nothing worth noting, was a fine hostess.

"Why, Mr Darcy," she said with a blush, "coming from one who is no doubt accustomed to the very best, that is high praise indeed."

"Not at all, Mrs Bennet. The entire meal was delicious."

"And lovely to look at, as well," Mr Bingley said from his seat beside Jane. "The pattern on this silver is exquisite."

Miss Bingley's ill-concealed sneer made it clear she was not nearly as impressed with the victuals or their presentation as he and Bingley were, although at least she had come; Mrs Hurst had claimed a sick headache and refused. Darcy had expected such a response, as the lady had refused half of what she was offered, and what was on her plate, she seemed to but push about with her fork.

"Yes, well, we shall make use of it while we can," Mrs Bennet answered with a theatrical sniff.

Darcy's brow must have puckered at her statement, for Elizabeth leant towards him and explained, "Longbourn is entailed away from the female line. As my mother was so unfortunate as to bear only daughters, this, as you can imagine, is a constant affliction."

He nodded in genuine sympathy and contemplated what this would mean in practical terms. Five unmarried daughters would be a burden on any mother, but having so many in one's charge along with the prospect of living out one's dotage in the hedgerows or dependent on the charity of family members must affect a woman acutely. No wonder Mrs Bennet was so eager to place her daughters in the paths of Bingley and himself.

Darcy was not surprised when Mr Bennet chose to forgo the separation of the sexes after their meal was cleared away. He did not seem eager to converse while there were ladies about; why should that change upon their removal? Darcy was glad of it; he did not wish to give the teasing man any more fodder for his sport.

As cards had yet to be announced, Darcy stood near the entrance, observing the Bennet ladies and pondering the regrettable circumstance of having their home entailed away to a distant relative. They were worse off even than he had assumed. He felt pity for Mrs Bennet, living each day with the knowledge that much of what surrounded her belonged ultimately to another, that even her knives and forks might be taken from her upon her husband's demise. It was a sorry state of affairs.

He hoped Miss Elizabeth's betrothed would indeed find success in his career, for he had heard of some naval men bringing home tens of thousands of pounds in prize money. The Bennet family would certainly need that kind of security.

Miss Elizabeth must know how fraught her circumstances are, he thought. *Perhaps that is why she has agreed to this unusual engagement.*

The youngest Miss Bennets, on the other hand, seemed not to have a care in the world, laughing and teasing and giggling over the militiamen they had encountered on the High Street that morning. He shuddered as he heard them speaking of getting up a flirtation with one or the other of the redcoats. If they only knew how vulnerable they were to the machinations of immoral men, they might be more circumspect. But, perhaps, that was just his own unhappy experience speaking. Not all young ladies became the object of unscrupulous men, he was sure. Perhaps these young ladies were better protected than...

"I can see where your thoughts lie, Mr Darcy," Miss Bingley said, her intrusion both welcome and not. He did not wish to give himself over to contemplations of betrayals and heartbreaks, but he wished they had been interrupted by anyone else. "Allow me to say I agree completely. All this talk of officers—so uncouth. How unbearably tedious I find this company. As do you, I am sure."

"No, indeed," he replied, eager to disabuse her of the notion that they shared any feelings whatsoever in common. "I was simply deciding with whom I might partner when the card tables appear."

"You need wonder no more, Mr Darcy, for I—" she began, but just at that moment, Elizabeth passed before them, and he lifted an elbow towards her.

"Might I engage you to partner me at whist, Miss Elizabeth?" Darcy asked, relieved to have had such a pleasant alternative present itself before he was forced by politeness to bend to Miss Bingley's wishes.

Miss Elizabeth's eyes sparked as they moved from himself to Miss Bingley and back again. She must have seen the pleading in his countenance, for, with a gracious smile, she accepted his invitation.

ELIZABETH WAS PLEASED TO TAKE HIS ARM IF FOR NO other reason than to rescue him from his pursuer. He had displayed no little dismay at Miss Bingley's efforts to catch his attention at the Longs' dinner party the week before. Even during her short visit to Netherfield, she had thought she had seen some irritation at the woman's conspicuous proximity.

"Whom shall we play, Miss Elizabeth?"

"That depends upon you, Mr Darcy," she said with a smile in her eyes. He raised a brow in question. "Do you play for amusement, or do you play to win?"

"We shall win no matter our opponents, as I am observant and you are clever," he said evenly, as if he had not paid her a rather weighty compliment. To be thought clever by a man of such sense and education was no small accomplishment.

"You wish to play for amusement, then? Now I must ascertain what you would consider amusing. My youngest sisters are lively and boisterous players, who exclaim every victory and lament every loss. My mother is never so agreeable as when she is winning at cards, giggling and wriggling with glee all the while. But, if you are sure we shall triumph, perhaps we should choose someone else, for she is most vexed when she loses and has no compunction in making the whole world aware of her having been very ill-used."

"Perhaps we shall play Mrs Bennet," Mr Darcy answered after some contemplation. Elizabeth was set to protest, for he could not know the depths of misery her mother might sink to—or put them through—were they to indeed be clever enough to best her, but then he added, "for one who can win easily can also lose easily enough, is it not so?"

"You propose that we lose on purpose?"

"In return for her kindness, it is a small sacrifice, is it not? If it will truly give her such joy."

"I suppose that it is," she said, unable to keep the smile from her face. "Though we may not need to throw the game, for she is a deft hand at whist."

"Then she shall be able to take full credit for her victory."

He walked his accomplice towards Mrs Bennet, made a slight bow, and solemnly requested her presence at their table, telling her he had heard she was a most formidable opponent. Mrs Bennet blushed, fluttered her handkerchief, then took Mr Darcy's other arm with a great beaming grin and allowed him to lead her to her chair.

"Oh, but I shall need a partner," Mrs Bennet exclaimed. Looking about her, she lifted her hand towards the lady standing sour-faced near the wall and fluttered her kerchief once again. "Miss Bingley, you must join our table. Come. There is a seat for you just here."

Elizabeth could see the chagrin on the faces of both Mr Darcy and Miss Bingley, he at having been thrust once again into the close company of one whom he wished to avoid, and she at having been so crassly summoned from across the room, Elizabeth was sure.

This shall be an interesting game, Elizabeth could not help but think.

And it was. She and Mr Darcy spent an enjoyable hour and a half trumping one another's aces and laying down losing cards, criticising the other's playing and pretending to be injured by the crows of their opponents.

"Oh, Mr Darcy," Elizabeth groaned as he once again threw the trick with some small card or other. "I thought you were more observant than this. You should have known my mother had the king."

"I do apologise, Miss Elizabeth. It seems whist is not my game this evening," Mr Darcy said with feigned contrition.

"It would appear not," said Miss Bingley. "What is the matter, Mr Darcy? You are usually the expert at the card table. Indeed, at Netherfield, it is an unspoken understanding that when one plays against you, we vie for second place, as first must always fall to you."

"Is that so?" Elizabeth asked, not unaware of how discomfited he was by such assiduous praise.

"Hardly," he answered, though she suspected he was being more polite than honest.

"No use dissembling, Mr Darcy," Miss Bingley said with a possessive pat on his arm before turning to the others. "Why, when my brother or I challenge him at cribbage, our only goal is to pass the skunk line before he defeats us. He is quite merciless, I assure you."

"Oh, cribbage," Mrs Bennet said with a scoff. "That is Lizzy's game too. None of us will even sit down to the board with her excepting her father. She is so sharp with all those fifteens and double-runs, I cannot keep up with it all. No, no. I much prefer whist."

A squeal from another table brought their attention to Lydia and Kitty as they played against Jane and Mr Bingley.

"La, you two," Lydia said in happy exasperation. "We have taken all the tricks while you two have attended to nothing but one another the entire game."

Bingley's eyes shot to the few cards left in his hand, a sheepish smile playing upon his lips, and Jane suddenly found her own cards intensely interesting as a blush crept up her cheeks.

"Lydia," Elizabeth said, hoping her warning tone would garner some decorum in her youngest sister. When she turned back to her partner, the genial openness that had graced Mr Darcy's face all evening was replaced by a glare of consternation as he took in the occupants of her sisters' card table.

Is he only irritated at Lydia's wild behaviour? Or is that a scowl of disapprobation? Surely he cannot disapprove of his friend's preference for Jane. Who could find anything objectionable in sweet Jane?

CHAPTER EIGHT

"Jane Bennet? Charles, you cannot be serious," Miss Bingley drawled as they were breaking their fast the next morning.

"What?" Bingley asked, pretending he could not possibly divine her meaning.

"We could all see it. In fact, I have seen it since we first stepped foot in this horrible place. You have found yet another angel and have devoted yourself to her every time you are in company."

"Your attentions have been rather marked, Brother," Mrs Hurst added, as if she had even been present at half the gatherings they had attended since their arrival. She had been feeling poorly most days, but her sister had undoubtedly kept her abreast of the happenings at each supper and party.

At Bingley's refusal to answer this accusation, Darcy added, "Do be careful. This is not the Season, where every beautiful debutante is pursued by a dozen beaux, and you can flirt as much as you like without creating expectations." As he spoke, he thought of his own attention to Miss Elizabeth, thankful their association had not drawn the same notice.

Miss Bingley nodded in vehement agreement. His congruence with her gratified her far more than it ought, but in this they did, unfortunately, agree. Bingley did not even truly know this lady, and none of them knew the lengths to which a mother of five unmarried daughters whose prospects were so tenuous would go in order to secure her future. There was no telling what arts she might employ to catch a wealthy man. And the serenity of character Jane Bennet displayed might make her just pliable enough to accept the task of making her family's fortune.

"You are quite right, Darcy. It would not do to raise expectations before I am sure of my own inclinations," Bingley replied slowly.

"Or of hers, naturally," Darcy said, hoping his friend was not blind to the fact that Miss Bennet bestowed the same tranquil smiles upon himself and Sir William Lucas as she did upon him.

"Naturally," Bingley replied with yet less enthusiasm.

"It is always prudent to be more circumspect than is one's wont in these matters."

Thank heavens Miss Elizabeth is engaged, he thought. He would hate to have to limit his association with her in fear of giving her false hope. When he was with her, all past trauma and regret fled, and the future felt promising. Indeed, her friendship had become quite essential to him.

It had never occurred to him how safe he could feel in the company of a female. And he had certainly not expected to feel safe with this one—*Lizzy*, the daughter of that wretched jokester. Yet, he did. She had proved that, while she certainly did have a sharp wit, she was not inclined to use it as a blade to injure.

No, she used her perspicacity to dignify others. She did not assume his quietness was arrogance, nor his pointed words conceit. More than once at a card table or over after-supper coffee had she interpreted for others some comment or another of his that came out differently from what he meant. If he were truthful, some of the barbs he *had* meant but, he realised afterwards, should have been left unsaid. Darcy was thereby happy to have them turned into something more innocuous by her gracious efforts. He had always assumed the reason women never understood him was because he had never allowed them to get close enough to do so. But Miss Elizabeth had fathomed him out from the first moment.

And the fact that she was engaged meant he had no reason to worry he was raising false expectations or conjuring in her heart any tender feelings.

Darcy, on the other hand...

IN JANE'S ROOM THAT EVENING, SHE AND ELIZABETH were discussing their new neighbours. Jane had been singled out at the Meryton Assembly, having been asked to dance twice by Mr Bingley, and his attentions had not abated. This was not the first time Jane had received special attention from a gentleman; she had been the belle of every ball since she was fifteen. But to be given such attention by an amiable, even-tempered, respectable young gentleman—one whom she could actually like—this was novel indeed.

"He is just what a young man ought to be," Jane said as Elizabeth listened in pleased silence. Jane continued to praise his sense, his good humour, and his lively temperament, all such Jane-like things to approve of.

"He is also handsome, which a young man ought to be if he possibly can."

Jane laughed at her sister's teasing, then became quite serious. "Speaking of handsome, you seem to have been quite singled out by his friend. Is this a trial for you? He does look so very severe."

"It is no trial at all. I shall not deny that he has a certain amount of pride, which keeps us unwashed commoners at bay, but I think most of his distance stems from being reserved by nature. I would conjecture that the reason he tends towards an open character like mine, or indeed his friend's, is because it is exactly the opposite of his own. Yet, upon hearing him in more candid moments, I can discern something lively and amiable concealed behind that furrowed brow. Of course, you heard how miserable he was after his riding injury; why, I am surprised he took the trouble of coming to the assembly at all. Do you know he has a love of farming? Apparently, much of his property in Derbyshire is farmed by tenants, yet he sees to the crops and inspects the piggeries. He even attends every lambing he can himself. Can you just see him in his frock coat and doeskin breeches assisting a ewe as she— What?"

Elizabeth had not realised how long she had been speaking about Mr Darcy, or how admiringly, until a mean-ingful smile had spread across Jane's face and the smallest giggle escaped her. "Lizzy..."

"What? Do not look at me like that. What is it you are thinking?"

"I think you like Mr Darcy. And I believe he may very well feel the same towards you."

"No. No, I do not like Mr Darcy," Elizabeth replied quickly, unwilling to allow her mind to ponder such a supposition. "He does not look at me in any way that compares to how Mr Bingley looks at you."

Jane's eyes brightened with hope. "Oh, do you really think so? I do not want to allow my heart to become engaged if he is not truly interested."

"He hardly leaves your side when you are in company together, and when he does, his eyes never stray from your position. He is certainly interested."

"I had not noticed that. I have tried to be discreet and not attend his every move," Jane said.

A pause ensued as Elizabeth rallied her courage to speak.

"May I say something? Something you may not desire to hear?" Elizabeth asked, gently taking her hand.

Jane nodded cautiously.

"Dearest, I love you so, and it is my heart's wish for you to find happiness. I believe, given Mr Bingley's character, you could do so with him. What I mean to say is, I was speaking to Charlotte Lucas recently, and she asked me if you were truly enjoying Mr Bingley's attentions. I know it was an impertinent question, but when I began to ponder it, I realised that if such a close friend as Charlotte could not discern the state of your heart, perhaps Mr Bingley might be unsure as well."

"What are you saying, Lizzy? Please speak plainly."

"Charlotte suggested, and I concurred, that if you want Mr Bingley to consider you seriously, it might do for you to demonstrate your affection for him in a way he can understand."

Jane's cheeks blazed. "I could *never*—"

"No, nothing improper Jane. I would never have you behave in a manner that might wound your conscience. I only worry that your serenity of countenance and your natural modesty might be confused with...indifference. Perhaps you might allow yourself to smile more when you are in company with him, be so bold as to seek him out and tell him how delighted you are to see him. You might touch his arm when you are speaking."

"I do not think I could do that," Jane whispered, almost panicked. "I cannot be expected to show more affection than I feel. Before I know his character? Before I know whether I really even like him?"

"Of course. You should not pretend more interest than you feel. But I do know you have more interest in him than you show. You ought only to hint at the effect he *is* having on your heart, nothing more. And besides, I think you do like him. I only want him to understand that as well."

"I believe I apprehend your meaning. You are worried that if he does not see that I return his regard, he might be persuaded to look in another direction. And I might lose my chance to secure him."

"I do not want you to secure *him* unless doing so would secure *your* happiness. But if you are to secure him, I do believe you must show more of what you feel, yes."

Jane's cheeks had begun to cool, but her brow creased at this revelation, and her silence told Elizabeth she would be lost in thought for the rest of the evening. She kissed her sister and left her to her ruminations.

CHAPTER NINE

"All the officers," Kitty exclaimed, her eyes shining with anticipation as she and Lydia took in the multitude of red coats before them.

"Do not get carried away, you two. We do not know these men, and not all of them are gentlemen," Elizabeth warned.

"Oh pish," Lydia answered with a scoff. "The officers are gentlemen, Lizzy. They had to have some money to purchase their commission, after all. As far as I am concerned, there are no finer men in England."

It clearly fell to Elizabeth to correct her sister's ignorance. After all, one could acquire a commission in the militia with far fewer assets to his name than was required in the regulars. Gentlemen and their heirs had no reason to join the militia, and anyone in need of such a paltry income was in no position to care for a wife.

Before she could undeceive them, however, Kitty and Lydia were off. Their insistence on being in their best looks for the officers' supper had caused the entire family to arrive late, and no doubt they were eager to make up for lost time. Elizabeth tried to relax her jaw, which had tightened as she watched her youngest sisters plunge themselves into the sea of red, lost all but for their giggles and the turned heads they left in their path.

Where other young ladies saw eligible beaux, Elizabeth saw only a troupe of extremely young men, wanderers who roamed from town to town and lived on tuppence. Unless some of them were second sons with terribly ill elder brothers, she imagined few of them to be genuine marital prospects for herself or her sisters.

With no dowry of note, she thought, *none of us would be considered a great catch, either.*

These considerations eased her mind a little. Hopefully their relative poverty would prevent any of the militia men from forming designs on, or even starting a serious flirtation with, Lydia or Kitty, provocative though they might be. Perhaps, too, her warnings might resound at some point, and they might spare themselves the pain of disappointed hopes or worse, a bad match.

Knowing she could do no more to check them, Elizabeth determined to make the most of the evening. She sought out Jane, but it was clear she was in deep discourse with Mr Bingley. Smiling, she allowed them to continue without her interference. Charlotte, she noted, was attempting to draw out that man's sister—and failing. Elizabeth supposed she should rouse herself to assist her friend, but as Miss Bingley appeared to be in acute torture at speaking with a mere country miss, Elizabeth concluded that taking Charlotte away would end that suffering prematurely. She could not bring herself to desire that. Mary sat alone under a sconce with a tome of some girth, while Maria Lucas fidgeted with a flounce on her skirt at her side.

One person she did not see was Mr Darcy.

As Elizabeth was scanning the crowd, Charlotte appeared at her elbow. Her efforts, it appeared, had been for naught, and she had finally given up on the impossible object of holding an engaging conversation with Miss Bingley.

"What has you so preoccupied, Eliza?"

"I cannot imagine what you mean," she answered.

Had the room become warm all of a sudden?

"You have been spending an awful lot of time upon Mr Darcy's arm these last weeks. I understood him to be a proud, disagreeable man. Indeed, after he slighted you at the assembly, I imagined you would scorn him altogether. However, he seems to have earned your good opinion at some point." Charlotte's gaze was a penetrating one.

"He is pleasanter than he seemed at first," Elizabeth began, attempting to keep her voice and her expressions as neutral as possible. "I happened to come upon him at a vulnerable moment and offered to assist him. We seem to...understand one another."

"I am not shocked that you two have some...understanding," Charlotte said, her implication clear.

"Nothing like that," Elizabeth replied, her pitch elevated in something like panic. "He simply requires my assistance. Mr Darcy feels ill-qualified to recommend himself to strangers."

"Hmm," Charlotte chirped. How so much could be communicated without articulating a single word, Elizabeth would never know.

"Hmm?"

"Why is it, I wonder, that a man of sense and education, a man who has lived in the world, might be ill-qualified to recommend himself to strangers? Perhaps he simply will not give himself the trouble."

"He has certainly taken the trouble the last several times I have been in company with him," Elizabeth protested, perhaps a touch too ardently.

"Indeed," Charlotte replied, facing away, then darting a glance back to Elizabeth.

"I believe there is more to him than the man who owns half of Derbyshire. Throughout our acquaintance, I have seen glimpses of something...softer. I am simply interested in seeing what truly lies beneath that proud exterior."

"As you are a keen student of human nature," Charlotte offered.

"Precisely," Elizabeth replied quickly.

Did Mr Darcy not come this evening?

Not that she had been looking for him. She had certainly not been seeking an excuse to remain free in case he needed her. Elizabeth had too much self-respect to put herself so wholly at his service again, naturally. Of course, Christian charity would dictate that, if her fellow man was in need, she should do all in her power to give him relief, would it not?

If said fellow happened to be tall, handsome, clever, and well-spoken, it did not follow that her motives in helping him must be attraction. He could not be attracted to her, certainly, for he must find her beneath him. When he saw to her comfort with a glass of wine or a warmer seat, such consideration was only due to his good breeding. When he stood so near that she could feel his breath on her ear as he whispered questions or observations, he was just being polite so that others might not hear themselves being discussed. And when he smiled at her as they bantered and joked across the card table, that was simply a manifestation of his growing ease amid Hertfordshire society, she was sure.

Yes, absolutely sure.

A warmth crept up her neck at the recollection of his delight in watching her mother triumph over them at whist and the conspiratorial grin he had gifted her. That his gaze had lingered upon hers longer than it ought meant nothing. It could not. He knew about Freddie. As far as he was concerned, she was just an accommodating friend with whom he happened to be rather comfortable.

Besides, had she not decided that any agreeableness on his part was the exception and not the rule? Despite her claims to Charlotte, at his core, he must be the disdainful, conceited man she had first been introduced to, must he not?

Elizabeth found him.

No wonder she had not seen him, tall as he was. Mr Darcy —proud, imperious Mr Darcy—was almost kneeling at the side of her precious Colonel Ashe-Benning, listening jovially to his stories and smiling, asking questions and volunteering his thoughts as if it were the most natural thing in the world.

She might have gaped at such a scene if she were not smiling so broadly.

DARCY TRIED NOT TO SEARCH OUT ELIZABETH AS HE and Bingley entered the soiree. Nevertheless, a weight of disappointment made its home in his gut when he did not immediately see her. He had to force his gaze forwards as he greeted Colonel Forster and was introduced to his new, surprisingly young bride. Harriet Forster caught his attention by her coy smile, the brazen cut of her gown, and the way she fiddled with the pendant on her necklace, clearly flirting with him whilst hanging upon the arm of her husband. She could not be eighteen, and Darcy wondered what the colonel, who was easily two decades her senior, could possibly see in such a vixen.

A cub, more like, he thought, disgusted.

Again attending to his expression, he gave the couple what he hoped was a respectful, if curt, bow, then wandered further into the room. Several of the higher-ranking officers of the militia had dined at Netherfield when Bingley had first come into residence, so many of the faces floating above the crimson coats were familiar, but Darcy was not inclined to converse with any of them. As he and Bingley had had no occasion to ride past Longbourn since having visited to thank Mrs Bennet for the excellent card party, Darcy had not seen Elizabeth in nigh on five days.

He felt like a child denied sweetmeats.

Her company had turned out to be just the invigoration he had needed after his harrowing ordeal at Ramsgate. When he was listening to her tinkling laugh, all thoughts of Wickham's treachery fled. Looking into her bright eyes reminded him that light and goodness still existed in the world, erasing all traces of the bitterness he had harboured since having seen his old friend fall and feeling the man's bullet rip into his flesh. Without her, that storm began to gather, and he had no desire to continue living under the dark cloud of Wickham's betrayal.

Resigning himself to her absence with a sigh, he perused the room, searching for one of the men about whom she had spoken. She would expect him to continue on in the vein they had established, striving to become interested in the affairs of those about him, even those beneath him. He espied an elderly gentleman sitting on a hard-backed chair across the room. Elizabeth had introduced him as an army colonel, Darcy recalled.

Colonel Ashe-Benning, yes. What was it Elizabeth said she admired about him?

"Colonel," Darcy said, crouching with bent knees to speak to the bushy-browed man eye-to-eye. "Might you wish for a softer chair, sir? I cannot imagine this one to be very comfortable."

"Not at all, my boy, not at all. If I were to sit in a soft chair, I should not be able to arise again," the colonel replied with a smile. "Mr Darcy, is it not? You are from Netherfield, yes?"

"I am staying there with my friend Bingley, who has leased the estate. I hail from Derbyshire."

"Ah, Derbyshire. Pretty county, very pretty. My Prudie was from Surrey, you know."

What relation there was between Surry and Derbyshire, Darcy could not conceive, but his mention of a lady reminded him of Elizabeth's reason for loving the old man. Prudie must have been his wife.

"Surrey is a beautiful place as well," Darcy said with a smile. "Mrs Ashe-Benning grew up there?"

The colonel needed no more prodding to lead the conversation, describing his love in exquisite detail: her face, her fair hair, her sweet nature, and the fiery spirit his darling Prudie displayed over any injustice she witnessed. Darcy listened for several minutes in delight. It was easy to understand why this gentleman held such a place in Elizabeth's heart. The colonel had just come to the point of how glorious his sprite of a wife looked while heavy with child when he heard the scrape of furniture behind him. The appearance of the footman holding a chair made him keenly aware that he was still crouching at Colonel Ashe-Benning's side.

What has Elizabeth done to me? A Darcy does not squat!

Standing to allow the footman to place the chair next to the colonel, he met the beguiling eyes of the woman he had been seeking. Darcy bowed. As Elizabeth rose from her curtsey, before her skirts could right themselves, a fleeting vision flashed through his mind of *her* heavy with child, more magnificent than Prudie Ashe-Benning could ever aspire to be.

"Do not forget to tell Mr Darcy what brought you to Hertfordshire, Colonel, for that is my favourite story of Mrs Ashe-Benning," she said, smiling at Darcy with what he could only interpret as a sense of pride.

His efforts to converse with strangers made her proud? Why did that hold such meaning for him? And what was this swelling in his chest?

What *was* Elizabeth Bennet doing to him?

CHAPTER TEN

"I do not know how you bear it, Lizzy," Lydia said as she slathered strawberry jam upon an already buttered scone. "Mr Darcy is so severe, so often staring and frowning. I should not show him half the consideration you have, especially not after what he said about you."

"Indeed," Papa said with almost a scoff. "If you were not handsome enough to dance with, I wonder he bothers to seek out your company at all, much less at every function in Meryton."

"Well, if he has changed his mind, I shall not be one to discourage him," Mama chimed in. "He is no card player, but I suppose he cannot help that. Still, ten thousand a year and very likely more. Why, that alone ought to pluck at some chord of mercy in our hearts. It is clear Lizzy has forgiven him, as well she should. Indeed, I would not hold such thoughtless trivialities against a man of his stature. Besides, though he does stare a great deal, I do not believe it is only to find fault. I have more than once sensed a bit of admiration in those long looks he gives you, Lizzy."

Elizabeth, upon rising from her bed, had not anticipated being bombarded with her family's many and varied opinions on Mr Darcy over porridge. Evidently, she was to be served a heaping helping of unsolicited advice alongside her eggs. Her cheeks warmed at her mother's conjecture, and she was unsure of how to respond. As it turned out, she was not expected to, for the confabulation went on merrily without her.

"I do not care how wealthy he is, I could never attach myself to such a silent, unpleasant man," Kitty said.

"I believe he simply follows the age-old advice to restrain his lips and thereby show prudence. Some of us would do well to imitate Mr Darcy and be swifter to hear and slower to speak." This was high praise indeed, for while Mary could always be relied upon to quote holy verses, not often did she employ them as accolades.

"Perhaps he is not so affable or demonstrative as his friend," Jane put forth in her usual quelling manner, "but I believe he must be truly amiable beneath his reserved exterior. Miss Bingley and her brother certainly value his friendship, and I cannot imagine they would allow someone truly disagreeable into their intimate circle."

Elizabeth could not fully agree with Jane in this, as she did not know anyone quite so disagreeable as Caroline Bingley. But she supposed Mr Bingley had little choice whether to keep company with his unmarried sister, unpalatable as her presence might be. No doubt he was her guardian until she was of age, and he thereby must suffer her presence until he could hand her over to a husband—especially as the Hursts were of so little help in entertaining her.

Poor man.

However, she knew what her sister supposed of Mr Darcy was true. Elizabeth had seen more and more of the considerate, captivating man behind the scowl. They had shared knowing looks and small confidences. He had seen to her comfort as much this last week as she had ever seen to his. Why, he had even deliberately lost at cards just to please her mother.

Yes, she believed there was a truly amiable heart dwelling in his broad chest. Against her will, Elizabeth's own heart was growing quite fond of it.

THE PARTY AT LUCAS LODGE WAS A LARGE ONE. THE gentleman and his lady had spared no expense as they entertained not only the local gentry and their families, but also several of the militia officers. It was not long after their meal was cleared away that the drawing room carpets were rolled up and the lid lifted on the spinet that sat in the corner. It appeared an impromptu dance was in order.

"What a charming amusement for young people this is, Mr Darcy." Sir William had accosted him yet again. "There is nothing like dancing, after all. I consider it one of the first refinements of polished society."

Darcy's initial inclination was to deliver a set-down that would rid himself of the man's attentions, informing him that every savage could dance. Presently, however, he saw the fine eyes that had become his solace coming towards him, and he answered instead, "Indeed. And now that I am well-healed from my...riding accident, perhaps I might try dancing in Meryton myself." By this time, Elizabeth was near enough to be drawn into their conversation. "If Miss Elizabeth would agree to be my partner."

Elizabeth's expression betrayed surprise at his request, and Sir William goaded, "Oh, yes. Miss Eliza, why are you not dancing? Allow me to present this young man to you as a very desirable partner. Come, now, you excel so much in the dance, you cannot be so cruel as to deny me the pleasure of seeing you take to the floor."

"Mr Darcy," she curtseyed in greeting, "I did not think you were inclined to dance."

"I am not, in general, but as my leg is feeling so much better, it would be a shame to stand aside when there is such a partner to be had." He held his hand out, and she smiled as she accepted it. Darcy led her to the makeshift dance floor and skipped her into the set while Miss Mary played a lively Scotch air.

Darcy's enjoyment of dancing had never been what most young men felt. He was always convinced of the mercenary intentions of his partners or put off by fluttering eyelashes and false smiles. He discerned none of these things from Miss Elizabeth, so he enjoyed her conversation and company even while moving through a crowd, going through the movements of the dance, and enduring the lingering ache in his thigh.

He was enchanted.

In truth, he found himself in constant awe of this dark-haired beauty with sparkling eyes and an ever-knowing arch of the brow. Watching the way she floated through every room and made each and every soul in it feel *seen*—how could something so foreign to himself be so natural in another? He wondered whether Georgiana would have made better choices if she had had the interest and example of one so kind and good. Could Elizabeth's influence help her to do so in future?

She was truly lovely.

As he gazed at her across the line of dancers, a laugh escaped his throat. Just a few weeks before, he had hardly allowed her to be pretty, and now he considered her one of the handsomest women of his acquaintance. More than once had he lamented to himself that she was already spoken for. And that she was so poor. And lacked sufficient connexions.

No.

He was most assuredly not falling in love with her.

Darcy was in no danger from this country maiden; he was far too honourable to set his heart upon a woman whose hand had been promised to another. He was simply taking her as a model for his ideal. It was a refreshing thing to know such a woman existed, and now he knew he would settle for nothing less when he chose a mistress for Pemberley.

No.

He was decidedly *not* interested in Miss Elizabeth herself.

He did not more than once of an evening become lost in the thought that perhaps, after such a long engagement, her heart was no longer as strongly attached to this naval captain as it once had been. He never wondered whether she was genuinely in love with the man in the first place, nor if she had been forced into the match by her parents just because he had offered for her.

And he never, *ever* had momentary imaginings of being in the room to comfort her upon receipt of the unfortunate news that her intended was secretly a rogue with a girl in every port...

A gentleman would never contemplate such things.

CHAPTER ELEVEN

Caroline Bingley wished she had never sent that invitation.

The week before, she had sent a missive to Longbourn at the request of her brother, inviting Jane Bennet for lunch at Netherfield. She knew Charles to be besotted with this quiet, fair-haired maiden, but as Miss Bennet had never shown any particular regard for him, she had not fretted about furthering her own acquaintance with her, especially if she could do so in such a way that her brother and Mr Darcy—and indeed Miss Bennet's upstart sister—happened to be absent.

However, in the week since the invitation, this very same Jane Bennet had begun nigh on flirting with Charles.

Such pretensions!

Half the time, she was the first to greet him when he walked into a gathering. Then they would walk hand-on-arm through the crowd until he seated her comfortably and set himself beside her. And when they were separated, she had developed the habit of brazenly smiling at him from across the room. More than once had she tapped him on the arm as she laughed at one of his 'clever' quips.

It was enough to make Caroline sick.

"Mr Darcy, what shall we do?" she hissed to him the morning Miss Bennet was expected.

"We? Do about what?" he asked in his usual high-born apathy.

"Charles and that Bennet girl."

"What should *we* have to do with that? Bingley is his own man."

"A man who believes himself in love. *We* are to be saddled with that woman and her family for the rest of our lives if we do not do something." She did not quite realise she had vocalised her fantasy of joining her own life with his until after the words had left her mouth.

Ah well, perhaps he will take the hint and act on it at last.

"This situation does not affect us equally, Miss Bingley, but I see why *you* might be concerned," he answered pointedly. "On one hand, Bingley might marry a woman who brings you no connexions and adds neither to your brother's fortune nor his place in society. On the other hand, you would gain as a sister a fine gentlewoman from a respectable family, who, while she may not add to your brother's consequence, could add very much to his happiness."

Caroline growled her frustrations aloud, unable to believe what she was hearing from the usually sensibly-proud gentleman. If anyone saw the necessity of preserving rank and standing in the eyes of society, it was Mr Darcy. Why would he answer in such a way?

"She has relations in trade," she cried.

"That is a common malady, Miss Bingley," Darcy answered drily, never looking up from his newspaper.

His refusal to satisfy her rankled.

And why does it feel as if he is implying something?

Surely *her* relations in trade were so far in the background they would not put a dent in her own social standing. Would they? They could not affect her chances of marrying well, she was sure. Her father had made his fortune before she was born, and had not his death severed that connexion? She herself had been raised from the cradle to be genteel and accomplished. Her Italian was flawless and her proficiency on the pianoforte was as fine as any young lady in England. Why, she had been finished in Switzerland! He could not possibly be lumping her in with these Bennets, could he?

Rather than setting her down, the notion only raised her ire to the point that, when Miss Bennet appeared on her doorstep not a little damp from the downpour that had over-taken her on her journey, Caroline could hardly countenance the woman. Of course, she and Louisa put on the airs neces-sary to play the gracious hostesses. They asked all the correct questions, shared all the correct stories, offered all the correct victuals, and very correctly called for the apothecary when their guest swooned at table.

While a little shocked at the event, she could not say she was sorry. Caroline did not want to give this self-seeking chit any more encouragement than she had already received from her gormless brother.

She was sorry, however, when Mr Jones came and made it clear the young lady should not be removed from Netherfield. And she was positively vexed when Miss Bennet's sister, the very sister who had been the grit in Caroline's eye since the moment they had set foot in Meryton, showed up the next day with her hair tousled and her hem six inches deep in mud.

In truth, it was not the muss or the mud on Miss Elizabeth's person that particularly irked her. It was the smile on Darcy's face as he openly admired the muss and the mud.

CHAPTER TWELVE

"I do not know who is happier at you being here, Mama or your Mr Bingley," Elizabeth said to the terribly ill creature lying before her. Jane's fever had not broken, and at times, she let out a quiet moan of pain, which Elizabeth knew to stem from more misery than the volume indicated.

Her poor sister.

Despite her aching bones and unconquerable chill, Jane smiled at Elizabeth's attempt to make her feel better. "He is not my Mr Bingley," she said through the soreness of her throat.

"Oh, I believe he is...or he very soon will be."

Jane's smile brightened, then faded as her head lolled and she fell back into an uneasy sleep.

Elizabeth had been with her all morning and had neglected to bring a book from Longbourn. She decided to stretch her legs and have a walk through the halls of Netherfield, intent on availing herself of its library. She knew it to be quite a large space, but she was not sure how full its shelves were. After a turn which brought her near the drawing room, where she nodded to her host and hostess, the former of which asked anxiously after Jane and listened raptly to her report, Elizabeth finally came upon the library, which was quiet and rather dark.

The number of books was not great, but there seemed to be a decent selection in different genres and periods. Milton. Shakespeare. Even novels. She almost laughed when she saw *Camilla*—how she had wanted to throw that book across the room as the naive girl got herself into one bind after another.

And yet, she could not help but think, *look at the quagmire in which I find myself.*

With a bit more sympathy for the young lady, she pulled it down and, walking towards the window to get some light, began leafing through the pages as she thought about her own conundrum.

Oh, if only I had never mentioned Frederick, her heart lamented.

It had always been the family joke, nay, the neighbourhood joke. She had used the excuse of their 'understanding' many times to ward off odious suitors or to set down haughty female acquaintances; it had seemed so harmless to use the convenience of it to put Mr Darcy at ease. But now he was altogether *too* at ease in her company, and she was altogether flustered.

She had refused Frederick outright the first time he had asked for her hand. He had done so whilst dining at Long-bourn, in front of both of their families. Her father had not been impressed and had told the young man that, as he wished to join the Navy, he would see that his daughter was not allowed to accept his offer until he had a living suitable to support a wife. As that would be several years off, Mr Bennet had figured that would be the end of the matter.

Young Frederick was undaunted. "That'll do, sir. As we are so young, I assumed it would be a long engagement..."

"A long engagement indeed. She is six years old!" her mother had cried, half vexed at the boy's presumptuousness, half joyous at almost having a daughter betrothed. Mr Bennet had picked little Freddie up off his bended knee by the ear and set him solidly on the couch as far removed from his Lizzy as the room allowed. Her smile at the remembrance gave way to a giggle as she pictured poor Frederick, all long legs and knobby knees, rubbing his ear and glowering at her father the rest of the night.

It had been his next proposal that had put her into the scrape she was in now.

Still staring into the pages of *Camilla*, Elizabeth made her way to a chair near the fire and took a seat. To her surprise, she was at once accosted by a long-haired, striped cat of indeterminate breed. She exclaimed as the creature stood on his hind legs with his front paws on her chest so as to nuzzle her face cheek to cheek.

"Get down, you mongrel. That is not how a gentleman behaves towards a lady." Mr Darcy's voice surprised her as she returned the feline's affections. Looking up, she discovered he was seated right across from her.

How did I not notice him? Has he been here all this time?

THE MORNING HAD BEEN A TRYING ONE FOR DARCY. Before he could break his fast, Miss Bingley had accosted him on the subject of Jane Bennet. She had yet again been overly familiar, assuming her brother's actions would affect him the same way they did her, as if their lives would forever be entwined.

He shuddered at the thought.

Then, when the household had been blessed with more pleasant company, in particular the delightful sight of one muddy and rather dishevelled Miss Elizabeth Bennet, Miss Bingley and Mrs Hurst had wasted no time in berating the whole Bennet tribe to him and their brother.

He had welcomed the sight of Miss Elizabeth, he told himself, because Bingley's nerves were in a state of high agitation, and it would calm his friend to know Miss Bennet was being so lovingly attended. If he was also anticipating more engaging conversation than Bingley could give, and a more pleasing visage than Miss Bingley's, he did not admit it to himself, for such meditations would be ungenerous.

However, his preferred companion had left them directly to see after her sister. He baulked at being given the hope of some relief from Miss Bingley's attentions and then having such hopes dashed so suddenly. His hostess's vituperations did nothing to ease his irritation.

"I should be careful if I were you, Mr Darcy," she said as soon as Elizabeth was out of her hearing. "It is clear to those of us who care about you that she is scheming for, shall we say, a better betrothal."

"Unfaithful *and* mercenary—so disgraceful," her sister added with a tut.

Unable to bear such company a moment more, he fled to his usual hiding place. A rather weighty ball of fur bounded upon him not ten seconds after having seated himself. Darcy dutifully ministered to the demanding feline whilst trying to assemble his thoughts. He attempted to lose himself in the silkiness of the cat's dark coat, to distract himself from thoughts of the lady upstairs—the glow of exercise upon her cheeks, her sincere concern for her sister, and the adorable state of her petticoats—but it was futile.

Darcy heard the library door creak as it opened behind him, then his breath caught in his throat as the object of his thoughts passed right by without seeing him and began perusing the tall shelves of Bingley's mediocre library.

Elizabeth chose a volume and shifted her position closer to the window, where the light streaming in allowed her a better view of its pages. The beams of sunshine through the glazing were illuminating every streak of auburn in her curls, highlighting every curve of her feminine figure. Her face became a perfect cameo of cream as one side was illuminated in brightness and the other shrouded in black. He was struck by the alluring picture she made, mesmerised really.

Then, she laughed. Darcy was caught off-guard by how delightful it was. It was brief, just a giggle, but its effect on him was a cascade of joy, inspiring a broad grin.

She walked towards the chair across from him, still reading, obviously unaware of his presence. Without warning, his furry friend abandoned him for what Darcy had to concede were sweeter pastures.

The smug beast, he grumbled inwardly.

He was not jealous of some random library cat, certainly. However, when the cat had gone from alighting upon her lap to outright cuddling her, caressing her cheek with his own, Darcy could not but scold the reprobate for taking such liberties, thus alerting Miss Elizabeth to his presence.

"Mr Darcy, I did not see you there," she said with a gasp. "How do you do?"

"Sitting before a fire with an engaging book, a happy cat, and now, pleasant company, I am quite well, thank you," he answered, smiling down at the feline in her lap. "How does your sister do?" he added more seriously.

She replied that Miss Bennet was not any better, but was resting, which gave her some peace at least. The cat continued rubbing his face against hers and gifting her roars of bliss. Elizabeth nuzzled back and kissed the bridge of his nose, instinctively baby-talking and cooing to the lucky rascal as he drank in the new attention. "And what is your name, you handsome fellow?"

"Fitzwilliam Darcy. I thought we had established that," he answered, mimicking her arch words with the slightest upturn of his mouth.

She was clearly dazed at his small flirtation. Indeed, he astonished himself.

"That hidden sense of humour emerges again," she said with a smile. "I quite like it. You should employ it in public some time. And who is *this* handsome boy?" she asked as she nuzzled and kissed the begging animal.

"Ah, the cat. That, I am told by Mrs Nicholls, is Italics the Library Cat. It seems he moved in at some point during the tenure of the last leaseholder and made his home in front of the fire here in the library. The servants feed him and tend to his needs, and he knows Netherfield better than anyone. His sole purpose in life, it appears, is to make reading practically impossible."

"Hmm, how curious."

"Yes, nobody knows where he came from or how he gets in, but he is always here when I come. Friendly little thing, is he not? He has become the bane of my valet's existence, I can tell you. Apparently, there is not a brush in the Kingdom capable of removing cat fur from wool." He swiped at the offending patches of fur on his coat and his lap as he spoke.

"I am surprised Miss Bingley has not had him consigned to the stables," Elizabeth said, not imagining the lady much of an animal lover.

"Perhaps she would," Mr Darcy replied, "but I do not think he would stay. He clearly believes himself the master of Netherfield Park and chooses to come and go as he pleases."

She looked into the eyes of the sweet little man and knew Mr Darcy to be correct. Italics was completely at ease, and that was because this was unquestionably his domain. Miss Bingley was simply a guest in his house, and no guest would relegate him to the cold, damp stables.

"I have to wonder how many hours Mrs Nicholls has spent in these very chairs tending to his needs over the years Netherfield has been vacant." She could envision the older woman pulling back the holland covers and inviting the boy onto her lap, enjoying his purrs in the silence of the empty manse.

"Mrs Nicholls is a highly competent woman. She runs Netherfield much as my housekeeper, Mrs Reynolds, does at Pemberley. One cannot overvalue an intelligent and responsible servant. If she chose to rest here and attend this monster after having seen to her other duties, such repose was probably well deserved."

"That is a surprising way to look at it, Mr Darcy. You must think highly of your Mrs Reynolds."

"I have known her since I was a lad of four. She has grown old in the service of my family, having been housekeeper to my great uncle Darcy before she came to us. She has practically had the running of Pemberley since my mother's death, and she shall continue in our service until she takes her last breath, I am sure. And I shall allow it if it makes her happy. That will not be for many years, however, as she is still lively and quite competent." Pemberley ran like a Genevese clock-works, mostly owing to Mrs Reynolds's tireless efforts, and no slowing down on her part would affect its efficient operation.

"That kind of thoughtfulness is rare among your set, I should think," she said, and he detected some softness in her eyes. He could get lost in those eyes if he was not careful.

"My valet will not believe me very thoughtful for yet again bringing him trousers full of cat hair," he said after a sharp intake of breath, breaking their gaze. "But in all seriousness, it is true. We are born to privilege and must maintain a certain manner of living to stem the tides of gossip in polite society. If one's living requires that he keep servants to furnish such a life, should he not respect them as being part and parcel to his position, to whatever greatness he achieves?" He noted a sparkle of wonder in her eye.

"I do not believe I have ever heard it explained quite like that. And, while I believe you are correct, I still contend your view is not a common one."

"It ought to be," he finished, settling himself back into his chair.

This was the easy conversation he had been longing for, and before he knew it, he was expressing his true thoughts to her again, as he had been doing more and more with each encounter.

He told her of his sister's antics as a babe, and Elizabeth laughed as she related those of her sisters, along with stories of her own mischief. He spoke of his father, how honourable he had been, and what a great hole his death had left in the lives of himself and Georgiana. She listened with true empathy, gently drawing him out with sincere interest.

When he told her of his annual sojourn into Kent at Easter to visit and assist his widowed aunt, her eyes lit up.

"My favourite thing about Eastertide is when the sallow branches burst with velvety catkins. I remember being a little girl and rubbing the silky nubs against my cheek, revelling in their softness." She closed her eyes as she spoke and reenacted the childlike contentment of such a simple pleasure, her hand moving over her face as if it were full of the blossoming twigs.

He was hypnotised by the beatific expression on her countenance and almost forgot to speak until the silence stretched, and she opened her eyes.

"We have always called them goat willows," he finally said, if rather throatily. "My mother would smack my hand if I so much as tried to cross the threshold with one before Palm Sunday."

"Well, naturally," she replied merrily. "It is bad luck to bring goat willows into the house before Palm Sunday. Though I confess I have been known to hang the budding limbs to dry and keep them in a vase until new ones emerged the next spring." Her eyes brightened with make-believe mischief as she betrayed her secret, and he could not but be caught up in her mirth.

Their intercourse was so effortless, three quarters of an hour had flown by before either of them knew it. Elizabeth stood abruptly at the realisation, apologised for her hasty leave-taking, and fled the room with quick steps.

When she had gone, Italics was once again upon Darcy's lap, nuzzling his face and purring. Darcy sighed.

"Oh, to be a cat," he began moments after her departure. "Kisses and sweet nothings from the loveliest of creatures—oh, to be a cat..." His forehead was butted against that of Italics as he spoke, his eyes closed.

He did not hear the footsteps creeping out the library door.

ELIZABETH FOUND HERSELF STARING AT THE MARVEL of a man across from her in amazement. How she had ever thought him heartless and cold, she could not now fathom. Sitting before her was a doting brother, a loving son, an orphaned boy left to fill the shoes of a man he had seen as a paragon of gentlemanly perfection. As he spoke, she sensed his pride—in his home, in his family, even in his servants— but none of the conceit she had attributed to him upon their introduction.

He had smiled as she had told him of the chaos at Longbourn when all five girls were small. He had laughed when she had imitated her mother's frantic howls over whatever small inconvenience might have vexed her. He had furrowed his brows when she had explained what she knew of Longbourn's entail, as though he fully understood how it troubled her.

When she had become carried away with her love of goat willows, he had listened with the ghost of a smile, his head cocked and eyes crinkled in what she might call fascination. It was as if he had been inside her mind, witnessing her four-year-old self experiencing the deliciousness of willow puffs against her skin for the first time.

She felt that Mr Darcy could truly *see* her.

One thing she did not wish him to see was how taken she was with him.

She paused, and a long silence fell between them. The interrupting chime of the clock caused her to start, and Elizabeth was overcome with the need to remove herself from their tête-à-tête.

With Jane as her excuse, she refused his offer of sending for tea and stood, leaving the cat to return to its previous station upon Mr Darcy's lap.

Halfway down the hall, however, Elizabeth realised she had left her book behind in her haste and turned back to retrieve it. When she came to the open door, she heard Mr Darcy's voice.

She leant her head in to see the great man murmuring to none other than Italics. What was it he was saying?

"Kisses and sweet nothings from the loveliest of creatures —oh, to be a cat," he said as he stroked the animal and met its forehead with his own.

Elizabeth backed out of the room silently and practically fell against the corridor wall.

He cannot mean me, surely, she tried to convince herself. Could he really think of her so warmly? Can he have truly been jealous of the attention she had shown Italics? Could Mr Darcy honestly wish for her to bestow kisses and sweet nothings...upon *him*?

Elizabeth could hardly catch her breath as she stumbled back to Jane's sickroom with one thought playing over and over in her mind.

Why did I ever mention Freddie?

CHAPTER THIRTEEN

E lizabeth heard footfalls outside Jane's bedroom. It was well past midnight before her sister had finally succumbed to sleep, but it was fitful. Jane was clearly uncomfortable, even amidst the luxuriant bedding of her fine accommodations. Elizabeth wished there was something more she could do, and her helplessness made her restless.

Hoping the noise she had noted was a maid moving through the corridor, she opened the door to request fresh water for Jane's ewer. Instead, she was faced with the form of Mr Darcy, wrapped in a sumptuous silk banyan, tied at the waist and showcasing the breadth of his shoulders. She cast her eyes down and intended to shut the door, hoping he had not seen her, but she was too late.

"Miss Elizabeth," he said gently. "Is all well? Has Miss Bennet taken a turn?"

"No, I thank you. She is sleeping at last."

"Then should you not rest as well?" His tone of sincere concern touched her.

"I wish I could. I had coffee after dinner in expectation of a long night. I must have had rather too much, for Jane nodded off half an hour ago, and I am unable to even contemplate sleep."

"I am suffering the same affliction, though without your excuse. I was just going to fetch some cards in hopes of lulling my mind to rest by means of solitaire."

"Oh," was all Elizabeth could say in response. She was not fond of solitaire, but perhaps she could do the same by means of a book. Not *Camilla*, for that novel was far too engrossing, verbose though it might be. Perhaps Netherfield's library held tomes on plant husbandry or some equally wearying topic.

"I could," Mr Darcy began, clearing his throat, "bring the cribbage board."

She gave an involuntary gasp of joy at the thought before the impropriety of the suggestion struck her. Where would they play? In his chambers? In Jane's? A slumbering, feverish sister was no chaperon. She began to demur, but he must have seen her expression of delight at the prospect, for he insisted that he would fetch both the cards and the pegboard.

He returned in a trice and began moving items from the small console table just outside of Jane's door over to its twin along the opposite wall. Setting the cards and cribbage board upon it, he turned to her and gestured in a manner that invited her to admire his cleverness. She could not help but smile at his boyish expression of accomplishment.

The candlelight played with the dark shadow of stubble upon his jaw. Taking him in complete with his unshaven face, long night robe, and tousled hair, the sight was enough to make her blush. She hoped the low light shaded her in such a way that he would not see.

He disappeared into his room, which was three doors from Jane's, and came back with two small chairs.

How thoughtful, she mused. He had brought her a seat when she could just as easily have procured one for herself.

He shuffled and set the cards before them, motioning for her to cut the deck. She drew an ace, and he groaned in mock disappointment, surrendering all hope of having the first deal. She dealt them each six cards and set the deck in the middle of the small table. As she calculated which cards to keep and which to put into her crib, she saw him straighten the deck and line it up perfectly against the long wooden board. She had to stifle a laugh—perhaps he *was* a bit fastidious.

He set his two crib cards face down onto her own, and she took the trouble to straighten them and set them aside neatly, tossing him an arch brow. He cut the deck this time, which turned up a two, then began his play by laying down a four. It was a good play. Any number from ace to four ensured that she could not make a fifteen off his first discard. Perhaps he was as accomplished a player as Miss Bingley had asserted. She laid a six before her. He placed a three upon his four and proceeded to quietly claim, "Fifteen for two," before moving his peg.

"Fifteen?" Elizabeth cried in an astonished whisper. "Since when do four, six, and three make fifteen?"

"Plus the two of the up card," he said matter-of-factly.

"You cannot count the turn-up card," she rejoined incredulously.

"You most certainly can. It is common knowledge that the turn-up card counts as you are pegging."

"It does not," she insisted. "Who taught you that?"

"I learnt from my father, and he was an expert at cribbage," he said, lifting his nose and pushing his shoulders back.

"Only because he played however he chose," she cried in laughing disbelief, baffled by his smug serenity. "*I* happened to have learnt from Mr Hoyle. My father owns the book, and it states clearly that one cannot count the turn-up card whilst pegging."

Mr Darcy scoffed.

Then squirmed.

He sat up straighter in his chair, which was almost comically small for his long legs.

"You are certain?" he asked at length.

"Absolutely certain."

Another pause ensued.

"I shall have to procure a copy of Mr Hoyle's rules," he conceded without truly conceding.

Elizabeth could not conceal her glee at his discomfort, nor could she stifle the urge to say, "No wonder you never lose, Mr Darcy. You play by rules you yourself created."

He threw her a challenging expression, clearly attempting to display a sense of affront. This lasted several seconds before a smile broke through his stern features. He let out a low chuckle and bent his head to his chest in a clear admission of defeat.

"Very well, Miss Elizabeth. Perhaps we might finish this hand, and you can point out any other glaring follies in my gameplay."

"Gladly, Mr Darcy," she said with more delight than she probably ought to have. Indeed, this entire scene had them both behaving quite naughtily. She and Mr Darcy should not be in such a situation as this under any circumstances, though such knowledge was not enough to convince her to take herself away.

The rest of the game was quiet but exhilarating. She was alone with a lovely man in the dark of night, talking and teasing him mercilessly, and he was laughing with her. More than once had one of them had to remind the other that it was their turn as their gazes locked, eyes glimmering in the flickering candlelight.

Just as Elizabeth was set to crow in whispers over her victory, a moan came from the room behind them. *Jane.* To her shame, Elizabeth had forgotten to check on her. If she were truthful, she had forgotten that Jane was there, that anything at all existed outside of herself and Mr Darcy, this small table, the cards in her hand, and the candlelit glint in his eyes.

She gasped and almost tipped her chair as she shot up from it. Mr Darcy pitched forwards to catch it—and her—before either of them could fall. She looked over her shoulder towards her sister's door, and when she turned back, she felt his breath tickling her skin as it moved through the curls at her temple. His arm was about her waist, steadying her. Her mind commanded her to keep her gaze down, away from his smouldering eyes, but when it rested upon the open collar of his night shirt, she espied wisps of dark hair grazing the small patch of exposed skin. Shocked by a sight so intimate, her eyes darted to his, and she stilled.

She should have moved, backed away, insisted he unhand her. She did not. Elizabeth was not sure she could stand in her own power just at that moment. Darcy's eyes roved over her face, resting finally upon her mouth. She flushed with panic, her breathing became ragged, and the hand she had placed upon his arm in the melee tightened. He was so handsome, his face all perfect lines and noble features, and his scent was bewitching—shaving soap and citrus and wood smoke and something floral she could not name.

Elizabeth melted.

Releasing all tension in her body, she allowed herself to fall into him and raised her other hand so her fingers might brush against the whiskers emerging on his face.

Her touch must have brought him to his senses, for, at that moment, he released her as if she were a hot ember. If he could have seen her soul, she was sure it would have been glowing. Heat had been radiating from him, as well; she felt the loss of it as he stepped away.

"I apologise, Miss Elizabeth," he said breathlessly. "I should not have... You have your..."

"Yes, I must... My..." she agreed, trying and failing to remember her sister's name as her scattered thoughts fought for purchase.

"Your betrothed," he uttered, running a hand through his hair.

Her breath caught in her throat. Of course.

Frederick.

CHAPTER FOURTEEN

The arrival at Netherfield two days prior of the two Miss Bennets, and the sickness of the eldest, had had quite an effect on its master. Bingley had been walking about, wringing his hands in apprehension over Jane Bennet's condition since the moment they had arrived home from their luncheon with the officers. More than once had he attempted to ask after her at her chamber door, only to realise that the maiden was alone, and he thereby could not.

Why did the thought of Bingley's behaving so honourably niggle at Darcy's conscience? He would admit that he and Elizabeth probably ought not to be alone in one another's company, but that was different. Bingley imagined himself in love with Miss Bennet; he was concerned for her reputation and likely wished to preserve the honour of his desired courtship. Darcy and Elizabeth were friends; that was all. Surely two people with no romantic attachment to one another were not to be bound by the same strictures as courting couples. Though Darcy was sure that, if he were

Captain Wentworth, he would take exception to his betrothed spending too much time with another man.

If I were Captain Wentworth, he thought, *I would not leave a treasure like Elizabeth Bennet alone for months at a time where another man might steal her away from me.*

Not that he had ever dreamt of stealing Elizabeth away from her captain.

Of course not.

Darcy turned his attention back to Bingley. He could see that his worry over the young woman sprang from an attachment unlike that of any of the man's former 'angels', and he could not help but be concerned.

Miss Bingley had made it clear that the Bennets had an uncle who was in trade and lived near Cheapside, a less than fashionable part of town. Of course, he would not agree aloud to any of *that* lady's objections. However, her point had been a valid one.

It was times like these that Darcy was unable to regret that the pretty younger sister tending the sickroom was already spoken for; such a low connexion must be considered highly reprehensible. If only Bingley could see the folly of such a choice for himself...

"This is dashed difficult, Darcy. I feel, as I have an independent income, I should be able to choose whom I wish to marry without having to take into account the fortune or status of the lady. I am not from a landed family like you, and I do not have to answer to lady aunts and lord uncles."

"I agree that you do not have as much at stake as I do; and your fortune certainly opens up the opportunity for you to marry as you choose. However, as said fortune was acquired in trade only a generation ago, you must be careful to marry a gentlewoman if you desire to be accepted into the society of the landed gentry. Your lease of Netherfield, and eventual purchase of your own property, puts you on the path to social advancement, without question. But your choice of bride will have a definite effect on how smoothly you travel that path. If you wish to continue towards this goal, you must choose the right lady."

Darcy knew that Jane Bennet was a gentleman's daughter from an old family, but he also knew how those of the *ton* would respond at seeing her on Bingley's arm. Bingley had been known to attend every fashionable ball of the Season, to dance with heiresses and peers' daughters. To appear in town with an unknown beauty without connexions or dowry—the *ton* would tear them both to shreds.

"However, as far as a lady's fortune is concerned, it is a natural consideration. Choosing a woman with a suitable dowry does two things at once: firstly, it adds to your own fortune and thereby your consequence in the eyes of society, and secondly, it ensures that you are not the object of a fortune hunter who might pretend all manner of affection in an effort to deceive and gain her object."

"Darcy, you cannot believe—" Bingley shot to his feet.

"I am not making accusations. I am only saying, better men than yourself have been blinded by such women and set in their shackles...I simply speak as I have found."

Inwardly, he knew it was wrong to ascribe anything insincere to Miss Bennet, even indirectly. Indeed, if he were in Bingley's shoes, he would see only a beautiful woman from a respectable family who received his attentions with pleasure and returned them in her own quiet way. But if Darcy were to show him true kindness, he would do all in his power to discourage this match. Up until a week ago, he had felt he could convince Bingley that she did not care for him, but to his great surprise, Miss Bennet had suddenly begun showing a distinct preference for his friend. *Was this sincere? Was this her mother's doing?* Darcy did not know, but either way, he did not want Bingley to be swept up in her attentions to the point of declaring himself.

Bingley's ire deflated a bit as he fell back into his chair with a sigh. "I have so much to learn..."

"Is that not why you asked me to accompany you? To help you navigate this new stage of your life? While it is true that I am not an expert in matters of the heart, I do have some experience being the bowl of cream in a room full of hungry tabbies."

"My, but we do think highly of ourselves."

Both men laughed lightly before Bingley became serious once more.

"What about you, Darcy? You certainly do not need to marry for a large dowry, and none of the heiresses of the *ton* have ever caught your attention. I imagine you can wed where you like."

"In theory. But with my name being an ancient and respected one, my family has certain expectations of me." He stated this matter-of-factly, though in his heart he resented such constraints. More than one relation had, because of these, assumed an eventual union between himself and a cousin for whom he had not the slightest inclination.

"So, what be the strictures upon the Master of Pemberley?"

"If I am to keep my family's favour, I must marry a highly-bred gentlewoman with a hefty dowry and every conceivable advantage of education and accomplishment," he answered, trying to keep his tone even to conceal the bitterness he had come to feel. He stared into his drink for several silent moments. "But, in all seriousness, my situation is unique. I must find, not only someone of whose upbringing and connexions my family will approve, but one who will be a capable mistress of a great estate, as well as a dozen other holdings throughout England and Scotland."

"A dozen?" Bingley sounded truly shocked.

"Indeed. Thus, while she would naturally be raised for a life of wealth and ease, she must not be averse to hard work."

Not to mention she would have to elicit from me the deepest affection and respect, he thought. Not wishing to encourage Bingley to follow his heart, however, he decided to leave his own out of it.

Darcy was quiet for more than a moment as he pondered what he wished for in a bride, lord uncles and lady aunts be hanged. *A helpmeet with whom I am comfortable, whose conversation is rational and engaging. Someone naturally kind; my household and tenants have been accustomed to being treated with dignity, and that must only be magnified with the addition of a mistress. She, of course, must be a fitting role model for Georgiana, a true friend to guide and assist her.* Darcy stared off a bit as he thought about the precious girl who was becoming a woman before his eyes— a young woman he knew not how to direct through the maze of temptations and emotions that besets a girl of fifteen.

"And she must be beautiful, I am sure."

"Of course." Darcy smiled at the singular bent to Bingley's thoughts. "Which is why I am still unattached and may well remain so for decades." The laughter the two then shared faded into a contemplative silence before Darcy added earnestly, "There are many kinds of beauty, Bingley. The serene English rose is not everyone's ideal. In truth, I find that as I come to know a woman, my opinion of her beauty shifts with my knowledge of her character."

A vision of Elizabeth in his arms the night before flashed in his mind, so innocent and alluring. He could still feel her fingers upon his cheek; she had wanted him as much as he had wanted her, he was sure of it. The pain of pushing her away still gnawed at his stomach. She had looked as crestfallen as he, and his mention of Captain Wentworth had seemed to startle her. Had she so thoroughly forgotten her intended? Could Darcy possibly have the hope of supplanting that man in her esteem? In her heart?

How could he reconcile such a thing with his own unyielding sense of honour?

Was it so unyielding? *Perhaps for Elizabeth*—

"But," Bingley began haltingly, interrupting Darcy's wayward thoughts, "having a fortune from trade would rule out even the loveliest of ladies?"

"For me, I am afraid it must." Darcy left it at that. He knew not whether Bingley harboured the same hopes Miss Bingley did, but honesty was always best in situations such as these.

Acting honourably was always the best course.

He was sure that if he reminded himself often enough, he would begin to believe it.

CHAPTER FIFTEEN

"I am no longer surprised at you knowing only six accomplished women. I rather wonder at you knowing any," Eliza Bennet argued after Mr Darcy clarified what made a woman worthy in his eyes.

The rudeness. To contradict a man such as he—Caroline had rather die! To be sure, if Mr Darcy said something was so, then so it must be.

To Caroline's dismay, rather than taking exception to Miss Eliza's pert opinions, Mr Darcy actually smiled. No doubt, he was diverted by her rustic ignorance.

"You are very severe upon our sex," Caroline chided.

"I speak as I find," Miss Eliza answered insolently. "I have certainly never seen a woman possessed of such taste, application, capacity, and elegance united."

Caroline could not tolerate this nobody sharing the passionate conversation with Mr Darcy that belonged to herself alone. She wished to be sharing different words with him altogether. Not that she would ever taunt him. What was

Miss Eliza thinking? To do aught but pander to such a power-ful, wealthy, landed gentleman was societal suicide. In fact, if she could get rid of this country chit, she might be able to engage him in more pleasant conversation right now.

Mr Darcy returned to writing his letter, and Miss Eliza was again directing her focus upon the book in her lap.

"Miss Eliza Bennet, do join me for a turn about the room. You must be hot sitting by the fire—your cheeks are fairly aflame. Come, it is so refreshing to walk after sitting so long in one attitude."

She knew the young lady could not refuse such a request, and when Miss Eliza stood, Caroline placed her slender fingers in the crook of her arm. She led her in silence for several moments before inviting Mr Darcy to join them.

He replied that he would not, as they might have only two motives for their activity—either they were in one another's confidence, and he would only get in their way if that were so, or they were aware that their figures appeared to best advan-tage by walking, in which case he could admire them much better from his current position.

Miss Bingley gloried in the comment, for it showed how astute his mind was, and it let her know that he was indeed admiring, even comparing, their figures from his writing table. Several inches taller, far more finely dressed, and certainly more svelte, she bested this Bennet girl in every measure.

Yes, Mr Darcy, admire on...

He soon went back to his quill and paper, at which point she drew Miss Eliza towards his table whilst complimenting him on what a skilled letter-writer he was. His hand was so even, she told him, his lines so close. And how attentive he was to dear Georgiana, always in constant correspondence.

How was dear Georgiana getting on with her music? She hoped he would send dear Georgiana her love.

Caroline placed Miss Eliza standing against the table, while she herself bent over it and noted how dull his quill was getting.

"I am excellent at mending pens. Indeed, Charles always entrusts me with the mending of his pens, do you not, Charles?"

Over the protestations of Mr Darcy and the muddled response of her brother, Caroline took the quill out of Mr Darcy's hand and, while ostensibly reaching for the pen knife, knocked the inkwell on its side where it splashed and spilled all over Miss Eliza's gown. It had worked exactly as she had hoped.

Miss Eliza stood in stupefaction, her arms outspread and her mouth agape, looking in astonishment between Mr Darcy, herself, and the pool of black seeping down the entire front of her apricot muslin.

"Have a care, Caroline," Bingley shouted from the sofa beside them.

"Elizabeth," Mr Darcy cried as he flung his body across the desk and caught up the offending pot, as if he could mitigate the damage by righting it quickly. He could not.

Naturally, Caroline was *mortified* that she had *accidentally* done such a thing.

Really.

Mortified.

"Oh Miss Eliza, look what a fright I have made of you! I do apologise. Your gown is completely ruined. I hope it was not a favourite, although it is probably one of your best. Wherever shall you find the five shillings a yard to replace it?"

It was while thus comforting her guest that she realised

there was ink pooling on the wood of the writing desk. Turning her attention to the corpulent young parlour maid who had begun clearing away the refreshments, she barked, "Quick, girl. Yes, you, you stupid girl. Do you not see what has happened? Clean this up now before it ruins the finish."

"I do apologise, Martha, it seems there has been an accident," Mr Darcy added kindly. "Would you please have Jepsen come in to inspect this stain and see whether he has anything that might remove it?"

See how well we complement one another? Caroline reflected as she watched him take charge of the situation. They would do so well together as master and mistress of Pemberley.

ELIZABETH COULD HARDLY BELIEVE WHAT HAD JUST happened. Her beautiful gown was besmirched with a large and growing blotch of thick black ink. She just stared, mouth open and eyes wide, first at her ruined dress, then at Miss Bingley, then at Mr Darcy as he lurched towards her, crying out her Christian name.

"Oh, Miss Eliza," Miss Bingley uttered some apology alongside her usual epithets, then began abusing poor Martha, the parlour maid, as if the resulting blot on the tabletop was somehow the girl's fault.

Elizabeth could see clearly what the jade was trying to accomplish, and she would not let her succeed. Elizabeth was not as volatile as her hostess; she would not scream or quit the room as if such destructive devices had pained her. She decided to hold her head high, knowing that her replying graciously would irritate Miss Bingley more than any fit of temper could do.

"It is no matter, Miss Bingley," Elizabeth replied, pasting on a wide smile. "It is only fabric and lace."

"You must let Yardley see to that stain. You know these country-born maids—they can work miracles. You must go upstairs and change directly. Borrow one of my gowns if you like. Oh, but that will not work. Of course, my gowns would be much too long on you. And rather tight, I dare say," Miss Bingley said, patting her flat belly with a false expression of concern.

"I have no doubt you are right," she replied with forced serenity. "Some women are blessed with lithe frames, while some of us have other...endowments."

Elizabeth could not believe she had said such a thing in front of two gentlemen. She glanced at Mr Darcy, hoping he had not heard her petty reply. The colour in his cheeks as he shifted his gaze from her *endowments* to the paper before him confirmed that he had. Dipping her head to her hostess, she then took herself and her wrecked gown back to the couch, picked up her book, and strove to resume her reading. She would not let Caroline Bingley have the satisfaction of seeing her flee to her room.

Though Elizabeth would not admit it, she was a bit heartbroken. She found her eyes falling from the pages in front of her to the ink stain more than once. Mr Darcy must have noticed her doleful expression, and perhaps he understood the events as plainly as she did, for he took a seat quite near her on the couch and apologised for what had just happened.

Casting them a glare, Miss Bingley left the parlour in a huff.

Goodnight and good riddance.

"I am sorry about your gown."

"It is nothing, sir," she replied in little more than a whisper.

"You need not prevaricate with me, Miss Elizabeth. I can see that you are distressed."

Her eyes met his and darted away. The warm affection in them made her stomach tighten, and she could not respond.

"Perhaps I should have been more vocal about her not being welcome to mend my pen."

"It is not your fault, Mr Darcy. I am sure Miss Bingley would have carried her point one way or another," she said.

"It is a lovely gown; was it made in London? Or is there such a talented modiste lurking in the wilds of Hertfordshire?"

"The pattern was a gift from my aunt in London, but its construction was accomplished here. Mrs Molland has a dress-shop in the next village over and is quite skilled. That is where we all have our gowns made. Have done for years." She was not as eager to put words together now, growing more and more forlorn as she gazed down upon the damage.

"I am very sorry, Miss Elizabeth," he repeated, his regret evidently growing apace with the fall of her spirits. "Was it a favourite?"

He was being so kind, and it reminded her of the words of admiration she had overheard earlier in the library. She swallowed hard before answering.

"It was, yes. Of course, my mother had charge of the packing of my trunk, so she chose my best gowns," she said with a woeful chuckle. "This one used to be Jane's, but she became ill last year and grew too thin for it. I had always admired it on her—such a lovely fabric—so when she asked if I wanted it, I did not hesitate to claim it. And hem it, of course. As time went by, vitality returned to her, but by then the gown was a full two inches too short, so she could not take it back."

His obligatory huff of laughter died on his lips as he watched her. He did not appear to be fooled. How could he be? He must know her better than to believe her unaffected by Miss Bingley's machinations.

But could he sense the effect his solicitude was having on her heart?

CHAPTER SIXTEEN

Behind her bedroom door, Elizabeth shed a few tears over her beautiful gown, but determined that it was still in good enough shape to be torn apart and pieced back together into a fine garment for her young cousin. So, with hopeful optimism, she folded it and set it atop her trunk so that it would not be taken to launder. Besides, no matter how skilled the lady's maid was, there was no way she would be able to remove this blight.

The cause of the other tears she had shed, Elizabeth would not admit even to herself.

She was shocked when morning came, and the dress was no longer there. Perhaps Miss Bingley had asked Yardley to take a look at it after all. Elizabeth wished to tell her in no uncertain terms that she had done enough, but she knew that gracious thanks would discomfit the malicious woman more completely.

As she arrived at the dining table, Elizabeth plastered on a syrupy smile and said, "Miss Bingley, I do appreciate your offer to remedy the disaster from last night. You did not have to ask poor Yardley to add to her workload in such a hopeless cause. The gown is beyond repair, I think. In fact, I had determined to tear it to pieces as soon as I was home. But, if you have so much faith in your abigail's abilities, I shall echo it and hope for the best. Thank you."

Elizabeth's words caught the woman mid-bite and completely off-guard. Miss Bingley coloured, looked about as if to ascertain if anyone else was as in the dark as she, and then, apparently understanding that she was being credited for doing something kind, simply accepted her gratitude. "It is the least I could do, Miss Eliza…"

Elizabeth was all smiles towards her hostess, but her mind was working out the details on a plan she had spent all night hatching. She had determined to utilise what was at her disposal to convince the conniving woman to desist in her abuses. This would require her to engage in a little connivance of her own, but the resulting peace would be well worth it. Therefore, after breakfast, she made her way to the library to await Mr Darcy.

"I THINK YOU HAVE FOUND OUT MY SECRET, MISS Elizabeth."

Elizabeth looked at Mr Darcy with one raised eyebrow, not appearing to comprehend. Darcy was glad she did not comprehend too much, for he realised after speaking that he had more than one secret regarding the dark-haired maid before him, and only one of them was appropriate for her to find out. He had walked in moments before and found her sitting in her accustomed chair in the library, stroking Italics, and failing to read.

Taking his seat across from her, he began to expound when she stayed him with a quiet, "One moment," and a finger raised in the air between them. Italics had hopped off her lap, and she sprang up before the cat could alight onto Darcy's. Stepping over, she picked something up from the table beside him and held it up. Spread between her two ivory hands was a large linen napkin. Without saying a word, while gently pushing the cat away with a foot, she motioned that it should be put over his lap.

"Hmm," he exclaimed, impressed, as he spread the fabric over his trousers and halfway up his torso, tucking it in at the sides. "My valet thanks you." *Why have I never thought of this?* Italics took his place on Darcy's lap and proceeded with his customary affections.

She bowed her head in a quick 'you are welcome', before saying, "Secret, Mr Darcy? I believe I have. In fact, I am glad you mention it, as I believe that bringing everything out in the open will save much frustration. You can tell your dearest love that I perfectly understand the lay of the land and have no intention of coming between you two; she has nothing to fear from me."

Darcy looked up from the cat's ministrations in consternation, his head jerking back as he strove to comprehend her meaning.

"I am sorry, what?" This was decidedly not what Darcy was expecting her to say, and he was genuinely apprehensive about what was coming next.

"I believe the reason Miss Bingley is behaving so…uncharitably towards me is because she is dispirited that you will not make your understanding known. If you were to make your engagement public, then she would be assured of your affections and would not need to continue this campaign of deni-gration as if I were some sort of threat to her."

As the full magnitude of her words dawned on him, his face twisted into a grimace of the sourest sort.

"Wait," he demanded, lunging forwards in the chair, prac-tically spilling the cat onto the rug. "Are you saying you believe me to be secretly engaged to Caroline Bingley?"

CHAPTER SEVENTEEN

"Miss Bingley is behaving this way because she is unsure of your commitment, sir. And really, it is cruel to keep your arrangement a secret, especially when anyone can see by the way she treats you that you have a long-standing attachment," Elizabeth scolded Mr Darcy as he paced towards the fire, his hand flying up to his forehead, his napkin—and one chagrined feline—falling to the floor and landing upon the ornately knotted rug.

She had known the insinuation would disconcert the gentleman, but to see him react by flying out of his chair and fairly shouting in disbelief was more than she could have expected. She regretted causing him such distress, but she comforted herself in the fact that, if he felt so strongly about such an idea, then perhaps he would act quickly.

She would then be able to leave Netherfield with the rest of her wardrobe intact.

"This is preposterous. I can assure you, madam, there is no understanding, or arrangement, attachment, however you phrased it, between Miss Bingley and me. Never. How could you even...?" His raised voice turned into the croak of a throat deprived of all moisture.

"As you have witnessed many of her worst actions with nary a rebuke, I assumed you were simply blinded from her incivility by your heart's affection." She understood it to be Mr Bingley's office to rein in his sister's malice, but Miss Bingley had made it clear that any efforts on her brother's part to check her were to go unheeded. Elizabeth had decided that it would require Mr Darcy's disapprobation to move the woman to better manners.

"Affection? For her? Can one have affection for a viper? A poisoned arrow? A red hornet? Never!" He spoke this quick and vehement response, but immediately seemed to realise how ungenerous he was being. "Forgive me, Miss Elizabeth. I should not have spoken thus, but you must believe that there is nothing—that there never will be anything—between Miss Bingley and myself."

"I am afraid she might not know that, sir. I am fairly certain she believes you to belong to her, and that by spending time in your company, I am invading territory that is decidedly hers."

"Well, if she has that idea in her head, she is *decidedly* wrong. I have never given her any special attention, nor shown even the slightest inclination towards her. Can she not see that I only answer her with one word unless I can help it?"

"Perhaps she believes that is how you communicate," Elizabeth said, straining to keep her expression free from the mischievous glee he was creating inside her.

"Impossible. She has seen me in animated conversation with Bingley; she knows I can string more than three words together when I am so inclined." He was still pacing, his brow furrowed in almost angry frustration.

"How you communicate with the fairer sex, then?" she offered.

"Extremely unlikely. She cannot help but see how I get on with you, how we converse so freely. She cannot be under the impression that if I admire a woman, I should speak to her *less*. No, you are imagining things, surely." He was rubbing his face now, and Elizabeth's eyes briefly widened at the truth he had laid bare.

"Why should she unleash her ire upon me if she has no claim on you?"

His distress was beginning to niggle at her conscience, but she was determined to see this through to the end.

"As I said," he answered, finally sitting again, though at the edge of his chair, leaning in close, "she must see how well we...get on together. Perhaps there is a bit of jealousy there. But, she is aware that you are engaged; she should know there is no danger of anything...happening...between us."

Elizabeth had to steel her resolve to continue, no matter how pitiful—or adorable—he was as he stumbled over his words.

"All I know is that she stares daggers at me the entire time we are in company together and spits fire with every word she says to me—and about me I dare say. The only logical explanation I could think of was that she was responding to the hurt she felt at seeing her betrothed pay attention to another."

"I am not her betrothed!" He was shouting again.

Then he was silent.

Elizabeth could see the gears turning in his head as he finally leant back in his chair, not sitting like a proper gentleman, but almost slumping, his long legs still stationed in the middle of the rug whilst his torso sank into the seat. He steepled his fingers before him for several moments and finally said, "You are correct about one thing. It is unacceptable for her to treat you as she does. I will not pretend that I can control her, but I shall do what I can to see that it stops."

"I thank you for that. I apologise for making you uncomfortable; I suppose I simply jumped to the wrong conclusion."

Mr Darcy bowed his head in acceptance of her apology and sat up properly. Spying the square of linen on the ground, he picked it up and replaced it on his lap. Upon seeing the man settling back into his seat, Italics forgave him freely and resumed his vociferous adulation.

Elizabeth hoped Mr Darcy did not see the satisfied curl forming on one side of her mouth.

AFTER SEVERAL MOMENTS OF SILENTLY TAKING IN Italics's purr, Elizabeth asked, "What was the secret, then?"

Darcy had been lost in his thoughts, absentmindedly stroking the appreciative feline. A long list had begun to compile itself in his mind of how inferior Miss Bingley was in every way to the woman sitting across from him. Miss Bingley was critical, cynical, supercilious, haughty, and heartless. Some might call her pretty, he supposed, and indeed that had been his first impression of her, but as he had hinted to Bingley, her beauty had diminished as her character had made itself known.

Elizabeth—*Why do I not think of her as Miss Elizabeth?*— he had to admit was truly a superior woman. She was gracious with the follies of others, humbly dignifying each person she touched without lowering herself. Yeoman, servant, and squire alike loved her. Even his own inexcusable silence in regard to the denigration he had witnessed Miss Bingley heap upon her, she passed over by assuming him blinded by love.

Love? Caroline Bingley? His body convulsed in an involuntary shudder.

"Secret?" he finally replied, oblivious as to what she could be speaking of.

"You said I had figured out your secret. If it is not regarding Miss Bingley, then I cannot guess what it is."

"Actually, it does have to do with Miss Bingley, and perhaps if I had shared it sooner, you would have been more quickly undeceived. I thought you had found out why I take solace in the library so often; Miss Bingley has severe sneezing fits...*near cats*."

Neither was so uncouth as to laugh out loud at such a disclosure, but they shared the joke with their eyes, each shining towards the other with knowing mirth.

"I feel rather sorry for her. You are all too aware of her faults, while she sees you as possessing none at all," she said.

"I have faults enough, believe me. My temper I cannot vouch for. It might be called resentful," he confessed, his brow becoming stormy as he thought of the betrayal he had endured in the last year.

"In what way?"

"My good opinion once lost is lost forever." The words left his mouth before he could think to lessen their severity, and she frowned at his brusque statement. He could not discern whether he read pity, sadness, or pique in her expression.

Finally, she enquired, "What might occasion the loss of your good opinion? For I hope it is not something you withdraw lightly."

"It is not," he assured her. "However, disguise of every sort is my abhorrence. There is nothing I condemn more than deceit. I have been betrayed by those whom I trusted most, and such sins I cannot find it in myself to forgive."

Silence reigned for several moments, the air becoming decidedly heavy between them. He could not banish the image of Wickham falling to the ground atop the cliffs of Ramsgate from his mind. Even now, he could not grant the blackguard absolution.

At length, Elizabeth cleared her throat.

Darcy loved hearing her begin conversations; she always amazed him with her wit and humour, and he was never bored in her company. He considered her expectantly.

"Mr Darcy, there is something I must tell you." She seemed nervous all of a sudden, which Italics must have sensed, for he promptly returned to her lap, forcing her to pet him with the hands she had begun wringing.

"You may tell me anything you like, Miss Elizabeth," he said earnestly. Darcy had never seen her so discomposed. He swallowed hard. What could she possibly wish to confess to him?

"It is regarding—"

Why is she hesitating so?

"Captain Frederick Wentworth," were the only words Darcy heard as the butler swung the library door open. Evidently, the man was awaiting Elizabeth in the drawing room.

CHAPTER EIGHTEEN

Wentworth was being waited upon cheerfully in the drawing room by Mr Bingley and not-so-cheerfully by his superior sisters. He saw in Miss Bingley a mirror image, only somewhat younger, of his beloved Anne's eldest sister, Elizabeth Elliot. Part of him desired to deliver her a set-down that would wipe the sneer off her arrogant face. Part of him wanted to laugh at how self-important these wealthy people and peers were in every part of the Kingdom. Another part wished he could run back to Kellynch Hall this minute and carry Anne away from the misery of that house, finally and forever.

He could not wait to tell his own Elizabeth his joyful news. She had always been his good friend; what rascals they had been together, bounding through the fields all those summers he visited his aunt in Meryton! How dirty they would be when they came home, she to the scoldings of her mother and he to the horror of his aunt. Mrs Westerbourne only kept a maid-of-all-work, and that woman was fully employed running the household without having stockings to mend and breeches to scrub day after day for their little guest.

Wentworth asked his host how the shooting was at Netherfield, and that led to an animated back-and-forth between Mr Bingley and himself, which evidently cemented him in the young gentleman's esteem. His brother, Mr Hurst, joined the conversation, and together they laughed as they exchanged stories of untrained dogs and poorly-loaded rifles until the object of his visit finally walked into the room, led by a striking gentleman, finely dressed.

"Ah, Lizzy...*ahem*...Miss Elizabeth," Wentworth said as he strode towards her, "you are still as lovely as ever." It was true; he was taken afresh with how captivating she was. No wonder he had been so devoted all those years. Of course, there existed now naught but a deep and abiding friendship. It was an admiration he felt for her alone, but it had never really been love.

He now *knew* love, and it came only in the form of one Anne Elliot.

Wentworth clasped both of Elizabeth's hands in his and offered a firm kiss upon them before looking up. Standing before her, still holding onto her, nigh on exploding with his happy news, he just knew she could read his thoughts. He looked into her face as if to say, '*Well? Can you guess?*'

It was only when another pair of eyes began burning into him that he realised he had been in that attitude so long. He met the gentleman's gaze, which was trained on him from under a stern brow.

Her genuine joy at seeing him was evident as she laugh-ingly said his name. Her companion's feelings, however, were of a demonstrably different nature. Wentworth released Elizabeth from his grasp and turned to that gentleman so she could introduce him. "Mr Darcy, may I present my good friend, Captain Frederick Wentworth? Captain Wentworth, Mr Fitzwilliam Darcy. I see you have already made the acquaintance of Mr Bingley and his family."

"Mr Darcy," Wentworth said with a bow, "your servant."

The tall gentleman was assessing him, taking in his form and dress no doubt. At length, Mr Darcy returned his bow with a polite, if cool, "Likewise, Captain."

Wentworth immediately turned back to Elizabeth, offering her his arm as he said, "Oh, how I have missed you. I have just come from Longbourn. When I heard that you and Miss Bennet were staying at Netherfield, I set out at once. I do hope your sister is feeling better." He peered down at her again as he set her upon the sofa. She mumbled a flustered affirmation, and concern overwhelmed all other objectives. "And how are you? You are well? You look flushed. You have been attending Jane in the sickroom, I hear; I hope you have not become ill yourself?"

"No, I am well, Freddie. Only a bit warm—we were...I was sitting quite close to the fire in the library when you were announced," she said, her hand floating up to cover one rosy cheek.

Fire indeed, he could not help but think as he glanced over to her equally *warm* escort.

"I am only surprised. I did not know you were coming. Was your journey a pleasant one?"

"It was uneventful, thank you. No highwaymen or broken wheels. But I must say the horses I hired in Bristol barely made it four miles before they were spent. Nothing I hate more than seeing good horses overworked, calling them fresh before they've been properly rested. That was *vexing,* as your dear mama might say, but that is the only thing I can think to complain about."

The gentlemen nodded with brows furrowed in silent consensus as Wentworth lamented his misused horses.

He did not wish to speak about the journey; he wanted to speak to his Lizzy about the *purpose* of his journey. As they were in company, and among strangers at that, he did not feel it was appropriate to proclaim to all the strong personal feelings he wished to make known. A man in love is exceedingly difficult to silence, but he reminded himself he was a trained military officer, a paragon of self-control, raised to the rank of captain at the tender age of four-and-twenty, entrusted with his own ship even.

Ah, *that* he could speak of.

"Perhaps you have heard they have given me command of my own vessel, a fine old sloop called the *Asp*," he started. It was not the ship he dreamt of—he knew he would need a frigate before he could start capturing ships and bringing in real prize money—but it was a start, and he was glad to have it. How comfortable Anne would be on board was yet to be seen, but if all went well with Aunt Westerbourne this evening, he would find out soon enough.

Mr Bingley eagerly chimed in, telling him how keen they all were to see the posting in the Navy List after Miss Elizabeth had told them of it.

This led to another lively conversation, one which occupied all four men for the remainder of his visit. Wentworth passed Elizabeth a glance or two, smiles of amusement at the puppy-like enthusiasm the elegant gentlemen were displaying.

As he stood to leave, he thanked his host for his hospitality, bowed to the man's sisters, and walked over to Elizabeth.

He offered her his arm in a request that she see him to the door, which she accepted.

"I am so pleased you have come," she said as he donned his greatcoat and gloves. "It was wonderful to see you. How long do you plan to stay in Hertfordshire?"

"Just long enough to see my aunt...and you. I must make a very important request from her before I head back out to sea." His eyes sparkled as he said this, thinking about the ring the old woman had promised him when he had written to inform her of his engagement to the baronet's daughter. "Oh, Lizzy," he nigh on whispered, "there is so much to say. Can we not take a turn in the garden?"

She pinked, unable or unwilling to meet his eye all of a sudden.

"I am afraid I have been away from Jane too long already this morning," she said with hesitation and regret. "Shall you be leaving so soon that you cannot call again?"

"May I call tomorrow?"

"I believe my sister is improving, and I was hoping to take a walk tomorrow. Shall we meet here at twelve?"

"Twelve o'clock, then." With that, he squeezed both hands again, swept his hat onto his head, and took his leave.

In the carriage on his way back to Meryton, Wentworth wondered why Elizabeth had been so reticent, so flushed. Then, a harrowing thought occurred to him—*what if she is still awaiting a declaration from me? What if she thinks I am coming to claim her hand?*

CHAPTER NINETEEN

From an almost hidden corner near the doorway, Darcy watched Elizabeth bid farewell to Captain Wentworth then hie away to her sister's sickroom. He wondered why she was not willing to spend a quarter of an hour with her beloved in the garden after such a long absence. She said herself that her sister improved; why should she hesitate? The man was obviously over the moon to see her and to be in her company, but why was Elizabeth suddenly so subdued, almost repressed? Did it have something to do with the secret she had been about to reveal?

"Impressive gentleman, is he not?" Bingley asked the room.

Miss Bingley sighed aloud and replied that she had seen more sophistication at that horrid assembly Bingley had dragged her to on their first week here. "Oh, Charles, I hope you do not take him for a model; I should hate to see you walking about as brown as a filbert."

"So tanned and weather-beaten," Mrs Hurst concurred.

Miss Bingley then turned to him. "Do you not agree, Mr Darcy?"

He uttered an almost silent humph, unwilling to yet converse with the lady, not until he spoke to Bingley in private about the matter Elizabeth had presented to him in the library.

"And to think, making captain at four-and-twenty," Bingley put forth. "How diligent and capable he must be. Of course he is. Just imagine being in battle, running guns on a man-of-war, carrying trunks of Spanish coins across a gang plank from a disabled ship..."

"One can hardly carry a trunk full of doubloons, Bingley. Gold is incredibly heavy," Darcy said.

"Yes, as Mr Darcy would know. I wish you were not so ignorant, Brother, as to these things," Miss Bingley added, passing a long-suffering smile his way.

"Just because Darcy is as rich as Midas does not mean he walks about carrying bags of gold, Caroline," he rebuked her. Turning to his friend, he asked, "So, what did you think of Miss Elizabeth's captain, Darcy? Did you like him?"

"There is little not to like, I think. Miss Elizabeth is an astute judge of character," *except when it comes to the leanings of my heart, it seems,* "and she esteems him, so I dare say we shall find him agreeable. Though I think his visit will not be long enough to become well acquainted."

Darcy did try to find something not to like about the man, but Wentworth was just as Elizabeth had portrayed him: engaging, friendly, and open, while at the same time discerning and careful not to say too much. If Darcy had met him in any other circumstance, he would have been just the kind of man whose acquaintance he welcomed. In fact, his military manner and agreeable mien reminded him much of his own cousin, Alec Fitzwilliam, a colonel in His Majesty's Army.

"That is too bad," Bingley lamented.

"I believe he is to walk with Miss Elizabeth tomorrow. Perhaps you might invite him in after," Darcy suggested. "I should like to hear more about his exploits myself."

"That is a fine idea, Darcy; I believe I shall. In fact, I will send a note around to Mrs Westerbourne's directly and extend the invitation."

Darcy was glad of the opportunity to get to know the captain better. He had often thought how much he would like Elizabeth to meet his sister, what excellent friends they could be. A less-than-exuberant part of him conceded that this would eventually mean introducing this man to her as well, so it behoved Darcy to gauge the suitability of his company. Wentworth seemed an honourable fellow, as much a gentleman as Bingley, well-spoken and genial; Darcy was glad of it. If the man were raucous or uncouth, he would not be able to countenance his company, and this he would regret, for it would mean losing Elizabeth's friendship, which he had so come to value.

For Georgiana. Yes. The friendship he valued for his sister.

Bingley stood to leave the room, and Darcy followed, asking, "May I join you, Bingley? There is something particular about which I should like to speak to you."

ELIZABETH HAD BEEN MORTIFIED AFTER MR DARCY'S declaration.

"There is nothing I condemn more than deceit."

Any argument she had had in mind had been lost in the constriction of her throat as the gravity of his words sank in.

She could not contemplate how fallen she would be in his esteem should he discover her prevarication. Was she, too, to one day be the object of his implacable resentment?

The thought of losing the friendship they had developed over the past several weeks caused her physical pain such that she clutched her stomach and began to feel hot.

Oh, who was she trying to fool?

She did not only dread losing his friendship; her dismay sprang from the fear of losing what she secretly hoped they might one day become. His company was becoming very... important to her. How could she have known at the Meryton Assembly that the coming months would throw them together so often, or indeed that he would seek her out and make her his solace from the discomfort of disagreeable or unfamiliar society? How could she have foreseen that they might become increasingly dear to one another?

Upstairs, Elizabeth had to catch her breath before entering Jane's room. How shocked she had been to see Frederick, and how discomposed she had been in his company while her deception hung over her.

What must Mr Darcy think?

Watching Frederick commandeer her attention immediately and kiss her hands twice, even openly requesting a private audience on the morrow—of course, he would think they were a couple in love. How on earth was she to explain that they were only friends now? What kind of wanton must she be to allow a gentleman, not her lover, to take such liberties? How low she must be to behave so familiarly with a man to whom she was not betrothed. Even if she could somehow keep Mr Darcy's good opinion after the truth was revealed, how would she convince him that she had no feelings for

Frederick after what he had seen today? How would she ever regain his good opinion?

Elizabeth could not lie to herself. She did not desire just his good opinion. Her horror at Mr Darcy discovering her pretence and the terrible shame she felt as she sat next to Frederick while that gentleman looked on brought forth a staggering revelation:

I love him. I am in love with Fitzwilliam Darcy.

CHAPTER TWENTY

When Elizabeth entered Jane's room, she was heartened to find her sitting up, sipping tea, her cheeks having gained some colour. On the side table was a plate whose crumbs indicated that Jane was eating again.

"You look better," she told her as she sat on the edge of her bed.

"I thank you, I believe I am. I should like to return home tomorrow; I have trespassed upon Mr Bingley's kindness long enough."

"I am sure Mr Bingley thinks no such thing," Elizabeth rejoined, attempting a levity she did not feel. A smile flitted across Jane's face before being replaced by a furrowing of her brow.

"Oh, Lizzy, you have cared for me so diligently. You look fatigued. I hope you are not overtaxing yourself."

"I am fatigued, Jane, but not from caring for you," she answered, taking her sister's outstretched hand in her own. "It is my conscience that wearies me. I have acted so foolishly, and now I fear I shall not be able to bear the consequences." Her face was aflame, and tears pricked her eyes as she spoke.

Jane set her cup down and leant in to offer her other hand to her beloved sister. Her brows were knitted and her eyes held deep concern. "What could you have done that is as bad as all this?"

Elizabeth closed her eyes for a moment, then told her all that was weighing on her heart: how she had deceived Mr Darcy; how he had made it clear that he could not forgive dishonesty, that he felt it was an irremovable blight on one's character that he could not look past; how she now knew that if she could not keep his friendship, it would be as if she had no air to breathe.

"Dearest Lizzy, if Mr Darcy is all that you say he is, then certainly he will forgive you once he understands the whole of the matter. Surely, he is charitable enough to extend such basic Christian kindness towards one for whom he has so much regard."

"He may regard me now, Jane, but no. Once he discovers that I misled him, any respect he has for me will wither; he will set me down as another one of those women who will engage in all manner of subterfuge to gain the attention of a wealthy gentleman. I have heard him speak with undisguised abhorrence of the tactics tried on him by the young ladies of the *ton*."

"I am sure he will not lump you in with such mercenaries. He certainly knows your character well enough to understand that your motive was pure."

Sweet, sweet Jane. She sighed. *If only I could be as sure that Mr Darcy would be so forgiving.*

"BINGLEY, IT SEEMS I SHALL HAVE TO DISABUSE YOUR
sister of the notion that I shall someday attach myself to her,"
Darcy stated plainly, unwilling to allow any room for misunderstanding. "It would be a shame for her to lose another
Season reaching for something she shall *never* have."

He spoke this as kindly as he could, while assuring his
friend by his tone of the absoluteness of his statement. Elizabeth's mistaken conclusion that he and Miss Bingley had a
secret understanding had unsettled Darcy greatly, and he
could not allow another day to pass without addressing it.

"No, no. I should be the one to tell her," Bingley said after
some amount of squirming. "I ought to have been more frank
with her before now. I shall speak to her today and command
her in no uncertain terms that she must desist in this...
endeavour."

Darcy was unsurprised at Bingley's frank acknowledgment of his sister's ambitions. He had given the young
woman no encouragement beyond the barest civility, yet she
simply would not be deterred. It was time Darcy's position
towards her was made perfectly clear.

"While we are on the subject of your sister, Bingley, there
is another thing I wish to address," Darcy began cautiously.
"Perhaps you have noticed that she is less than thrilled with
our current company."

"To say the least," Bingley replied. "Why, she is positively
beastly to poor Miss Elizabeth."

"If you have noted her spiteful behaviour, why do you
allow it to continue?" Darcy asked, taken aback. He had
honestly thought Bingley too distracted to have seen it, or else
his friend would have attempted to curb his sister's hostility.

"I do not *allow* Caroline to do anything," Bingley cried.
"You know she is ungovernable when she sets her mind on

something. She has decided that the Bennets are worthy of her malice, and so she treats them as such."

"Yes, but her ill temper shall have a detrimental effect on you and your reputation. If you do not take the trouble to check her, you will reap the bounty of her maleficence."

"And how do you suggest I do that? You know she holds only to her own counsel. Even Louisa can say nothing to direct her."

"If she will not listen when you speak, perhaps she will be more malleable in the face of action. Do you not hold her purse strings? Would not a threat to her allowance impel her to be more compliant?"

DARCY SPENT THE REST OF HIS DAY ATTEMPTING TO finish correspondence in his quarters. His writing desk was a comfortable and well-stocked one, thanks to Bingley. He was able to finish half a letter at a time before his thoughts were again and again drawn away from his task.

Why was Elizabeth so out of sorts? Should she not be ecstatic to be reunited with the holder of her heart? Could it be that Captain Wentworth, worthy though he might be, was no longer its keeper? Could it be that she was not as eager to be joined to the man as she once was? Or was he only seeing what he wanted to see?

He finished the letter to his steward and enfolded the instructions the man had requested regarding crop distribution and pasture changes, pleased to have that important business done in plenty of time for said plans to be implemented before his return in the early spring.

Ah, Pemberley in the spring.

His mind flashed forwards to sitting in his coach as it

rolled up the long drive through the park. He could see the old stone fence that once held beef cattle, but was now just a remnant of a past his father had not wished to forget. As the coach passed the orchard, he could smell the apple blossoms. He turned to the seat across from him into the beaming face of his sweet Georgiana. She loved the scent of the orchard in spring as much as he.

Soon, the trees parted and there it stood: Pemberley in all its glory.

In his vision, he heard a gasp come from beside him on the squabs. When he looked over, he revelled in the delight on the lovely face of his companion.

It was Elizabeth.

She was there, by his side, taking in the grand view of her new home.

No. He must not think such things. She was an engaged woman. Engaged, not to a despot or a blackguard, but to an industrious and conscientious captain in His Majesty's Navy —a man whose reputation and character were above reproach, and who was as good as his word. He said he would return when he had made something of himself, and here he was; no sooner had he been given command of his own vessel than he was here to claim his bride. He was a real man of honour.

Darcy could not even contemplate tempting this respectable man's intended away from him. He would not be able to live with himself. On second thought, then he would have Elizabeth, and what crime would not be worth such a prize? *No.* He simply had to control his emotions and his behaviour; he would not be the cause of a rift between these two lovers. At this resolution, he went back to his writing; he had never finished his letter to Georgiana, and there was no better time than now.

Darcy reviewed the contents of his missive thus far and was distressed to find that he had mentioned Miss Elizabeth several times. He had even omitted the 'Miss' once. He could not send this. No, he must start afresh and leave her out of it except for the barest mention of having been in her company. Then he recalled that he had sent his sister several letters since his arrival at Netherfield—what had he already betrayed? How often had he already spoken of the lovely woman who had so comforted and captivated him? What had Georgiana already concluded?

He could not help that now. He could only direct the course of her thoughts from this point forwards. He finished the letter he had started by informing his sister that Miss Elizabeth's intended was visiting Meryton, and that, since the captain would be much at sea in the future, he hoped the two ladies could meet someday. Yes, Darcy thought she would be just the right friend for his sister.

Just the right friend? Again, he was fooling himself. Who were Elizabeth Bennet's connexions? What were her accomplishments? Who were her aunts and uncles? How could a woman like Elizabeth be just the right friend for his sister, an heiress from the heights of society, to whom the most refined and noble ladies of the *ton* would one day look for inspiration and guidance? How could her friendship benefit his sister at all?

Reminding himself of her unsuitableness brought Darcy a measure of relief. Even if there was no Captain Wentworth, Darcy would never be able to bring the pretty Miss Elizabeth home to his relatives.

How Lady Catherine would scold him upon introducing

her; she would be merciless. Then again, if he were to marry anyone but his cousin Anne, that lady would be nigh on apoplectic, so perhaps her sentiment was not one to consider.

But Lord and Lady Matlock—they had made it quite clear what kind of woman they expected him to wed by throwing at him every well-connected maiden of fortune in London Season after Season, without regard to temperament or character. If he were to take this penniless country lass, their disappointment would be immense.

On the other hand, the earl and countess had great affection for him. Would they not rather accept an undesirable bride than risk alienating their most-favoured nephew?

Without a doubt, *ton* society would ostracise him were he to appear at Almack's with a complete unknown from the wilds of Hertfordshire.

What a punishment that would be, he thought, *to have to spend less time among the prigs and pretenders of London.*

He groaned aloud as he threw down his quill and rubbed his face with both hands. This was getting him nowhere. He could not focus. He needed a distraction, and the library was certainly out of the question. He could not risk meeting her again today; he might be tempted to say more than he ought. No, he needed to be out of doors.

A few minutes later, his valet arrived in answer to his bell.

"My riding clothes. Directly."

CHAPTER TWENTY-ONE

The next morning saw Elizabeth awaken early, unable to sleep as the inevitable visit with Frederick and her confession to Mr Darcy loomed over her.

How am I to tell him what needs to be said? What will be the consequences?

She did not wish to bother Jane with her pacing, so she slipped her dress on as well as she could without help and quietly made her way down to the library. Martha was stoking the fire and stroking Italics as he snaked between her legs. Requesting a pot of coffee be delivered to her there, Elizabeth set to pacing the length of the beautiful rug after Martha shuffled out, too agitated to be still.

She could only think of one reason Frederick would seek her out so quickly and insist on a private audience—he had made something of himself as her father had required, and now he was ready to secure her hand in marriage. Had he ridden all the way from Somersetshire to propose? Four days on the road, several changes of horses, wind and rain, and unpalatable inn food, just to propose to her? How could she say no? Had she not practically encouraged his suit all those years by continuing to run wild with him every summer until he left for the Navy? Was she not grown enough then to realise what his intentions were?

Here he was, ready to declare himself.

Her stomach plummeted at the thought of losing the respect of both the men she most regarded. Frederick, her beloved friend of old, would never speak to her again after going to such trouble only to be refused—for refuse him she must, as her heart belonged to another. And Mr Darcy would never see her again after learning of the subterfuge she undertook to gain his trust.

Elizabeth did not believe she could survive such a fate. But what could she do?

She began contemplating what she knew of the two men, determined to approach each situation in such a way as to cause as little pain to each of them—and to herself—as possible.

Frederick was her friend. Her true friend. He knew her. He knew she would never lead him on intentionally. His affection for her was born of a true and deep regard for who she was, and he would never wish her to change who she was just to bend to his will, not if it pained her. He would not be able to help seeing that her heart was leaning in another direction; he knew her too well. He would recognise the connexion she felt with Mr Darcy within an hour of being in their company, and he had too much self-respect to accept a woman whose affection belonged to another.

She knew Mr Darcy to be reserved and somewhat proud, but Elizabeth was sure he was genuinely good. Should she not have the same faith in him that Jane did? Jane always thought the best of everyone; of course she would assign Mr Darcy such Christian generosity of spirit. She had witnessed his restraint towards Miss Bingley, whose attentions thoroughly irked him, and she had also seen how he truly disdained the woman, often holding back sneers and groans in response to her observations. Would Elizabeth be relegated to such a position in his eyes when he learnt the truth? At least he could not accuse Miss Bingley of deceiving him to gain his favour; she was always her genuine, vitriolic self, for better or for worse.

Could he really be so implacable? Could he really reject such a friend as Elizabeth had become to him because of a... misdirection, the consequences of which she could never have foreseen? How was she to know they would become so close? Surely after all these weeks, she had earned some place in his esteem. Surely it would be as painful for him to extract her from his heart as doing so would be for her.

Surely.

She threw her head back with a sharp inhale just in time for Martha to return with the coffee. And Mr Darcy.

"I asked her to bring in an extra cup; I hope you do not mind," he said to Elizabeth as the maid set the hot kettle down with two cups and several scones on a platter. "Thank you, Martha, that will be all."

"Mr Darcy, good morning," Elizabeth said, her thoughts scattered. "Yes, yes, of course. I did not know you would be up so early. I hate to commandeer your refuge."

"Not at all, Miss Elizabeth," he said softly after the maid departed. "May I?"

He crossed the rug towards her.

This was the first she had seen of him since her revelation the morning before. He had been absent when she had gone down for tea with Jane, and she and Jane had chosen to take supper in their room in order to begin packing. He was also absent when Mr Bingley came to the door to bid the ladies good night and tell Jane once again how elated he was to see her doing so well.

Darcy's tall frame and handsome face struck her anew, and she found herself unable to move. She was rooted to the floor, and he was coming nearer and nearer.

Soon, he was standing mere inches from her with his feet planted among the ornate flowers of the hand-knotted rug. He looked from the fireplace down to her face, which had tilted up to meet his as he had drawn close. Her heart thrummed in her ears, and her stomach became a torturous knot.

What is he doing?

"Miss Elizabeth," he whispered.

"Mr Darcy." She swallowed hard at hearing her name on his lips. *His lips.* She could not keep her gaze from them; they were so close.

"May I?" he repeated, his eyes moving from hers to her parted mouth.

She could not answer. Her throat was too dry. Her chin began to tremble as the emotion she had been labouring to quell came crashing over her.

Can he really be here with me, alone, about to—

"Black?"

She blinked, confused. "Black?"

"Or do you prefer cream and sugar?"

Coffee.

Of course.

She was standing directly in front of the coffee tray.

CHAPTER TWENTY-TWO

D arcy met Martha on his way down to the library, and when he asked her to bring him coffee, he was taken aback to hear that she had already ordered some for Miss Elizabeth and would he like some scones as well? Unwilling to be a source of gossip for the household, he could not change his mind now, so he accepted.

He stood on the stair for some time, trying to decide whether to avoid Elizabeth for the rest of her stay as he had planned, or to gratify himself with the sweet torture of her company one last time before letting her go completely. When Martha entered his vision with the tray in hand, two cups catching his eye, he chose the latter.

Still, when he walked in behind the maid to see Elizabeth standing between the two chairs, arms crossed about herself in a hug, he was arrested for a moment by the sight of her as she threw her head back with some emotion. What was she thinking about? Could she be thinking of him? He wished he could watch her forever, but his hopes were dashed by

Martha's clanking the tray onto the table near the fireplace. She looked up startled.

"I hate to commandeer your refuge," Elizabeth said. If only she knew how much he needed a refuge from *her*.

"Not at all, Miss Elizabeth," he lied. He watched as Martha exited the room, and a sense of excitement began to grow in his chest. He was alone with her in a dark library, only lighted by the fire roaring behind her. Nobody else in the house was even awake, and the servant had left them. Was this the moment? Was fate giving him an opportunity to admit to her all he thought—all he felt?

No.

No.

Coffee.

"May I?"

She did not answer, but he knew he had to do something before he allowed his heart and mouth to take the helm. He strode towards the table, which sat just steps beyond the place she was standing. To his surprise, she did not let him pass, but stood still as he approached, her arms falling to her sides. Soon, he was directly in front of her, looking down into her sweet face, tilted up to his. He took another step, this time wholly into her space, and said, "Miss Elizabeth."

Still she did not move, only replied with a guttural, "Mr Darcy."

God she was beautiful. And her supple mouth was *right there.*

"May I?" *What was I asking permission for?* His thoughts had fled completely. *Where was I going before this moment? Did anything exist before this moment?*

Darcy swallowed.

Coffee. Yes, coffee.

"Black?" he finally choked out.

"Black?" she blinked.

"Or do you prefer cream and sugar?"

There. He had done it. He was a man. He had self-control, and he had done it.

She broke his gaze and looked about her to see the coffee pot and pastries on the table behind her. At that she stepped back, clearly embarrassed.

"Ah, ahem, just cream if you please," she answered. He complied, his heart racing at the thought that she might have desired his kiss as much as he had hers.

With his back to her, he was able to compose himself and school his features while he poured their respective cups. He turned about to deliver hers, only to find her in her chair, her hands occupied performing her duties to Italics. His composure fled, and he watched in delight as the two affectionately greeted one another.

"I imagine you are overjoyed to have your captain home, even if it is only for a short visit," he put forth, knowing that the subject of her betrothed was the surest way to keep their conversation in safe waters.

"*My* captain," she said on a sigh. "Yes, of course, I am happy to see Captain Wentworth again. It has been several years since he left to join the Navy, and his visits have been infrequent since."

She was quiet for some time, as if searching for the correct words. He waited silently.

"I find myself conflicted. You see, we were quite young when we made our...understanding. The first time he proposed, I rejected him firmly. My father set him across the room from me and told him that he was not to even think about marriage until he had made something of himself. Well,

Freddie was ten and I was six, so he simply said, 'That'll do, sir. I figured it would be a long engagement'."

Darcy joined in her light laughter, charmed by her little Freddie Wentworth voice as she reenacted the scene. The merriment soon faded, though, and her posture stiffened.

"Brazen little lad, eh?" Darcy forced a smile, hoping it would urge her on to the rest of the story.

"You have no idea. We ran wild through the fields every summer, always the very best of friends. He was like the son my mother never had. It was so natural to just see my life going on so with him in it forever."

"And when he proposed again..." he prompted. *Why do I feel the need to know every circumstance of their attachment? What am I hoping to learn? Am I looking for some circumvention, some way to nullify the whole thing while leaving Elizabeth free, honourably?*

Yes. Yes, he was.

"He was refused again. It was after church one Sunday, just before he was to leave Meryton to report to his first post as midshipman. I told him I still felt I was too young, and I was not ready to marry."

"How did he change your mind?"

"He did not. As the vicar came out to see the parishioners off, he pulled me to him and kissed me square on the mouth in front of the whole congregation, declaring, 'There, now you *have* to marry me!' You can imagine how my father reacted to that scene."

Darcy's eyes flashed with anger at hearing this confession. She was *forced* to attach herself to this man? Surely, she could not be expected to marry such a scoundrel.

"I see that you can," Elizabeth offered, no doubt noting the fury in his brow. "We can laugh about it now; it was so long ago. Suffice it to say, Freddie spent the better part of the afternoon behind my father's library door being told exactly how he was to treat me from that day forwards. As is to be expected, it has since been understood throughout Meryton that we are destined for one another."

"You never actually accepted him? Yet you can think on him with affection?" Darcy asked in disbelief. He had leant forwards in his chair again, so eager was he to understand the situation. How could a woman like Elizabeth Bennet acquiesce to such a farce of a proposal? She who mesmerised all whom she met. She who could have her choice of men among the highest set of society with her glittering presence and sparkling countenance. She who had unlocked the vault in which lay his guarded heart and gently come to possess it so completely.

Elizabeth was silent. Her mouth kept opening as if she would speak, but soon it would close again without saying anything. In her face was the same worry he had seen there the day before, after she had bid Captain Wentworth farewell.

Is she trying to reveal the secret to which she has been alluding? What can it be? How can it concern me? Will she ever say?

CHAPTER TWENTY-THREE

Elizabeth was attempting to find the words to explain herself, but they would not come. How could she tell him that their supposed understanding was cemented by Frederick 'compromising' her when she was all of nine years old? How could she tell the great Mr Darcy of Pemberley the whole circumstance without him feeling himself the victim of some elaborate practical joke? That, she knew, would hurt him more than anything. Tears began to well up as she tried to force herself to speak.

Her expression, the worry and fear in it, must have pricked Darcy to the heart, for it seemed he could not allow her to continue in such misery.

"Miss Elizabeth," he said soothingly, "I can see that you feel you must explain yourself to me in some way. Please, be assured you owe me nothing. However, if I can be of any help by hearing you, know that it would be my honour to do so."

"You will despise me," she was finally able to whisper.

"Despise you? *You*?" At this, he leant into the space that

separated them and reached out his long arm to place a hand on hers. "Elizabeth, nothing you could say could make me despise you. We have not known one another long, but I believe you may be the truest friend I have ever had. You have my full and complete trust." His consoling declaration only increased Elizabeth's wretchedness, making her watery eyes begin to pour.

She looked at their hands, and the images she had begun to entertain of them sharing such intimate touches, his bare hands on hers, struck her with a regret of such force that she felt she might be sick. She could do naught but flee from the library and from his company before she made even more of a fool of herself than she already had.

Upstairs, Elizabeth took several deep breaths before entering the bedroom she shared with Jane, only to see her beautiful sister being attended by Miss Bingley's lady's maid. Her colour had returned. In her fine gown and with a blooming countenance, Jane was lovely. Elizabeth could not help but think about how enraptured Mr Bingley would be upon meeting her this morning. At least her Jane still had the hopes of winning the heart and hand of the man she loved. *She* would not suffer heartbreak from this visit.

Elizabeth was not inclined to go down and sit at the break-fast table as if nothing had happened, but she knew it would be rude to miss the meal on their last day. After all of Mr Bingley's hospitality, she had no wish to give offence.

Yardley touched up her hair, Elizabeth dressed herself properly, and she and her sister walked to the dining room.

Awaiting them were the gentlemen. All three rose, then bowed their good mornings, but only Mr Bingley walked about the table to greet them personally. The chair next to Mr Darcy, he pulled out for Elizabeth, clearly not imagining she would wish to sit anywhere else. Then Mr Bingley offered Jane his arm and escorted her to the other side, pulling out the chair nearest himself so that he might dance constant attendance upon her. Though contented to see this, Elizabeth dreaded her own circumstance.

Mr Darcy was an accommodating neighbour at breakfast, serving her and not demanding conversation. He simply smiled encouragingly and endeavoured to make small talk. He could not know how his kind solicitude stung.

BREAKFAST WAS A QUIET AFFAIR, WITH THE BINGLEY sisters joining them halfway through the meal. Miss Bingley nodded a formal greeting to Darcy, dripped a syrupy good morning to the Bennet ladies, and shot Mr Bingley a cold glare replaced quickly by a false smile. She mercifully refrained from either attacking Elizabeth or flattering himself.

Evidently, his conversation with Bingley had had some impact.

"I have just been informed you two are leaving us today. We are simply desolated to be robbed of such pleasant company. How we have enjoyed having you," Miss Bingley said with exaggerated feeling.

"We are indebted to you and your brother for your kind hospitality," Miss Bennet replied, clearly taking the woman's words as true expressions of friendship.

"It was nothing. You must know it was no trouble at all, Miss Bennet," Bingley assured his angel.

The lovers gazed at one another for a moment as if the room, nay the world, were devoid of all but themselves.

Darcy was not fool enough to deny that the two shared an affection, but something in him still held to the conviction that the match would not be a good one for his friend. Watching them regard one another put him in mind to hie Bingley off to London for a week and reintroduce him to some of the more suitable 'angels' with whom he was acquainted. He must do so soon—before his friend became so besotted that he made a declaration he would come to regret.

Darcy was so distracted by this line of thought that he was startled by a knock on the door and the butler's voice as he introduced Captain Wentworth.

"DO FORGIVE ME, MR BINGLEY; I DID NOT INTEND TO encroach upon your breakfast. How do you do?" Captain Wentworth made a cheerful bow, which was acknowledged rightly by all at table. "Miss Elizabeth," he said with a nod before turning his attention to her sister. "Miss Bennet, how relieved I am to see you looking so well. I promised Miss Elizabeth that I should accompany her on a walk later today, but I find myself unable to keep my word. However, as you are both here, I should like to tell you my happy news. That is, if your host does not object."

He turned towards Mr Bingley expectantly.

Bingley stood, entreating him to share anything he wished and implored, "By all means, have a seat."

"I thank you, but I cannot. I have time only to tell my dear friends that the year twelve is looking to be a very good one for me, for by February, I shall be a married man!"

The gasps from the ladies were as expected and satisfactory, but the one from the taller gentleman came as a surprise. Frederick noted Mr Darcy staring hard at Elizabeth. Turning his eye to her, he noted a fierce blush as she attempted to force a smile and join Jane in her congratulations.

"Miss Elizabeth, I am sure, will be glad to have my ill-timed advances come to an end," Wentworth said as he took her in, "and I shall relish the thought of never being dragged anywhere by the ear again. I hope you will forgive me for breaking our *engagement*."

"I release you," Elizabeth said in less than buoyant tones whilst still attempting sanguinity, "with all my heart."

"You have been desiring to say that since you were nine years old, I am sure. I did not give you much choice then. What an undisciplined rogue I was—how you could ever deign to remain friends, I cannot fathom."

Both Bennet women stood to shake his hand and wish him joy. Mr Darcy, however, left the room without a word, and Elizabeth watched him go with an anxious expression. Mr Bingley soon chimed in with his own well-wishes, while Miss Bingley and Mrs Hurst simply sat, exchanging a triumphant glance before smirking in the general direction of Elizabeth. Wentworth took all this in, but was lamentably too behindhand to investigate.

"I am told that we shall meet again this evening at Long-bourn. I will be able to tell you all about it over supper, I am sure."

And with that, Captain Wentworth was off, wondering what could make Elizabeth so miserable. She could not still be holding a candle for him, could she? No, she seemed genuinely happy for him behind her troubled eyes.

What, then, could it be? *And what can it have to do with Mr Darcy?*

CHAPTER TWENTY-FOUR

U pon arriving home that afternoon, Jane and Elizabeth were introduced to their cousin, William Collins, who had been recently ordained and was serving a parish in Kent. This was the dreaded heir, the one to whom Longbourn would pass upon their father's demise. He had always been 'that odious man' when mentioned; Elizabeth could not imagine what circumstance could have made him welcome in their home.

She was soon enlightened.

For many minutes, he beamed at Jane with admiring eyes, as had any number of men before him. But, after a short conference with Mrs Bennet, those same admirations began to be directed towards that woman's next eldest daughter. Elizabeth had noted this shift with acute horror; she was in too much tumult of emotions to deal graciously with the attentions of the obsequious man intent on stalking about after her. She soon claimed a sick headache and, begging Mary to entertain their guest in her stead, fled to the solitary comfort of her chambers.

With the doors closed behind her, she continued to contemplate the implications of what had occurred that morning.

Freddie is engaged.

She no longer had to fear him asking for her hand and the pain she might have had to inflict by refusing him. How that weight had been pressing upon her hour after hour since his arrival, and now it was lifted.

But another weight, the weight of Mr Darcy's disapprobation—no, more than that, his feeling of betrayal—began to oppress her. She would never forget his expression when Frederick made his announcement; he was shocked, then confused, then tragically not confused at all. It was as if he were the last one to understand the joke, and he felt it was on him. Her duplicity had been exposed, and it had hurt him. Bricks were being laid between them, a wall going up that would prove too high to surmount. The hurt on his countenance, though fleeting, had wrenched Elizabeth's heart. The true pain, however, came when that affliction was replaced with the stony, practised indifference he wore for those about whom he cared nothing.

She could not trust his words of the morning.

"Nothing you could say could make me despise you," he had sworn. He had called her his truest friend, and now she would be considered his falsest. Their entire relationship, their place of trust, was founded upon a lie, a deception that sketched her as scheming and mercenary. And there was nothing she could do to make it better.

Promises made in absolutes are rarely kept.

Elizabeth remembered almost saying to Miss Bingley at

Netherfield that the surest way to rankle Mr Darcy would be to tease him, to laugh at him. But even voicing that, recognising aloud this chink in his armour, this fault of his pride, felt too much like a jest at his expense, and she could not mortify him so. How hearing Frederick laugh about their 'engagement' this morning must have struck him thus! If he did not dismiss her as mercenary, he would surely brand her a heartless harlequin intent on making a mockery out of him.

After turning the situation over in her mind for far too long, Elizabeth's head truly did begin to ache. She had not slept the night before, and her early rising and the subsequent events had taken their toll. Soon, she was deep in slumber, a black, dreamless place where neither concerned voices, nor fireplaces, nor striped cats, nor dark eyes invaded her peace.

Elizabeth was just opening her swollen eyes when she heard the snick of her chamber door closing. Jane had entered, her face showing genuine worry, and informed her that Frederick was asking for her. Elizabeth looked at the clock, disoriented and confused; she could not have slept through to supper. No, it was only half past three. What could he need?

Entering the drawing room, it was obvious from his dishevelled appearance that he was in some great distress.

"Freddie, what can be the matter?" Elizabeth ran to him and grasped his hands, searching his red-rimmed eyes.

"She has thrown me off. My Anne. Broken our engagement because I do not live up to her pompous father's standards." He reached into his coat and withdrew a letter, which seemed to have been crumpled and abused before being finally folded and placed there. Handing it to Elizabeth, he said, "Here, see for yourself."

Elizabeth opened the letter and read while Frederick

looked on. She saw an elegant hand and evidence of tears blotching the ink before it was dry—*her* tears. The woman, Anne Elliot, wrote of her undying affection and respect for him, then explained that after having endured the censure of her family and trusted friends, she did not feel that it would be prudent to follow through with their engagement. Her father had made it clear that he would do nothing for his daughter and had been treating her icily since their announcement. Her friend Lady Russell, it seemed, had begged her to look at things from a standpoint of reason, and Anne could not but agree that becoming attached to a man, however brilliant and deserving, who had only himself to recommend him, who had not an income to support a wife, nor yet a place to keep her, could not be capable of success.

Elizabeth's anger at Miss Elliot's lack of resolve softened a little as she read the last paragraph, wherein she explained that she could not be persuaded to relinquish him were she not convinced that it was in his best interest, that he would ultimately be happier because of her decision. Bidding him every wish of success and assuring him of her lasting affection, Anne Elliot closed the missive with a signature hardly legible for the tears it had sustained.

No longer capable of meditating on her own affliction, Elizabeth threw herself into the comfort of her friend. She ordered them tea, then sat near him on the sofa while he told her about his Anne: how they had met, what had attracted him to her, how he had courted her and convinced her of the certainty of success they would have together, how she would help him on to greatness, and he would care for her with every breath. Listening to Frederick—once all knees and elbows, now a well-formed Captain Wentworth of the Royal Navy—as he spoke in his deep voice things so tender and hopeful, Elizabeth could not help but feel what a distinction it would be to be pursued thus by a man of such worth.

How could Miss Elliot break his heart so? Elizabeth was determined not simply to share his pain but to ease it. Thus, she sat with him and commiserated with him and cried for him until it was time to dress for supper.

IN HIS CHAMBERS AT NETHERFIELD, DARCY WAS AGAIN attempting to finish some correspondence, and again, his tasks were interrupted by thoughts of Miss Elizabeth Bennet and what a fool she had made of him. Was she even now teasing him, laughing at him with her sister? How much of the supposedly sanguine Miss Jane Bennet's serenity was put on? Was she, too, a cunning mercenary, triumphing in her victory over his friend's heart?

Well, Miss Elizabeth would not crow over *him*. Her designs had been found out, and he had escaped her wiles. He wondered how she had planned to extricate herself from her supposed 'engagement' if the man had not conveniently shown up. Would she have pretended to receive a letter from this Wentworth, calling it all off? Would she have claimed that the captain had been lost at sea and looked to Darcy for comfort in her grief? There was no telling to what depths such a practised beguiler would stoop in the effort to gain her objective.

No doubt his poor sister had felt the same connexion to George Wickham. Georgiana had been fully convinced of his sincerity and his heart's affection. His friendship, like Elizabeth's, had been a worthless counterfeit, a paste diamond, pernicious and deceptive and brilliant.

Some part of Darcy pleaded with him to be more generous. Had he and Elizabeth not spent many hours conversing, sharing stories of their upbringings, laughing over anecdotes of silly sisters and meddling mothers, relating on a level of intellect and insight that could not be feigned? Could he really have been just an object to her, something to be gained no matter the cost? A life of luxury and ease—silk gowns, pin money, carriages, and the consequence of his exalted name?

That generous part also pleaded: whatever she may have been at the start, what if she had developed true feelings for him? She certainly seemed to be genuinely overcome as she tried to tell him whatever it was she had struggled to say. She could have been attempting to tell him how young she and Wentworth had been when their sham of an engagement had come about, that she had lied to him and now felt regret. Even then, if she were attempting to confess her dastardly designs and profess a change of heart, could that wash away the avarice that had given rise to their relationship?

No. This was his own fault. He had fallen for the schemes of a fortune hunter. Or worse, a bored maiden interested only in making him a laughingstock. Perhaps she had had a change of heart when she had thought she might actually win him, but the facts remained.

She was false, and he was a fool.

CHAPTER TWENTY-FIVE

Frederick, having spent the afternoon at Longbourn in a state of acute misery, imposed upon Mr Bennet that he might make use of his rooms to clean up before supper. After some personal time with a basin of steaming water and a freshly stropped razor, he was ready to present himself to his hostess as the genial naval captain once more. As he had passed the blade over his face, stroke after stroke, the rhythm had soothed and lulled him into a state of peace he hoped would last the evening.

His time with Elizabeth had been truly comforting. She had, as always, proved to be a most loyal friend. It was only after an hour of pouring out his anguish that he had begun to understand why she was so moved. She knew what he was feeling firsthand. Indeed, his heartache was hardly an hour fresher than her own.

When he had finally released every thought he had had of Anne and his pain, he had managed to cajole her own feelings from her. Just as he had suspected after the scene that morning, it was Mr Darcy over whom she was so forlorn. As it happened, he himself was indirectly the cause of their rift.

Elizabeth had insisted that the distance now existing between herself and Darcy could not be traversed. She had deceived him, and disguise of every sort was his abhorrence. His resentment was implacable, she claimed; he could never forgive her.

Wentworth could only think of how angry he was that Anne had forsaken him, and yet how desperately he loved her and how readily he would forgive her if she asked it of him. If this Mr Darcy truly loved Elizabeth, he would find it in himself to overlook this folly. And Frederick would do all in his power to bring them back together.

First, though, he had to get a measure of the man's feelings.

Not surprisingly, Mr Bingley came to supper at Longbourn alone that evening. Mr Darcy, it seemed, was out of sorts and unable to accompany him, and Miss Bingley generously stayed home to nurse her elder sister through a sick headache. Of Mr Hurst, not a word was said. This worked out well for Jane and Elizabeth, as Bingley was the one gentleman of the Netherfield party of whom both would welcome the sight.

Upon seeing Wentworth, Bingley greeted him with a cheerful, "Here is the lucky man. Captain Wentworth, how do you do?" As the captain drew nearer, Bingley's sunny countenance fell. "I say, are you well?"

"How very astute you are, Bingley. I have had a letter from Somersetshire, and I am afraid it has caused a breach," Wentworth answered quietly.

"Dashed bad luck," Bingley empathised, patting him on the shoulder. "I am more sorry than I can say."

"No great loss," he lied. "I am determined to think on it no more tonight. I am here among old friends and new, and I could not be happier." He donned his usual jaunty demeanour and strode with Bingley towards the dining room to join the ladies and their cousin, Mr Collins.

Wentworth had to admit that the parson was a wonderful distraction with his sanctimonious speeches on morality in the military and the constant comparisons of everything he saw, heard, or tasted to what he had experienced at the hand of Lady Catherine de Bourgh. His patroness was evidently a rather prominent personage in her native county of Kent. Upon Wentworth's declaration that he had never heard of the woman, Mr Collins went from a state of utter and almost angry shock to a conviction that he must acquaint the poor captain with all her amiable qualities, her kindly bestowed condescension, and the many favours she had in her gift.

In the midst of one of the man's long-winded speeches, Miss Lydia piped up to speak over him, beseeching Mr Bingley, "Did you not promise to hold a ball at Netherfield?" Affronted by such a rude interruption, it appeared Mr Collins's dignity would not allow him to speak further.

"I do not remember making such a promise, but I will do so happily. Pray, when would be a good day for you, Miss Lydia?" He smiled at Jane, and Wentworth noted the look of joyful anticipation on her face.

"Hmm...the twenty-sixth of November!"

"That is too soon, Lydia," her eldest sister chided. "Can you not give him more time to arrange things?"

"No, no, Miss Bennet, that is perfectly sufficient. I have long been desiring to entertain at Netherfield and to dance again with the lovely Miss Bennets. I shall have Nicholls prepare the white soup."

Cheers went up from almost all the females in the party, and the rest of their time at table was spent discussing the ball —meaning, of course, gowns, lace, and new white gloves. Bingley listened with clear delight as the young ladies gushed over the prospect of an evening's elegant entertainment. Elizabeth was a bit less enthusiastic, but wore a smile nonetheless.

As supper was being cleared away and the ladies retired to the drawing room, Frederick stared at the glass of port he held between himself and the fire. Bingley asked him what he intended to do now.

"I believe I shall stay in Hertfordshire another fortnight. Say, Mr Bennet, have you ever taken up shooting? Or do you still prefer hunting books to birds?" he asked the older man.

"In truth, I detest almost any activity that involves leaving my study. Of course, for God and country and all that," he noted, bowing his head to the parson who sat at the far end of the table. Collins gave him a solemn nod of acknowledgment in return.

"Well, I do not sail until the first week of December. I dare say I could convince Mr Bingley here to take me out."

"Of course," Bingley agreed enthusiastically.

"Besides, I cannot leave before the ball," he added with forced cheerfulness.

"Shall you stay with your aunt?" Bingley enquired.

"No, no, she cannot accommodate me. Meryton has a fine inn and a first-rate tavern. I shall be quite comfortable there."

"By no means," Bingley exclaimed. "You must come to Netherfield. The guest quarters are freshly made up, and your company would be much appreciated. Indeed, Darcy and I are both keen to hear about your escapades, and we shall do all in our power to make your stay pleasant, keep your mind off things."

"If you are certain you do not mind," Wentworth replied, nodding his acceptance, "I thank you."

CHAPTER TWENTY-SIX

D arcy, usually the first of their small set to awaken, was surprised to find the dining room already occupied when he entered. When the newspaper that had obscured its occupant was lowered, Darcy was nigh on shocked to meet the eyes of Captain Frederick Wentworth.

"Ah, Mr Darcy, good morning. I hope you like strong coffee; I asked cook to...intensify it, if you will."

"If she made it even stronger than I already take it, I wonder that your spoon did not stand up in it," Darcy answered, taking his seat, determined not to reveal his disquietude at meeting the captain again, and in such close quarters.

Darcy had spent the evening in, attempting to convince himself of his having been the victim of the schemes of a fortune hunter, not the innocent bystander of an unwitting injurer, as Elizabeth's tears had indicated. His heart desired desperately to absolve her of her trespasses, but history had taught him that deceivers and mercenaries could give every proof of innocence. His childhood friend Wickham had showed him that in a way that still pained him.

Literally.

And here was the man whom he had become so comfortable despising, the one who had been there first, the one who had upset all his dreams of future happiness. He could see now that Captain Wentworth was no villain; he was simply the tool Miss Bennet had used to wedge herself into his good graces.

"I would not know," declared Wentworth regarding the stir-spoon, "I take it black."

"A man after my own heart." Darcy raised an eyebrow and his cup in salute before taking his first sip of the black tar the Jack Tar had poured him. A hard swallow and a quick grimace, and his palate was acclimated to the point where he could drink the rest without revulsion. The captain laughed at his response, then nodded with respect as Darcy continued to imbibe.

"You were not expecting to see me here this morning, I dare say, but your affable Mr Bingley is a most generous friend. I found myself inclined to remain in Hertfordshire for a bit, and he was kind enough to invite me to stay at Netherfield," Wentworth volunteered.

"Indeed, I was not, but it does not follow that your presence is unwelcome. I must say, however, I had expected you would be eager to return to your betrothed."

"Ah yes, bad luck that. As I mentioned to Bingley, I find myself relieved of my obligations in that quarter. Received some information from Somersetshire which, unfortunately, meant I must sever the attachment." The captain, though disciplining himself to sound sanguine, was clearly brought low by this circumstance.

Darcy did not know how to reply and so remained silent, save for a concerned expression and a small grunt of empathy. How ironic, he thought, that the very man whom he had imagined had kept him from Elizabeth, the man whom he had wanted so badly to deplore, was now suffering exactly the same malady as himself. Their ladies had proved untrue, their characters not what they claimed. And he and Wentworth had both escaped their wiles before it was too late. He wondered if his companion would see it that way.

"Which is why I do not rush back westward as had been my intention. Instead, I stay on here, and I find myself quite aching to be out of doors," said Wentworth. "Shall we have any sport today, do you know?"

"I do not know. My only aim for the morning is to post some letters. I could send a servant, but I find it refreshing to ride out and do it myself. Are you a horseman, Captain?"

"I admit I am better at steering a ship than a steed, but I can hold my own."

"Perhaps we shall ride together, then?"

Hours later, with Bingley in tow, the three men set out from Netherfield towards Meryton on horseback. After Darcy's trying night, he wanted nothing more than a punishing run through the fields and hills, but his companions were interested in something more sedate. Thus, they trotted over the well-worn roads into town.

As if overnight, the main causeway had become practically flooded with redcoats. The small militia regiment appeared to have swelled with new recruits. Darcy thought of how giddy this might make the silly young Bennet girls, and no sooner had it entered his mind than the very creatures entered his line of sight.

Bingley, upon espying his angel amidst a small crowd, led them towards her directly. All five sisters were there, along with two officers and two other men, one of whom wore the black garb of a curate. From his seat high above them all, Darcy was unable to make out the faces of the gentlemen. When Miss Bennet saw Bingley, she offered him a dazzling smile, while her next sister cast her blushing face down, hidden from view beneath a straw bonnet.

Darcy was beset by clamouring emotions at the sight of her. He was awash with the usual gladness and relief he habitually felt at having her near. Almost immediately, however, he became laden with indignation over her transgressions against him. His gaze lingered only seconds before Wentworth dismounted and strode towards her, bowing over her hand and asking to be introduced to the gentlemen in their group.

The sensation creeping over him as the captain greeted Elizabeth so familiarly was new to him—it was uncomfortable, it was yearning, and it was almost angry.

I cannot be jealous, surely.

Darcy watched them. The captain was no longer engaged. Might he seek solace in Elizabeth? Might he wish to rekindle their former intimacy? The knot in his stomach forming at the thought only tightened as he listened to her next words.

"Captain Wentworth," Elizabeth's melodious voice began, "this is Captain Denny and his good friend, Mr George Wickham. Mr Wickham is to be a lieutenant in Colonel Forster's regiment. They are to be stationed in Meryton for the winter."

At the sound of that name, Darcy's full attention and the full height of his ire were immediately directed towards the man who owned it. *George Wickham.* He shot the man a look of such fury that it could not be mistaken by any in their two parties. In return, the blackguard had the nerve to smirk and tip his hat to him, casually brushing his hand against his left shoulder as he lowered his arm. That was the last straw.

Would that I carried a pistol, Darcy grumbled within himself.

Without bothering to take his leave, Darcy turned his horse and rode away, finding the edge of the town and fulfilling his desire for that hard and fast ride over the fields.

"WHO EXACTLY IS THIS WICKHAM FELLOW?" Wentworth asked Darcy as soon as the two were alone together that afternoon.

Bingley had chosen to stay in the company of the Bennet ladies, and Frederick had followed them all back to Long-bourn, staying just long enough to pay his respects to Mrs Bennet before returning to Netherfield. Bingley, however, was in no such rush to return.

He had found Darcy wool-gathering in the library. It seemed that the perfectly disciplined gentleman had already had a few fingers of brandy. His face was a month of wet Sundays. Naturally, Wentworth poured himself a glass as well, hoping he could get to know Elizabeth's beloved while his guard was down.

"He is an unprincipled rogue of the lowest order. A seducer and a slanderer and a thorn in my side," Darcy answered without hesitation, glowering unseeing into the flames.

Wentworth had assumed it would take a bit of liquid persuasion before the quiet man would open up; apparently he had imbibed enough, for Darcy soon continued. "He was the son of my late father's steward and a favourite with all. He learnt how to wrap people about his finger from a very young age, and even my father, wise though he was, was not immune to his wiles. My father left him a generous living upon his death, which the blackguard spurned in lieu of ready cash. And how has he repaid him? By injuring his children in a way I cannot even speak of." The hurt behind Darcy's sneer was unmistakable.

"I wonder if Colonel Forster knows he has such a rapscallion among his ranks."

"He cannot know. As I said, male or female, all are bewitched with the charming George Wickham. I am sure he has sold his hard-luck tale to his commanding officers to obtain their pity and favour, just as he has in every other area of his life thus far."

"Hard-luck tale? He has suffered much misfortune, then?" Wentworth prodded.

"Oh, yes, his misfortune has been great indeed. Educated alongside me, raised with every conceivable advantage, even supported through Cambridge by my father. Given the opportunity of an income that would have sustained him for life. But, no, he chose to spurn such generosity and spend every farthing of his inheritance—all told amounting to *four thousand pounds*—squandered no doubt in brothels and gaming hells. And when that was gone, he insinuated himself back into my life in a manner so painful—" Darcy's eyes were a storm beneath knitted brows, his mouth a grim line of fury as he contemplated the parts of the story he was unable to finish.

Wentworth could see no pretence in the gentleman's air, and there was clearly more to the account than Darcy was willing to share. Something roiled beneath the surface, and Wentworth recognised that he was not yet in a position to draw it up. He wondered how much of the defensive wall he had perceived in the gentleman had to do with this constant source of treachery.

And how could he use this knowledge to help Elizabeth?

CHAPTER TWENTY-SEVEN

The following evening, the Bennet family were guests in Mr and Mrs Philips's home in Meryton. Several officers, along with Colonel Forster and his young wife, had been invited to make up the party of dinner and cards. Elizabeth was glad of the distraction, though she was unsure how she should behave towards one particular officer in the party after having seen the reception he had been given by a gentleman she so respected.

As the evening wore on, she found herself again and again in company with Mr Wickham. He was the fortunate man to whom almost every female in the room directed her attention. He had all the best parts of beauty—a fine countenance, a good figure, and a pleasing address. Added to all this, he possessed a happy readiness of conversation. This combination of pleasant attributes eventually resigned Elizabeth to his company, and she found herself less and less inclined to evade his attention.

"Have you known Mr Darcy long?" he enquired when

they were outside of the hearing of others. "I only ask because...you must have noticed the coolness of our greeting."

"Indeed, I did," she said with a touch of embarrassment. "I have not known Mr Darcy long, perhaps six weeks, but we have often been in one another's company." She was not sure how much she should reveal to this new acquaintance, as it seemed evident that his views on the gentleman might be rather different from her own. Her expression must have betrayed her positive opinion of the man, for his next question was made in an almost incredulous tone.

"You do not find him arrogant and above his company as your sister Miss Lydia does?"

"Some might find him aloof, but I, myself, do not. We get on well enough. And, as far as wealth, rank, connexions, and education, I dare say he *is* above his company. In stature, indeed, for he is half a head taller than most gentlemen in the neighbourhood." She hoped her attempt at humour would discourage the gentleman from continuing along this negative path.

It did not.

"True, true," Mr Wickham replied. "I am glad you do not find him disagreeable. I suppose I am just speaking out of bitterness..." Thus, without taking a breath, the handsome lieutenant went on to regale her with what she could only call his tale of woe. Raised with love by Mr Darcy's father, even supported by him at Eton and on through Cambridge, Mr Wickham had every prospect of living a respectable and comfortable life. The elder Mr Darcy had intended him for the church and even promised him a valuable living as soon as it became vacant. Alas, when the father died, the son, jealous and vengeful, withheld the living from him and gave it to another man. "And so, here you find me. A poor foot soldier

with barely enough to live on," he concluded, clearly anticipating Elizabeth's sincerest sympathy.

"So, after his father died, he gave you nothing of what that
gentleman intended for you?" she asked, astonished that the
honourable Mr Darcy could even be accused of such baseness.

"A paltry sum, hardly enough to survive. Of course, he
was never intending for me to be around long enough to
receive it. Indeed, Darcy's last treachery towards me was
much worse than his first. He wishes me dead, you know.
Tried to kill me himself." His final words were whispered, but
Elizabeth could not restrain a loud gasp.

"He what?" she replied in a hushed, frenzied tone.

"That brute circulated a rumour about me, libel so diabol-
ical that if true, I would have deserved every ounce of his ire. I
shall not repeat it; it would not be proper for a lady such as
yourself to hear. Then, as soon as his slander was well-known,
he had the audacity to call me out."

"Mr Darcy challenged you to a duel over an accusation he
himself created?" She could not believe it. The Darcy she
knew—the man who so detested lies—would never commit
such calumny, especially not with a view to taking a man's
life.

"Oh yes, that was his aim all the time. He has wanted me
out of the way since I was a lad; his father favoured me over
him from a very young age, and he has always teemed with
jealousy. He missed my heart by just a few inches, and my
bullet caught him in the leg. I am surprised he was even
walking when he arrived in Hertfordshire—that was in
September, was it not?"

Elizabeth could not form a response; her thoughts were
too full of a miserable Mr Darcy, wincing in pain as he
hitched through the Meryton Assembly.

All of this.

Could it be that all of this was a result of an injury Mr Darcy had sustained in a duel?

No, she thought. *No, it cannot be!*

Elizabeth's head reeled with disbelief. She peered into Lieutenant Wickham's countenance in an effort to search out any indication of prevarication or malice. She saw none. The man was perfectly ingenuous, never grasping for words or weaving about details. There was truth in his looks as he proffered names and facts, all mentioned without ceremony.

This was disorienting indeed. She had always prided herself on her ability to read people, but this man was an enigma—how could he speak things so shocking, so out of character about Mr Darcy, of all people, and without the smallest hint of cunning?

Elizabeth felt compelled to defend the man who held her heart. "This does not sound like the gentleman I know, Mr Wickham. You astonish me exceedingly."

"I am sure it does not. Among those he views as worthy, he can be pleasant, generous, amiable even. You will have no such report from his servants or his tenants, for he values nothing more than the Darcy name, and with that name brings the obligation to treat those beneath him as his father did. Indeed, this familial pride often leads him to be liberal and generous; to give his money freely, to display hospitality, assist his tenants, and relieve the poor. And, as I said, his father was one of the best men who ever breathed, so he must maintain that outward show of liberality, no matter how he despises them internally. And I assure you, Miss Elizabeth, despise them he does. Every last one of them."

This, Elizabeth *knew* to be wrong. Had Mr Darcy not practically rhapsodised over his Mrs Reynolds and how pleased he was to have her in the service of his family? This claim must be false. Still, the look of unimpeachable verity in the lieutenant's countenance could not but abrade her confidence.

Elizabeth hesitated to advocate for the absent gentleman and risk hearing yet more vehement claims of his heartlessness, some of which might cause her resolve to totter. She therefore extricated herself from the uncomfortable conversation as elegantly as she was able and drew nearer her eldest sister. She longed to be home that she might acquaint her with these claims and have Jane's good opinion of Mr Darcy soothe her worries and put out the small flames of doubt Mr Wickham had so skilfully set.

And she *must* speak to Mr Darcy.

"SURELY YOU DO NOT CREDIT THIS TALE?" JANE'S FACE was wrought with the confusion that overcomes one who cannot allow either side of an evil to be truly guilty. "But, then, why should Mr Wickham invent such dreadful slander?"

"Can it be that Mr Darcy has been acting a part? Pretending to be a man of principle, claiming to abhor deceit, disguising his true character all the while?" Elizabeth gave voice to the worries she had been inwardly entertaining throughout the evening. She had related Mr Wickham's words as faithfully as she could remember, and they had affected Jane as they had herself—disbelief, astonishment, and anxiety for Mr Darcy's good reputation.

"I cannot believe that of such a fine gentleman," she answered. "Think of how well you know him. You know how honourable he is. You see the prodigious amount of care he takes of Mr Bingley and of his own young sister. You have heard him in unguarded moments. Surely your keen eye would have picked up on such inconsistency of character. No, Mr Wickham must be mistaken."

"Not about everything, I know. I saw Mr Darcy's agony the night of the Meryton Assembly. He was in real and true pain. He even told me he had been shot."

"He told you he was shot?" Jane cried. "You said he was injured in a riding accident—a horseshoe or some such thing?"

"He did. I thought it was a joke; indeed, I teased him over it. It was only after I made it clear that I would not believe it that he told me of the ill-shod horse."

"Poor Mr Darcy. This cannot be so. I hate to speak ill of anybody, but I simply cannot believe Mr Wickham's story to be true. No doubt he has been deceived himself."

Elizabeth loved that Jane would continue, despite all evidence, to attempt to acquit Mr Wickham of wilful perfidy. But Elizabeth could not. The more she thought about it, the clearer it was to her that the lieutenant's accusations were patently false.

Still, there *was* more to the story. She did not know if it was her place to ask for all the facts, but she had to bring this to Mr Darcy's attention—if for no other reason than to inform him of the rumours that would soon be circulating about him in Meryton. And to allow him to deal with his accuser in the way he would think best.

She had convinced herself that this was the only motive in her intention to seek him out the next morning. She had seen his expression, the frigid glare, and she knew he would not be receiving her attentions in the friendly manner to which she had become accustomed. Perhaps if he knew she had his best interests at heart, he would realise she truly was his friend.

If nothing else.

Elizabeth was ready to blow out the candle when Jane spoke up. "I need not fear that you are entertaining the thought of accepting Mr Collins, do I?"

"Mr Collins? Never," she answered in horror. "To what does this question tend?"

"He has been paying you marked attentions, and I am afraid you have been too distracted to notice. I wonder, if you were more vocal with him, might it dissuade him before he declares himself? I would hate to see him disappointed."

Could Jane be correct? Elizabeth had often over the last two days looked up from some abstracted reverie or another to see the parson hovering nearby or staring at her from across the room. At each meal, Mr Collins had contrived to sit next to her. She had not given him the least encouragement, but, considering it, he did not seem like the type of man who needed any.

"You are correct, I suppose; I have been doing my best to ignore him," Elizabeth said. Upon reflection, she added, "I thought Mary was meant to marry a clergyman."

"I do not think Mr Collins is aware of that, though I have seen them in conference over Fordyce more than once. That is an idea, though. Do you think she really likes him?"

"I think she would certainly accept his suit if it was given," Elizabeth offered. "Perhaps, with a little help, we could divert his attentions in hopes of a happier ending?"

Jane did not like anything that hinted at subterfuge, but if Mary were truly interested in their cousin, she was happy to help bring them together. As for Elizabeth, her thoughts were consumed with the conversation she must have with Mr Darcy on the morrow. She could only think she might need a distraction in the coming week should that interview not go as she hoped.

Hope. What was it she hoped for? The best she could hope was that he would apprehend her sincere concern for his good name. There was no reason to hope he would renew their friendship, nor indeed that he would ever respect her again. And there was certainly no hope that he would once more look at her as he had in the library only days before.

CHAPTER TWENTY-EIGHT

D arcy's only wish this morning was to leave the teeming market without being noticed, especially by one pair of eyes, however fine they might be. He had done his duty to the locals—inspecting each stall and handing over coin for anything he thought he might use—and now he desired nothing more than to retire with a book, a brandy, and an attentive cat. Ah, the library—what a sanctuary that had become for him. Always comfortable and warm, full of good wine and intelligent conversa— *Gah!* He could not even escape her without running right smack into her the next moment.

It was while he was looking over a sea of straw hats and silk bonnets and lamenting the sluggishness of his exit that he did just that.

He walked straight into Elizabeth Bennet, treading on her gown and pinning her to her spot. She had evidently been seeking him out, as his presence was not nearly as surprising to her as hers was to him. Still standing upon her hem, he looked upon her in distaste, despising the fact that, in all this crush, he could not deliver the set-down playing upon his tongue. Instead, he stared past her ear as he tendered a cold and clipped, "Miss Elizabeth."

"Mr Darcy, I am relieved that I caught you," she began before he interrupted her.

"No, Miss Elizabeth." He looked her squarely in the eye. "Mercifully, you did not."

At this, he forgot his gentlemanly manners and forced his way through the crowd and into a narrow alley situated between two shops. Darcy strode across a grassy clearing to reach the far tree where his horse was tied. The chestnut whinnied in the distance at his approach, clearly as eager to escape the vicinity of Meryton as his master. The din and clamour of bartering buyers faded with each footfall, and soon he was out of sight as well as earshot of the crowd. As he was mounting the beast, however, he heard Elizabeth's voice behind him call out, "Mr Wickham."

Darcy pulled his foot from the stirrup and strode towards her, careful not to give way to any feelings of concern for the wretchedness of her countenance. He looked about them, unwilling to become sport for curious locals. The trees hid them well, and it seemed most of the villagers would be returning home by way of the High Street. When his gaze shifted, he was almost face-to-face with his beautiful Judas.

"You take an eager interest in that man's concerns, do you?"

"No. But I do take an interest in yours, sir," she bit back, a battle raging in her eyes. "He has made such horrid accusations, Mr Darcy."

"*He* accuses *me*. That is rich. I suppose I should not be shocked that he gravitated towards you so quickly; peas in a pod you two are." He turned his head with a sneer, then looked back at her with mock curiosity. "Tell me, of what does he accuse me?"

"He told me that you dishonoured your father's wishes and refused him the living he was promised."

"I *refused* him the living? *He* refused to take orders. I will have you know I paid him the value of the living—out of respect for my father's wishes, not because the degenerate deserved it, mind you."

"A paltry sum, he claims," she retorted.

"A paltry sum? *Paltry*? I may not have the same perspective as others, Miss Bennet, but I believe most would find four thousand pounds a touch better than paltry." Now he was being sarcastic. He hated himself when he resorted to such pettiness, but his hackles were up; he was faced with a deceiver accusing him based on the word of another such. Both had hurt him, this one more deeply than he was willing to admit. "Now, if there is nothing else—" He gave a nod before turning back to his horse.

"That is not the worst of it," she said breathlessly.

"Dishonouring my father's dying wish and robbing an innocent man of his rightful living is not bad enough? I am to be accused of blacker deeds than this?" he asked, not ready to give up his intent to mount his steed.

"He says you wish him dead." She darted her eyes left and right as she spoke this, as if afraid others might overhear. "That you tried to kill him."

He fixed her with a hard stare, the rage he felt for the man glaring through stony eyes. "Then, for once, George Wickham has told the truth."

"You admit that you circulated a rumour so dastardly that you were able to call him out for it? You lied to everyone you knew so that you might have the excuse to murder him in a duel?"

"Is that what he told you?" He once again closed the distance between them, speaking quietly. "George Wickham was given everything. *Everything*! And it was never enough for him. It took him less than three years to squander his inheritance—I will not mention his preferred entertainments, but suffice it to say, he did not spend it on profitable pursuits—and when it was gone, he came back for more. Thirty thousand pounds more."

Elizabeth's brow wrinkled in incomprehension.

"Only last summer, Wickham engineered a plot to stumble upon my fifteen-year-old sister unprotected, convince her that she was in love with him, and elope to Scotland, thus securing her dowry."

"Of thirty thousand pounds," she breathed.

"When I caught him in the middle of this cruel, mercenary scheme, yes, I wished him dead. And, yes, I called him out."

Elizabeth stood in shocked silence.

"I would have got him, too, but the contemptible weasel had spent the night before rigging his boot so his heel would slip out from under him when he turned; lost us both a good two inches," Darcy explained with no little resentment.

"And his bullet caught you in the leg," she noted softly.

"Missed the bone and the artery, thank God. Still hurt like — At any rate, you observed how much pain I was in at the assembly," he said more gently, remembering how cared for he had felt when she had approached him and how every eye brightened as it met her that evening. Then, his countenance darkened. "Was that when you decided to make me your target?"

"My what?" Her brow was furrowed again, but her eyes were wild with outrage.

"I wonder Wickham should have tried to ply you with his lies; he should have recognised artifice like yours at first glance."

"You truly believe that? I have been only a friend to you, sacrificing my own enjoyment for your comfort, at your service at every party and assembly for weeks. And, why? Because I felt sorry for you. I thought you needed my help so badly that I was willing to be at your beck and call. I pitied you."

Darcy winced at that. It was a blow to his pride, which took the reins as he resorted to recriminations.

"Oh, I know your type. Simpering and flattering, making yourself indispensable," he said.

"Simpering and flattering? I believe you are confusing me for Miss Bingley. I would never," she claimed, her colour high and her delicate hands balled into fists at her sides.

Darcy had never seen such fire in her, and she was radiant. How he had enjoyed bantering with her. This would sadly be their last tête-à-tête; he would drink in her furious glare as long as she favoured him with it.

"And how convenient that, just when you think I might be reeled in, your sister becomes ill at Netherfield, and naturally, *you* had to come stay with her. Masterfully done, both of you." His volume was increasing as he spoke over her to make his sentiments clear.

"You accuse my sister of pretending? Jane would never do such a thing! And if I were guilty of what you are accusing me of, she would tell me plainly how wrong it was." Elizabeth scoffed, her face a study in disgusted disbelief. "You should have heard her defending your honour against Mr Wickham's claims, and this is how you view her." Her volume was rising to match his until, pleadingly, she concluded, "You know neither her nor me, sir."

"You are correct. I do not know you. I thought I did—you played your part exquisitely: sparkling and vulnerable and selfless, so charming and handsome, casting glances my way and nuzzling that blasted cat." This he punctuated with a mirthless laugh before going on. "Oh, you had me through and through, every fibre of my being. To think, I was about to go against my family, society, and I hardly need add my own better judgment. You must have seen how close I was; that is why you orchestrated that little scene in the library the morning before you left."

"*Orchestrated*? You were told I was there alone." She stepped towards him, lifting her chin. "You invited yourself into the library. *You* walked up to *me*."

"And you were completely innocent, were you?" He was towering over her again, only now in a stature of anger rather than the longing he had felt in the library that morning. "Standing in the middle of the floor, the light of the fire glowing through your skirts, revealing your shape to me so brazenly." He stepped closer and spoke quietly, intent on calling her out for her shamelessness while she listened, mortified, her colour rising. "Drawing me closer, fluttering your eyelashes, your lips inviting me to..."

"I did not— I was— I thought you—"

"Oh yes, I am sure you hoped I would," he said, his face so near hers he could feel the heat emanating from her flushed cheeks. "And you would have let me too. That would have played right into your devious little plan. Tell me, was Martha stationed outside the door to conveniently walk in and see us?"

She turned her face away sharply before turning back to him and spitting, "You blackhearted cur. If you think I could devise such a thing—"

Her nearness, her lavender scent, her fierce gaze undid him.

"And even now, now that you know what a bitter, mistrustful wretch I am," Darcy continued throatily, as if he had not heard her. Her shoulders were square in glorious defiance of his accusations, her head bent back in her refusal to relent, and her mouth—*her mouth.*

Time slowed as they observed one another, face-to-face, their bodies inches apart. The heaviness of her breathing matched his own. Her eyes went from afire with fury to wet with anguish as he bore into them with his own. Then, he made the mistake of looking at her mouth. Her full lips were parted as if in readiness to receive his, and he thought he felt her hand light upon his chest.

His ire deflated, his shoulders fell, and a yearning like nothing he had ever experienced overwhelmed him. He leant towards Elizabeth, her kiss less than a whisper away, and gave in.

"*For ten thousand a year...*" he breathed as he closed the distance between them.

The sheer force of her palm as it met his face jarred him from the daze he was in and left a ringing in his ear. His hand immediately rose to rub his red cheek, and he flexed his jaw in pain. "I thank you, Miss Bennet, for saving me from my ill-advised passions."

"How dare you, sir!" she cried, stumbling backwards. He expected her to walk away from him without another word, but within five steps, she stopped, turned back, and stated with tears in her eyes, "I admit that I misled you, and I am

177

sincerely sorry. Though none of my words were untrue, I let you come to an erroneous conclusion, and in that I was wrong. Despite what you believe, however, I had no designs on your person. Or your despicable purse. Though my motive may seem insufficient to you, it was in the service of a friend."

"Oh, the service of a friend, was it? You thought you could gain my confidence by deceit and then lead me towards one of your Hertfordshire spinsters? Which friend, I ask. Miss Lucas? Miss Long?"

He chose not to regard the pricking voice in the back of his mind telling him he was being unjust. That, perhaps, *everything* he had said had been unjust.

"No, Mr Darcy, *you*. You," she said with a heavy exhale, her countenance falling as if something inside her were giving up, "needed a friend, and I wished to be that for you. My mistake," she added, clearly plucking up her shredded courage. "I should have left you to the solace of your bitterness and disdain. You deserve one another."

CHAPTER TWENTY-NINE

E lizabeth spent that evening walking alone. She had originally been invited along with her sisters and her cousin to walk to Aunt Philips's home in Meryton, but in her rage, she had soon outstripped them all, once again leaving Mary to care for the needs of Mr Collins. This was only half intentional, as she could scarce give full notice to anything happening about her.

She was too occupied with the cascades of shame, regret, embarrassment, and fury that continually washed over her as she picked apart every word of the conversation she had had that morning with Mr Darcy.

"That stubborn, pig-headed, odious man," Elizabeth cried to herself as she squeezed her hands into fists and stamped a foot on the grass. Throwing her head back to keep the tears from falling, she growled to the air, to the trees, to everything about her. "How could he? How dare he!" She bent down and snatched up a fallen leaf, only to tear it apart bit by bit whilst biting out vituperations against the man she thought she loved.

There were no thoughts of her overwhelming disbelief that such a lovely man—one who had sat cooing to a tomcat in a candlelit library, who had so gently tried to tease the truth out of her only days before with a light hand upon hers, and whose eyes had shone as he spoke of his sister as a baby— could commit such devilry as to attempt to take another man's life. She did not give a moment's consideration to Mr Wickham's assertions, nor to Mr Darcy's explanations in his defence.

She thought only of his allegations against *her*.

'*Fitzwilliam Darcy. I thought we had established that,*' she remembered him saying with a barely-there grin. She felt again the charge that had run through her at that moment, so unfamiliar and so thrilling. *He* had engaged in flirtation, not she. He had been the one to show her particular attention, seek her out, ask for her assistance, insist on her presence. She had only ever responded to him; she had followed the age-old rule for females of her society to let his behaviour be the rule of hers. When had she forced herself upon his notice?

'*The light of the fire...showing your shape to me.*'

Her whole being became hot with shame at the memory, just as it had when he had said it. She had had no idea her appearance had been immodest, but of course, in a dark room, standing before the glowing fire, how much might he have seen? Having slipped herself into her gown without chemise or petticoat, she wore just enough for decency's sake to hurry out of the room and have her time alone. The thought of being less than fully dressed had never entered her mind when she had heard Mr Darcy's voice at the library door.

He thought she had engineered this? That it was all part of a vicious scheme to seduce him and trap him into matrimony?

'Simpering and flattering, making yourself indispensable.'

Elizabeth gritted her teeth at that insult—*what was he thinking? When did I ever?* To be accused of the type of pandering she so despised in Caroline Bingley was too degrading. She had far too much self-respect to indulge any man with such fawning and adulation.

"You must have seen how close I was," he had said. The battle waging inside her had begun again in earnest as she heard him admit that she had really touched his heart, that he was, perhaps, on the verge of declaring himself. Hope soon lost ground, however, as his final allegation dawned on her.

He had somehow twisted their meeting in the library into some avaricious scheme on her part to claim compromise. As if that had been the culmination of all her designs since the night of their first acquaintance.

'And even now...'

She could see his eyes, full of yearning and fire as they flicked down to her lips. Her stomach had plummeted, and she had become weak in the knees as his voice, so throaty and sultry, had spoken those words. Her hand had begun to float up, as if disconnected from her powers of control, to lay upon his chest. They were both breathing hard from their passionate speeches, and their breaths were mingling as he drew nearer, ever nearer. Her chin had begun to tremble as he leant forwards, just fractions of an inch from the kiss she so longed for. The tear she had been holding in slid down the side of her face as she leant her head back to accept him, anger and pride dissolving as her heart took the reins and insisted that she melt into the arms of the man she loved.

Then thunder cracked and lightning struck, tearing them apart, perhaps forever.

'For ten thousand a year...'

How dare he test her rapacity in such a humiliating manner, as though she were a common wanton who would embrace a man in wide open view merely to secure his fortune!

What did he take her for?

Looking down at her hand, she relished the sting she had suffered upon so deservedly slapping him. She only hoped her handprint made a lasting impression, literally and figuratively. She hoped he was suffering; she hoped he was bruised.

Elizabeth certainly was.

What must he think of me?

No. She refused to dwell on such questions.

He had refused to listen to her explanation and had proved how meanly he viewed her. She must not allow his wrongful accusations to influence her behaviour or her self-control. She sniffed and sighed and straightened her shoulders in a physical display of her emotional resolve. She was not made for melancholy, and she certainly would not let this fleeting sojourner tear her spirits down completely.

'Sparkling and vulnerable and selfless, so charming and handsome.'

Yes. She would regain her dignity and focus on caring for others the way she always had, without worry that he might assign her selfish motive.

She would eventually be herself again. For her own sake.

And he...would eventually leave.

CHAPTER THIRTY

The next day dawned bright and clear, a crisp chill in the November air. The men had decided to get up a small shooting party this morning, but only Bingley and Wentworth were present at the breakfast table. Indeed, Darcy had been in a brown study the entire day before, unwilling to be drawn into any conversation and unable to lift his stormy brow, and now it seemed he would not be keeping their sporting appointment.

Wentworth knew it had something to do with Elizabeth, but now was not the time to investigate.

His aim today was to find out where his host stood with regard to his childhood friend, Jane Bennet. Bingley's eyes tended to wander off to a confusing and unhappy place at any given time, and Wentworth felt that, for Bingley's sake, and Jane's, he should offer his services. Perhaps an outside perspective might help the couple see their way to joy.

Someone deserved a happy ending amid this turmoil.

Soon, Hurst joined them, the men Bingley had invited

arrived, and the party set out, dogs, guns, and servants in tow, in hopes of bagging enough birds to make dinner worth their while.

"It seems you have a favourite in Miss Bennet," Wentworth said when he and Bingley found themselves alone behind a blind. Bingley was no crack shot, and indeed did not seem much interested in becoming one, so Wentworth felt free to make conversation amidst the dogs running, the birds winging, and the other men's rifles cracking.

"She is an angel. I cannot imagine the man for whom she would not be a favourite," Bingley answered enthusiastically, setting down his gun as the captain had anticipated.

"That is true; her beauty is beyond compare. It is rumoured that you have a habit of singling her out. As her oldest friend, standing almost in the seat of a brother to her, I feel I must enquire as to your intentions." He knew he was stretching things a bit, but Bingley did not.

The gentleman's open visage turned to one of consternation.

"What is it, old man?" Wentworth asked.

"She is the loveliest creature, in character as well as countenance, and I care for her deeply. But, you see, Darcy thinks she is all wrong for me. He is afraid that making a match with such low connexions would do me a disservice in society, and I shall ultimately come to regret it."

Wentworth's fists clenched reflexively. With some effort, he relaxed and asked, "And how do you feel?"

"I feel that, having an independent income, I should be able to marry whom I choose. And my fortune—do not tell my sister I told you this—my fortune was acquired in trade, so it is not as if I have the respect of society in any case. Why should I throw away my chance of felicity for the good opinion of people who give it so unwillingly?"

"All good questions, my friend. I see that Mr Darcy wishes to protect you from being bound to a woman who would not make you happy, and I cannot but respect his concern for you." Conceding this much was painful, but Wentworth did not wish to create a conflict between Bingley and himself by straight away calling Darcy out as a presumptuous interferer.

"He is a most loyal friend. His guidance has been invaluable, and I usually take his opinion very much to heart. On this, however..." Bingley trailed off, evidently deep in thought over this matter that touched him so profoundly.

It was only moments before the man himself caught them up, and Wentworth's interview with Bingley was forced to come to an end.

So, Wentworth thought, *it is Mr Darcy who is holding Bingley back from declaring himself. And over social class.*

Anyone who knew Wentworth well would have recognised the pulsating clench in his jaw at this revelation. The same disgusting pride that had forced from his grasp his one true love was again thrust into his vision and in a situation so similar to his own that it riled him to the core. He had seen the way his childhood friend looked at Bingley, and indeed, the way he looked at her; there was no question in his mind that this was a couple very much in love. And, unlike Wentworth, Bingley had every resource they could ever need to have a long, comfortable life together. Why should Darcy be so high-handed as to separate two people so wholly unconnected to himself?

Careful not to betray his irritation towards the latecomer, he called out cheerily, "How now, Darcy?"

CHAPTER THIRTY-ONE

Jane entered the small parlour to which her father had consigned the old pianoforte. There, as usual, she found Mary practising before breakfast. They and the servants were the only ones yet about this morning, and Jane decided this would be her best chance to have a relatively private conversation with her younger sister.

"Mary, dear," she began as she took a seat upon the bench next to the purposely plain girl.

"Jane," she said with some surprise. "Good morning. You do not usually awaken this early. Are you well?"

"I am well; I only wished to speak to you on a particular subject, and I knew I would find you here," Jane assured her.

"You wish to speak to me? Why?" Mary was incredulous, and Jane was rightly chastened. She had not shown the interest in Mary that she did in Elizabeth, and it was wrong. No matter how little they shared in common, they were sisters, and Mary deserved her attention and affection just as much as the others.

"Am I mistaken, Mary, in believing that you enjoy Mr Collins's company?" she asked carefully, not wishing to embarrass her.

"Excuse me?" Mary choked, clearly shocked that her sister would speak to her on such a matter.

"I only ask because I have seen you often in conversation with our cousin, and as his purpose here has been made clear to Mama and Papa, I wonder if you are beginning to entertain...*hopes*...towards him."

"I confess that I have allowed my mind to wander to that possibility, yes," she answered guardedly, her gaze intent on her hands, which had left the ivory keys to sit firmly in her lap.

"So, if Elizabeth and I were to attempt to...help things along in that vein, would you have any objections?"

"Do you think I need helping along? Should not a sensible man, a man of God, know a sensible, God-fearing woman of education and application when he encounters one?" Mary looked earnestly into Jane's eyes as she made this argument.

"Ideally, he should. And indeed, if *you* were looking for a friend, you would see such estimable qualities and value them above all things. But men are men. They see what is on the outside before they bother to look at what is on the inside."

"Are you saying I am not pretty enough to attract him?" she fairly huffed.

"I know you are beautiful, Mary. I am saying that you are logical and pragmatic, and I believe because of these qualities, you have convinced yourself that your beauty does not matter. I am saying that, along with your talented fingers and brilliant mind, you should let him see the glory you so strive to hide." At this, she lifted a hand and pulled a taut strand of hair from her sister's severe bun and placed it to fall gracefully over her face.

"But if that is all he cares about, then is he the kind of man I should wish to marry? Someone so superficial?" Mary contested.

"Appreciating a fine face and figure does not necessarily make one superficial, my darling Mary. We were created to enjoy lovely sights, were we not? It is natural for a man to be taken with a woman's appearance, as well as her inner excellence. Did not Adam, upon first seeing Eve in all her perfection, take to waxing poetic? It is no sin. But if it makes you uncomfortable, dearest, then you must be true to yourself. And, you are right, if he cannot love you for who you are inside and out, he does not deserve you."

Moments passed as Mary seemed to contemplate her sister's assertions. Jane waited patiently, inwardly determining to show all her younger sisters more personal attention. Perhaps if she had done so for Mary earlier, she would not now be so hesitant to listen to her thoughts. At length, Mary looked up from her lap and responded.

"I take your meaning, Jane. And I know you only mean to advise me for my good. I shall meditate on what you have said," she promised. At that, feeling she had done as much as Mary would allow at present, Jane left her sister to her practise, noting that it was a touch more halting than it had been previously.

"Cousin Jane, have you seen Cousin Elizabeth? I hope she has not become ill, for she seems to be taking exceedingly long to come down." Mr Collins's grating voice could not but catch Elizabeth's ear as she strode towards the drawing room.

"I believe she will be down soon," Jane answered sweetly. "She and Mary were almost finished when I checked on them a quarter of an hour ago."

At that moment, Elizabeth stepped into the room. Starting towards her, Mr Collins's welcoming smile turned into a grimace as he saw that her hair was pulled back in a tight bun and her neck, bare of jewels, was covered by a thick chemisette, pulled high and tucked in neat, so as to hide every inch of feminine skin. Her dress was a simple linen shift, rather shapeless and a drab tan, which tended to wash every trace of colour from her complexion. Jane, too, was dressed plainly, and her face was, by design, lacking the smile that usually brightened it. Elizabeth had tried to cajole her elder sister into dulling her natural rosiness with powder, but that was too much like guile to the ever-pure Jane. Elizabeth, however, needed no cosmetic assistance to appear wan, tired, and worn—her sleeplessness the night before had accomplished that.

Behind her, dressed in a most becoming lavender muslin and with her hair in a lovely braided pile atop her head, a clearly uncomfortable Mary stepped into the room, blooming with a becoming blush, which brightened her rich brown eyes. Elizabeth gave her cousin a cursory greeting before stepping over to her elder sister. Mary, as they had rehearsed, opened with, "Ah, Mr Collins, how nice to see you this morning," and with a smile and an outstretched hand asked, "How do you do?"

"Cousin Mary? Eh," he began before the power of speech left him. Then, remembering himself, bussed her proffered hand with a kiss, swept her a most formal bow, and answered,

"I am quite well, thank you. You are certainly in looks this morning, Cousin Mary. I say," he began as he raised his arm to lead her to the sofa, "did you ever find the script you mentioned yesterday, the sermon by the Reverend Sir Matthew Grunyan?"

"I am afraid I did not," she answered, shooting her sisters a look of panic at this unexpected turn in conversation. This was not what they had envisioned at all.

"Sir Matthew's sermon?" Elizabeth volunteered. "You know that almost by rote, do you not, Sister?" Turning to her cousin, Elizabeth added in her best Lydia style, "La, Lord knows I have no use for such ramblings-on, but Mary always was more inclined towards religiosity than I."

"Religiosity, you call it, Cousin Elizabeth? No, I have observed that there dwells within your sister a genuine devotion, much more than just a *claim* to be religious. She is a true student of Christian capability."

"You flatter me, Mr Collins." Mary said, embarrassed by his attentions whilst appreciably revelling in them.

"Our cousin speaks only the truth, Mary," Jane told her with an encouraging smile. "I am glad Mr Collins has the good sense to recognise these amiable qualities in you. Your modesty simply baulks at receiving such praise."

Seated now, Mary demurred sincerely, and her two elder sisters retreated to a distant corner. Mr Collins, as if on cue, took the seat next to her and asked if she truly did know Sir Matthew's sermon by heart. Upon a rather bashful nod, he prodded her to regale him. After a slow start, she soon fell into a comfortable recitation, becoming engrossed as she evidently realised how thrilling it was to have as an audience one who actually wished to hear what she had to say.

CHAPTER THIRTY-TWO

"I say, Darcy, you have done a fine job avoiding us the past two days. Scarce said a word this morning while we were out. What's on your mind, old man?" Wentworth asked him as he poured two glasses of scotch. The other gentlemen were in the billiards room with Bingley, awaiting a dinner of pheasant and grouse, as well as a haunch of pork for those who preferred not to spit lead balls onto their plates as they ate. Darcy, having had a surfeit of polite attention from the country squires, had slipped away at his first chance.

He had been meditating without intermission on his conversation with Elizabeth. If he was honest, most of his thoughts centred on one moment, that moment where all his fears and doubts and misgivings and distrust were overruled by the magnitude of his attraction. He had found himself surrendering, knowing full well that it meant giving her his name, his hand, his fortune, his whole self. He had not intended it as a test of her avarice in that moment, but after she had walked away so furiously, he could not but admit that it was a test she passed.

"Avoiding you?" Darcy responded at length. "I suppose it would seem that way. I apologise; I have had much to think on of late. I had a rather disconcerting conversation yesterday, and it has me...distracted." He accepted the drink from the captain's hand and unconsciously rested it against his aching cheekbone. It was not black and blue, but he certainly felt it.

"Lizzy, I take it? I saw her trying to get your attention at the market. I assume she caught you up, then?"

"Oh, that she did," he replied drily.

Darcy expected Wentworth to enquire as to the nature of their conversation, but before he could form in his mind a circumvention to another topic, the captain spoke up.

"That woman can certainly get a man in a tangle. Why, I was in a tangle over her from the age of nine up until I met Miss Elliot, I would say. And I am not the only one."

"No?" This piqued Darcy's interest. How many men had she insidiously conquered and left writhing in pain in her path?

"Elizabeth is universally admired—and not just because of her beauty, like her sister. Elizabeth makes everyone she meets feel so heard, so appreciated. And her laugh; well, you must have noticed how her laugh can hypnotise. Problem is she does it so unconsciously that she often finds herself with admirers she would rather not have, like that canting prig of a parson, Mr Collins."

"Collins is in a tangle over Miss Elizabeth?" Darcy asked, of a sudden almost worried, while at the same time affronted that a man like him could dare to think he deserved such a woman.

"Oh yes, couldn't keep off her elbow at dinner the other

evening. She was out of sorts, but still, he was charmed. I suppose, taken in a prudential light, it would be a good match, as he is to inherit. It would guarantee her the estate of Longbourn."

"Never going to happen," Darcy replied, unwittingly voicing his condemnation of the ridiculous cleric aloud.

"Well, she does not have her standby excuse to refuse him anymore, so she will have to rely on her own resourcefulness."

"Standby excuse?" He was learning so much; of course he would from Elizabeth's oldest friend.

"When she was about sixteen, I came for a short visit, and she was being hounded by this septuagenarian with a fat wallet and eager hands. He would not accept her polite hints of refusal, so when she told me about it, I asked her, 'Did not *we* have an understanding?' I shall never forget the look of gratitude in her eyes when I said, 'You dare entertain the advances of another man? You are spoken for!' And from that moment on, she has had a ready means of deflecting any unwanted attentions."

Wentworth smiled broadly at the memory.

Darcy could not believe what he was hearing. Elizabeth's words came unbidden to his mind, 'You are in no danger from me, for I have long been spoken for.'

Feeling as though Wentworth was party to her deception, he asked, "You were amenable to her using your name to deceive respectable gentlemen?"

"It was never about deceit, *per se*. Just a gentle way to guide their attention elsewhere. She has never been in a hurry to marry—indeed I do not think she has ever met anyone whom she liked well enough. And you know her mother. Dear creature, but terribly anxious about her daughters' futures. If even the scent of an opportunity had made it to her keen nose, she would have insisted on Lizzy taking anyone with more than four hundred a year, be he a king or a cobbler."

"Was she trying to guide *my* attention elsewhere when she told *me* she was engaged?" Darcy asked, unsure whether Wentworth knew that he was one of Elizabeth's tangled men.

"Ah, yes, she mentioned that she told you of our *understanding*," he replied simply.

"She must think quite highly of herself, or quite lowly of me, as she informed me of it almost the moment we met. What a disgusting creature I must be for her to feel the need to so forehandedly reject me." He tried to laugh it off as a self-deprecating joke, but the plausibility of its truth stung, stunting his chuckle.

"No, she drew you up straightaway," Wentworth answered without hesitation, casting him a smile with an arch of his brow. "She knew you would not allow her to help you—something about you limping at the ball and needing her assistance. Never thought you would look twice at her—what was it you called her, *barely tolerable*? In any case, she knew you would lump her in with all the eye-batting belles and teasing tarts, so she decided to take herself off the market. It worked, did it not?"

Wentworth's speech was given so freely, it appeared that Elizabeth had related to him the circumstances of their acquaintance without compunction. Her conscience, it seemed, was perfectly clear where Darcy was concerned.

"Yes," Darcy said, his thoughts and emotions in a tumult. "It certainly did."

"Not that she is proud of it. Not in your case, at any rate. If you knew Lizzy, you would know, as playful as she is, she is never underhanded. It appears that after you two became friends, she worried that you would feel deceived. 'Course, I told her it was not possible—you are too honourable a man to hold something so innocent against her. You may not value her friendship as I do, but I am sure you would not give it up on such a slight offence."

Darcy strove to follow as Wentworth revealed truth after truth about the lady he had so determined to despise. Elizabeth had not accepted the fat wallet who had hounded her just a few years ago. She would not accept her cousin, who could guarantee her and her family a comfortable home for life. And she had not accepted his own improper, presumptuous attempt to compromise her into matrimony—not even *'for ten thousand a year...'*

His whole being was ablaze at the remembrance, only this time with scorching shame. How could he have demeaned and dishonoured her so?

In his anger and distrust, he had driven away the only woman he had ever loved. His scepticism had prevented him from even hearing her explanation. He had promised that nothing could make him despise her; yet, at the first test of the veracity of his word, he had proved faithless.

She was right; he deserved to be left to the company of his bitterness and disdain. He had earned every ounce of the self-recrimination he would yet suffer for having treated her so disgracefully.

She was no mercenary.

But, truly this time, he *was* a fool.

CHAPTER THIRTY-THREE

"You are right, Darcy," Wentworth said as they closed the door on the last of the shooting party that evening. "Anything you can do to keep that debauched lieutenant away from the respectable ladies of our fair county would be worth doing. I only wish I had the blackguard under *my* command —we know how to reform men like him on a naval ship,"

"And a thing worth doing cannot be done too soon. We shall have to arrange a meeting with Colonel Forster, but I have some favours to call in from London beforehand. I believe I have a plan that might answer all our ideas of retribution," Darcy replied. They were careful to keep their chatter in whispered tones, and to finish it altogether before joining the Bingleys and Hursts in the drawing room, where they met a very weary Miss Bingley sighing her relief.

"How pleasant it is to have one's home to oneself again," she proclaimed. "Well, almost..." she amended, casting a glance at Wentworth.

He had been the target of her petty darts since he had

arrived, though she usually waited until her brother was out of the room before shooting them. Wentworth thought perhaps she had become so comfortable disparaging him that she no longer worried if Bingley was present. Her next speech to the gentlemen confirmed this suspicion.

"How tedious is the company of these country ciphers. The insipidity and yet the noise. The nothingness and yet the self-importance of these people," she said.

"I confess I find it quite tiring," Mrs Hurst added, parroting her sister as was her usual wont.

"Why, when Sir William Lucas was droning on about St James's, I could hardly keep my countenance," the younger one continued.

"I find Sir William to be quite a good sort of fellow myself," her brother interjected.

"And I am sure he kept a very good sort of shop before his elevation to the Knighthood," she replied, joining Mrs Hurst in a titter at the kind gentleman's expense.

"As did our father, *Caro*," Bingley nigh on shouted, clearly tired of hearing her self-important shredding of their neighbours. She responded with a horrified scowl, her mouth fully agape, her wild eyes dashing from Bingley to Wentworth.

"That is not the same, Charles, and you know it," she cried.

"How, pray tell?" Wentworth finally chimed in, heated. "And please apprise me—at what point will *I* be admitted into your society without epithet?" With that, Wentworth stood, bowed to the ladies and informed the others, "If you will excuse me, gentlemen, I believe I have an appointment with Italics."

The look Bingley shot his sister at that moment would have brought a strong man to his knees. Instead, it brought her to her feet, and she left the room in a huff several steps behind Wentworth, not towards the library, but towards her own chambers.

Wentworth had not reached the library door before Bingley and Darcy had joined him, the younger one holding a decanter of brandy and three small-stemmed glasses. They were all silent as they took their seats. Drinks were poured and passed about. Italics, seeming to understand who most needed him, lighted onto Wentworth's lap and began his affectionate ministrations.

"I apologise, Bingley. I should have held my peace back there," Wentworth said as he stroked the feline's fur, staring at nothing in particular. "I simply have no patience left. I am done being reminded of how I have been weighed in the balances and found wanting. It has been deuced hard pretending that nothing is the matter when the one woman in the world I have ever truly loved has thrown me over. I just do not understand; Anne never saw me for my value in coin, but for my value as a man. How anyone could have persuaded her to view me otherwise is dumbfounding."

"She cannot have changed how she views you," Darcy assured him. "You said yourself she was put upon by her family. The pressure was likely just too great."

"You said it, Darcy. Though, I think she could have withstood the pressure of her family. It was Lady Russell whose entreaties she could not overcome. That lady used her position of trust, her close friendship with my Anne, to convince her to send me packing. Told her I was trying to gain consequence by marrying the daughter of a baronet; as if anyone would respect me more, knowing I was related to that fool father of hers. She was honour-bound to me; she had already accepted my proposal. Her father had even relented, as disgusted as he was by the prospect. And yet, Lady Russell still urged her to separate herself from me."

The two men sat, listening with empathy as he poured out his rancorous heart. Wentworth had planned to acquaint them with the situation at some point so that Darcy might see the pain he was causing by keeping two people apart who loved one another—and so Bingley could see the folly of being too malleable in the hands of his associates. This was not how he had wished to go about it, however. He had planned to be self-possessed, nonchalant, even light-hearted about it.

But that would have been a lie. The truth was, Wentworth was devastated.

He was devastated and indignant and bitter.

And pathetic and heartbroken.

And desolate without her.

Over the next hour, Wentworth told them all about his Anne, much as he had with Elizabeth. Grief oft finds peace in covering the same ground over, and a sense of comfort filled him as he relived the moments of joy and anguish he had experienced since knowing Anne Elliot. He spoke of how they had met and fallen in love, how they had seen their future in one another, and how he had assured her of the rightness of their union in the face of her family's indifference.

How he had thought her so steadfast.

"Did I not know how much she loved me, it would not pain me so," he said.

He bit out the account of his first meeting with Sir Walter and Miss Elliot, laughing mirthlessly at how precisely Miss Bingley's words described them: 'the nothingness, and yet the self-importance.' Anne's senseless, spendthrift father had left the family almost penniless after her mother's death, yet somehow his having been born into a baronetcy made him better than an industrious, serious-minded attorney or shop-keeper...or naval officer.

"You see Bingley here—I do not care that his fortune is from trade. He is a gentleman, a man of sense and education, and, I might add, great hospitality," Wentworth said, raising his glass in salute. "And Darcy—I do not care if you own half of Derbyshire. It would not matter to me if you were a fish-monger. You are respectable and good. And Lizzy likes you, which makes you agreeable in my book."

Another salute, and one returned.

"What hast thou that thou didst not receive? Why dost thou glory, as if thou hadst not received it?" Darcy quoted the scripture, explaining that his father had used it to remind him of the privilege to which he had been born and the humility with which he should view his station.

"Hear, hear," Wentworth agreed with another salute.

He then spun poetical tapestries as he explained to Darcy and Bingley the intricacies of Anne's excellence. Her applica-tion and perspicacity, her gentle way of loving and leading others, her selfless care of those about her, how delightfully bashful she was when he attended her in any small degree, and yet how strong she was in the face of the ridiculousness of her family.

For the most part.

If Mr Darcy drew any similarities in his mind between this woman and another, he did not say so.

Then, through gritted teeth, Wentworth snarled his final feelings on the whole matter:

"My only consolation is that, in the end, this will hurt her far more than myself. I will go on to take my prizes; I will make my fortune. Perhaps I will even find some pretty thing to put up with my ill humours in my old age. But she—she will never find someone who will love her like I do. After this humiliation, I shall not offer for her again. And Lady Russell will have to live with that on her conscience..."

No one in the room believed this idea brought Wentworth any consolation—himself least of all.

IN HIS ROOMS THAT NIGHT, DARCY COULD NOT HELP but think about what he had learnt from the captain. He had been separated from the woman he loved by the interference of well-meaning friends. He did not know whether he had told him this story by design, but Darcy could not help but draw the similarity between himself and Anne Elliot's Lady Russell.

Had he not strongly urged Bingley to rethink his intentions towards Jane Bennet? Did he not feel, at the time, that his reasoning was sound? Did he not attempt to persuade Bingley that Miss Bennet's social class was an impediment that could not be overcome? To his shame, Darcy had even suggested that Jane Bennet might be a fortune hunter.

Who was he to decide that for someone else? Bingley was educated, wealthy, and universally liked—he never met a man who was not proud to call him a friend within the course of an evening. Why should Darcy think that having an exquisite woman from a respectable but unknown family on his arm would damage Bingley's place in society?

This will not do.

If his interference could leave Bingley in a state resembling Wentworth's in any way, Darcy could not live with that on his conscience.

He would leave off warning Bingley of the possibilities of

evil associated with his choice of Miss Bennet as a bride. Darcy would allow his friend to stand on his own two feet, and he would support him in whatever he chose. Satisfied with this newfound generosity of spirit, he blew out his candles and settled into bed—*unsettled.*

Something was still nettling him.

It struck him in the dark of his bedchamber that Wentworth's story had more to teach him. Perhaps he was not only Lady Russell in this drama. Perhaps he also had a bit in common with Sir Walter.

Why else would he arbitrarily assume that any woman without a fortune was mercenary? Why should he think that Elizabeth's deceit must be associated with some sort of ploy to fool or compromise him into matrimony? Why could he not simply believe that she wished to make him comfortable for the sake of helping her fellow man? And how many offers of such kindness had he failed to benefit from because he, in his conceit, had rejected them as coming from a grasping heart?

No wonder she felt she must lie to him. He was, he now recognised, sorely in need of just such a friend as herself, but if she had tried to be that for him as a poor, unattached country lass, he would have grumbled and delivered her a setdown, just as he had so many other daughters of lowly families.

What makes you better than her? What do you have that you did not receive? And if you received it for nothing more than being born, why should you boast in it as if you have in some way earned it?

In that moment, Darcy suffered a crushing revelation: he, like Sir Walter, was eaten up with class-pride. It was not the kind of superiority of mind that, when kept under good regulation, need not be a weakness. This was a pride that was exclusive and haughty, founded solely on his name and fortune, two things he had done absolutely nothing to attain. This was the sort of pride that alienated those about him and made others feel inferior.

This was the sort of pride that just might cost him the love of a worthy woman.

SITTING IN A PLUSH LEATHER ARMCHAIR IN THE master's chambers, Charles Bingley was smiling. Sad though he naturally was for poor Wentworth, hearing the captain's story cemented in him the determination to be his own man, unmoved by the advice and opinions of those who valued society's approval more than he.

He had decided to offer for Jane Bennet.

He was determined.

He would.

CHAPTER THIRTY-FOUR

The previous day's revelations had nearly done Darcy in. He had much to think on, and he knew he would get no peace at Netherfield. Bingley's high spirits would be too much for him, especially if his friend had taken Wentworth's words to heart and decided to pursue Jane Bennet in earnest, as Darcy suspected. Wentworth's perspicacious gaze was more than Darcy could bear at this moment. Miss Bingley and her sister were never what Darcy would call pleasant company, and their constant, inane chatter would certainly not permit him to assimilate all he had learnt the night before.

He certainly could not enter the library. There were too many memories there to allow him to think rationally. Elizabeth was there. Her empty chair taunted him, and his imagination filled it with her lovely form. He relived every conversation, every sensation of awe and affection she had conjured in him, every moment of regret he bore over her being out of his reach. Even Italics's ministrations brought her back to mind.

'Oh, to be a cat. Kisses and sweet nothings from the loveliest of creatures,' he had said. He had meant it. He longed for Elizabeth, and seeing Italics only exacerbated his yearning.

No, he had to leave Netherfield Park. He needed some time with only his horse for company in order to work through the tumult of thoughts and emotions roiling in his heart.

Upon entering Meryton, Darcy noted several ladies and gentlemen milling about on the High Street. A flurry of skirts disappeared into Pratt's, the area's principal woollen-draper and haberdashery, no doubt in search of trimmings and gloves for Bingley's ball. A clutch of militia officers swaggered and postured for the maidens who passed them.

A sharp giggle seized his attention and, turning towards it, he noted the youngest Bennet girl being pulled into an alleyway by a tall redcoat. He instinctively rode towards the couple, unwilling to stand by as Elizabeth's sister risked her reputation for all and sundry to witness. Before he could see the face of the man, he noted another young lady standing with Miss Lydia. It was Mrs Forster.

While a married lady's presence ought to give some semblance of propriety to Miss Lydia's clandestine interview, this particular matron's being there did nothing to quell Darcy's agitation. Indeed, the coquette was probably more likely to lead her into mischief than protect her from it. Still, Darcy had no claim on any of the Bennet ladies, no right to act the gallant on their behalf. Thereby, he turned his horse and began to clop away, shaking his head as he did so.

Tying his horse in front of the post office, Darcy walked in to hand over his correspondence and was back out again in a matter of a minute. He mounted the beast, then cast another glance in the direction of the alley. The two girls emerged together arm in arm, whispering behind their hands and giggling. A moment later, the man with whom they had been in such close congress made his appearance.

Wickham.

What could George Wickham have to do with Lydia Bennet and Mrs Forster? Could he truly be toying with another fifteen-year-old child? It took every vestige of Darcy's self-restraint not to climb down from his horse, pull the miscreant's own sword from its scabbard, and run him through with it.

He scowled down at the villain, not caring what a shock it would be to the ladies pouring out from Pratt's. Let them observe his disdain for the man.

Darcy had devised a plan to deal once and for all with George Wickham, and he would not wait another day to put it into action. He would settle it all this evening at Sir William's card party—with Wentworth's assistance, of course.

As it was, he could not be in the rake's presence, not even within sight of him. In a rage of disgust, he turned his steed and headed in the opposite direction.

WHEN ELIZABETH WALKED OUT OF THE DRAPER'S SHOP with Jane, her first feeling was gladness at the continuing presence of blue sky. As she turned her face towards the light, however, she caught the sight of a tall man on horseback across the way. It was Mr Darcy.

The sun was shining behind him, shading his face beneath his tall beaver, but she could easily discern the scowl he wore as he turned towards her. He must have been watching her as she and Jane had exited the building, for he sat stock still upon his steed, his gaze fixed in her direction. The anger in his countenance turned to disgust before her eyes as he pulled his reins hard to the right, riding away faster than was strictly proper.

Her heart shot into her throat, creating a painful lump she could not swallow. She had hoped their next encounter might be civil. Never had she imagined he would be unable to refrain from revealing his animosity towards her in public.

How he must detest her!

Kitty followed her and Jane into the street directly, and Lydia appeared behind them with Harriet Forster a moment later. The three girls proposed to visit Aunt Philips and half-heartedly requested Elizabeth and Jane to accompany them.

Knowing she was in no state to be in company, Elizabeth begged her sisters to excuse her; she felt the need for a longer jaunt than they had set out for. Jane hesitated, but gave in at Elizabeth's insistence. The other three were happy to leave her to her ramblings; they had gowns to trim and gossip to exchange.

Upon reaching the edge of the town, Elizabeth heard hooves clopping behind her. Her heart caught in her throat at the thought that it might be Mr Darcy, but when she turned about, she found the kind, worried eyes of Frederick. Waves of relief washed over her, and before she knew it, she was releasing all the pent-up worry, anguish, and anger she had been suppressing the last several days. Tears flowed freely as her dear friend listened without interruption.

"You speak as if all hope is lost," Frederick finally said in quelling tones.

"I saw his face. He will never respect me again," she said, resigned. Breathing deeply, she worked to regain her composure. "No, Freddie, I have nothing to hope for from Mr Darcy. I shall just be relieved when his time in the neighbourhood is over. Then I shall be able to be myself again, and life will go on as it always has."

CHAPTER THIRTY-FIVE

E lizabeth watched as Mr Collins handed the other
Bennet ladies down from the carriage in front of Sir
William's fine house, purposely staying back to take a last
deep breath. After assisting his new favourite, however, he
seemed to forget there were any others awaiting assistance,
offering Mary his arm and leading her into the house without
a backwards glance. Elizabeth was not unhappy to be left in
the solitude of the coach. Indeed, she would rather have been
left in the solitude of her home. As Charlotte had been insis-
tent upon her attending the Lucases' soirée this evening,
however, she did not feel she could refuse.

In her readiness to bring Jane and Mr Bingley together,
Charlotte had assured Elizabeth that the Netherfield
gentlemen would be attending. This filled Elizabeth with no
small amount of dread, as her last sight of one of the
gentlemen had been so wrenching to her peace. Her project to
assist Mr Collins in his search for a bride by pushing Mary

forwards in the best light had been enjoyable, but not nearly as distracting as she had hoped.

She still found herself contemplating each moment of her association with Mr Darcy—from their first meeting at the Meryton Assembly to their last tragic interview on market day, to the furious look he had sent her way that very morning.

And she was exhausted.

She could not but blame him for having invited her into his company so often, and indeed inviting himself into her own, without really knowing anything about her. If he had known her true character, he would see that she had never had ill intent, that she had never wilfully hurt anyone in her life, much less someone who had become such a friend to her. And should he not also have seen how desperately she wished to tell him the truth, to clear up matters, with tears and trembling more than once? Could he not give her the benefit of the doubt as common charity might do?

That was not to say she did not blame herself at all—she had certainly been false of a manner, and just denying or misunderstanding the consequences of one's actions did not make those consequences unjust. She was the author of her own distress, she knew.

Thus her mind circled from ire to regret and back...again and again.

After several minutes of this, Elizabeth's grave reverie was interrupted by the appearance of the coachman at the carriage door. She gave a long sigh, raised her eyebrows, pasted on a smile, and allowed him to hand her down.

INSIDE, DARCY WATCHED AS BINGLEY ANXIOUSLY EYED the entrance hall. It had been a quarter of an hour, and it was starting to become comical watching his friend's eager ears prick up every time the door opened. Now that he had come to terms with Bingley's choice, he was able to share his joy. Within moments, Bingley was rewarded with the sight of his beautiful beloved, and in a breath, he was up and at the door, ready to lead her into the party.

Darcy expected to see Elizabeth enter behind Miss Bennet, but instead the two youngest sisters appeared, giggling to one another. Miss Lydia caught his eye and shot daggers at him, which he put down to her being poisoned by that pernicious Wickham. Though he knew it to be meaningless in the scheme of things, it disconcerted him to be treated with contempt because of Wickham's treachery—especially by an ignorant flirt of lowly origins—

No, I must not keep thinking of people this way.

His determination to refrain from looking meanly at others was tested afresh a very few moments later when the sanctimonious vicar walked in, escorting another of Elizabeth's sisters. Was this the plain one whose nose was always in a book?

Hmm, he thought, *it turns out there was a pretty face behind those tomes.*

As he was admiring Mr Collins's partner, the man himself approached and gave him a deep bow. Darcy waited to be addressed, prepared to answer with patience the obsequious attentions he knew he would be given, but was disappointed.

Instead, Collins turned to Miss Mary and began telling her about Mr Darcy's having the unequalled privilege of being a nephew of his noble patroness, Lady Catherine de Bourgh.

"As a close familial relation, I am sure Mr Darcy would not but concur with me when I describe her great condescension, her abundant favours, her kindly bestowed admonishments."

Darcy was given no opportunity to concur. He stood blinking silently as the couple simply continued walking into the fray with nary a pause from the parson. Though a strange occurrence, he thanked the heavens for not having to endure too much attention from that quarter.

Upon turning his head, Darcy heard his name in a hushed tone. He could not make out every word, but what he heard immediately soured his mood.

"Poor Mr Wickham," he heard one voice say.

"Cheated the man out of his inheritance," said another.

"Not as if he could not afford it," from yet another.

As his gaze travelled over the crowd, he saw several who refused to meet his eye or turned away. Not only did this uncouth behaviour rankle his sensibilities, he hated that he was the centre of attention, especially over something he knew to be false. Without realising it, he found himself moving towards the wall, then inching his way towards the corner.

He was contemplating whether he should defend himself before the condemning crowd—and becoming increasingly incensed as he considered the necessity of it—when Elizabeth finally walked in. That familiar, light sense of relief whelmed him when he saw her, and he reflexively began to walk towards her. Her sullen countenance recalled to him the crevasse that lay between them—a chasm he had created—and he retreated to his corner.

His worry over the other occupants of the lodge was abandoned as he focused almost solely on Elizabeth. From where he stood, he could watch her without notice, which had been his goal for the evening from the time he had accepted Sir William's invitation.

As the minutes wore on, she floated through the room, enchanting everyone just as she had the first night they had met. She helped the shy young Lucas girl to have the confidence to play for the party, whispering encouragement and turning the pages for her. She noted an elderly widow who was looking a bit neglected and pulled her into her conversation, brightening the woman's countenance. Nervous, skinny Mr Long—home from town where he was training to be an attorney—she took by the elbow and paraded about the room, finally leaving him in the company of a handsome young lady, whose blushes bespoke her heart's inclination towards him.

This was Elizabeth. Giving, loving, and self-sacrificing. He had been the grateful recipient of her selflessness, and she had become mistress of his heart.

He lost sight of her for a moment before her voice drew his attention. She and Miss Lucas stood quite near, evidently in deep conversation.

"Charlotte, please, take my word for it—Mr Wickham is a liar and an adventurer," Elizabeth declared. "Mr Darcy is innocent on every charge. I cannot in honour reveal details, but I do know that Mr Wickham refused the living and was generously compensated. Mr Darcy is blameless."

She was *defending* him? Could it really be? After all his accusations, could she still speak so charitably of him? If she had an untruthful bone in her body, now would be the time to use it to her satisfaction.

Yet, she did not. She could not listen to the lies being spread about him without speaking up and attempting to vindicate him. He, on the other hand, had allowed her character to sink in his estimation at even a perceived wrong, his trust in her like a dry rope that burned through at the scent of smoke.

She was so truly good.

And he was so truly *hers*.

CHAPTER THIRTY-SIX

D arcy had been so engrossed in listening to Elizabeth courageously defend him, he almost forgot that in his pocket was proof of his innocence regarding George Wickham. As soon as she and Miss Lucas had moved on, still speaking about him, no doubt, Darcy made his way out of his clandestine corner and over to his host.

"Sir William, may I say again how honoured I am to have been invited into your home this evening?" he began.

Sir William hesitated, doubtless having heard the rumours pulsating through the room. Ever the genial host, he replied, "Mr Darcy, it is I who am honoured that you have graced us with your presence."

"Over the last several minutes, I have been made aware of some rather nasty gossip, which paints me in quite the negative light," Darcy volunteered.

"I confess, I have heard some rather, ahem, preposterous accusations," Sir William affirmed uncomfortably.

"I am glad you see the ridiculousness of these claims.

However, I wish to assure you, as a fellow magistrate, that every word George Wickham has directed against me is false, and I happen to have documented proof. If you would join me in conference with Colonel Forster, I believe I might satisfy you on that point." The gentleman nodded dumbly and followed him to the table where Wentworth was already in congress with the colonel and a couple of young officers.

Wentworth clapped the younger men on the shoulder and bid them go find some female company, thus making room for the two newcomers. He raised an eyebrow at Sir William's joining them, to which Darcy gave him a look that bespoke its necessity. Darcy withdrew a packet from his jacket's inner pocket and laid the contents out before them.

Thus, the four men were engrossed for the better part of an hour.

"You have been such a kind friend to my brother and myself, Miss Bennet. Indeed, I do not know how we shall live without your society," Caroline purred as her brother departed to find them some refreshments.

"Are you leaving, Miss Bingley? Mr Bingley has said nothing about this," Miss Bennet said with concern.

"Oh, of course. After the ball, we shall hie off to London. I believe we have all had our fill of country manners...and country maidens. Poor Darcy—and Charles—beset by grasping beauties, all coy smiles and batting eyelashes. I assure you, though they might appear to enjoy such attentions, when they are behind closed doors, they profess their absolute loathing of it."

Her campaign to sow seeds of doubt in Miss Bennet's

mind and heart was apparently having its desired effect, for the lovely creature was unable to respond.

Caroline continued, "Naturally, Mr Darcy is eager to see his sister, who has been in London all this autumn. I do not believe Georgiana Darcy has her equal for beauty, elegance, and accomplishments; and the affection she inspires in myself is heightened from the hope I dare to entertain of her being hereafter *my sister*. Indeed, Charles admires her greatly already; it will only take some few evenings together to cement the match."

"Oh," was all Miss Bennet could say, which Caroline answered with a satisfied smirk.

When Bingley reappeared with drinks, Miss Bennet did not seem as eager to be in his company. Within a few short minutes, the lady claimed a headache and excused herself to find her sister.

"What is wrong with Miss Bennet? Did you say something to her?" Bingley asked, attempting to stare her down.

"I could not say," Caroline answered him innocently. "She said something about giving the wrong idea, and then you returned, and I could not ask her what she meant. She seemed quite distressed."

Bingley glared down at her, as if attempting to discern the truthfulness of her claim. Then, without a word, he went after the chit, leaving Caroline holding all three drinks.

ELIZABETH COULD NOT HAVE BEEN HAPPIER TO LEAVE the party. First, she had had to hear from one person after another the unjust indictments against Mr Darcy. This put her in such a conflicting position—should she speak up for him? How could she, without breaking his confidence? Did she even wish to defend his character after he had treated her with such disdain?

Finally, she chose to tell a select few all that her conscience allowed. Among these were her discreet friend Charlotte, as well as her not-so-discreet Aunt Philips, who would, Elizabeth knew, make short work of acquainting the whole room with her assurances.

It was insupportable that the target of the rumours was not there to defend himself, thus she had felt obligated to interject. However, after her interview with Charlotte, she looked up to see Mr Darcy walking across the parlour to speak to Sir William. He had arrived before she, it seemed, and had not even deigned to acknowledge her presence. After this, he had immediately entered into conference with Sir William and the colonel without so much as a glance her way. It was as if she did not even exist.

So it was that when Jane approached her, feeling faint and wishing to return home, she readily acceded. What Jane related to her of her conversation with Miss Bingley puzzled Elizabeth.

The whole party will leave Netherfield directly after the ball? Mr Bingley has been pretending to enjoy Jane's attentions, whilst actually hoping to wed Miss Darcy? It is all too fantastical!

Elizabeth knew it to be a calculated falsehood, designed to discourage Jane from attaching herself to Mr Bingley, and she said as much. Jane would have none of it. The sweet lady would not believe that her friend could invent such a hurtful story.

Elizabeth had no such compunction.

CHAPTER THIRTY-SEVEN

S aturday morning was rather dull. The Bennet family busied themselves with their usual chores and occupations. Mary was industriously practising at the pianoforte, whilst Mr Collins listened with infatuated sighs. Lydia and Kitty attended their mother in the drawing room, busily attaching new lace to their old ball gowns. Jane was speaking to Hill regarding the menu for the week. Elizabeth decided she would visit her father in his library.

"This is a rare privilege. What brings you into my undesirable company this morning?" Mr Bennet asked with raised eyebrows.

"You are right, Papa. I have sorely neglected you these past weeks."

"Why are you not trimming frocks with your sisters, pray tell? You cannot be prepared for a ball a full three days ahead of time."

"I shall not be attending the ball," Elizabeth told him with no little sorrow.

"Hmm, I find that rather interesting. My only two daughters of marriageable age and sense shall forgo dancing and flirting and dazzling the crowd to stay home and mope?"

"Two daughters?"

"Indeed. Jane told me the same thing this very morning. It turns out her hopes towards young Bingley have been in vain. Poor Jane. Oh well, a girl likes to be crossed in love once in a while. When is your turn, Lizzy?"

She winced as the barb hit. Her father had a penchant for making jokes that hit the most tender points without realising the pain he was causing. Ordinarily, it was Elizabeth who checked his sharp wit on behalf of others, but today, there was no one to check his tongue at her expense.

Without warning, the door to the book-room flew open, and, before her father could voice the protestation such villainy warranted, Kitty cried, "Lizzy, there is a package arrived for you. Come see."

Elizabeth followed her sister with intrigue, her brow only becoming more quizzical as she eyed the large, soft parcel wrapped in brown paper and tied with twine. The whole female set gathered round the dining table, where it had been laid. Elizabeth did not know what to expect as she pulled the string to untie the twine, but what faced her when the paper splayed itself open only wrought more confusion.

There, folded neatly, was her gown—the apricot muslin she had adopted from Jane.

Miss Bingley's maid must have been able to work a miracle on that ink stain, and she is finally returning it, she thought.

But, no, as she lifted it by the shoulders, the thick, matted black unfurled before her eyes.

"Your gown, what happened?" asked Jane, who knew her sister's fondness for the garment.

"*Caro* happened," she answered simply, still staring in wonder at the dress as she held it up.

"What is this?" Lydia exclaimed, snatching another parcel from under the first. It, too, was wrapped and tied, but the paper was a delicate tissue infused with lavender blossoms, and it was bound in a pale peach satin ribbon more fit for tying about a bonnet than a bundle.

Laying aside her ruined frock, Elizabeth pulled the parcel from her youngest sister's grasp just as the ribbon was loosened and the paper fell open.

Before her was, again, her gown. It was nearly the same pattern, but in a paler shade of apricot and a rich silk, delicately embroidered with glittering ivory vines and flowers to match the motif on the muslin of the original. This was no day dress. This was an exquisite ball gown. She could not help but run her hands over the opulent, shimmering fabric, feeling the threads of the vines beneath the tips of her fingers. It was so lovely.

"Oh, Lizzy," was repeated by all five women, along with various tones of "ooh" and "ahh" as they all absorbed the beauty of the work of art before them.

Finally, her mother asked, "Where did this come from? Surely you did not order this?"

"No, Mama, I did not," she replied breathlessly. "It must have been Caroline Bingley. She must have felt remorse for ruining my muslin and ordered this to replace it. In truth, I am shocked; I did not think she possessed such kindness."

Elizabeth pulled the gown up completely from the table and walked it over to the window to examine its exquisiteness in the light. Why would Miss Bingley have done this? Why would she wish to favour her with such a lush, resplendent costume for their simple country ball?

It makes no sense. She so dislikes me.

Elizabeth heard her sisters and mother, almost in a chorus, cry, "There is another package!" She was relieved of the gown by one of its young admirers as she approached the last parcel.

Her heart was racing as she stared at it. Like the gown, it was wrapped in delicate paper, but this one was much smaller, bound with long white ribbons. Pulling them loose, she was met with the sight of several delicate sprigs of gold decked with small tufts of white enamel in the style of sallow branches. She willed her hands to stop shaking as she reached down to pluck one of the shining hairpins from the pillow into which they were stuck.

Goat willows.

"Well, now, Lizzy. I believe you shall be attending the ball at Netherfield after all," came a male voice from behind her.

"I suppose I must, Papa," she replied dumbly, twirling the bauble in her fingers, wondering if the package truly had come from Caroline Bingley.

Could it be...?

Her cheeks warmed as she thought of stories she had heard of men who outfitted their mistresses with beautiful gowns and jewels. Indeed, it would be quite improper for Mr Darcy to have sent her anything other than flowers without an understanding having been established between them.

No, it could not be Mr Darcy. He would never do something so improper!

But, the *goat willows*. Only he knew about both her wrecked muslin *and* her love of goat willows. Perhaps that is why there was no evidence of the giver; he simply wished to replace the gown Miss Bingley had ruined—as it was clear that that lady would never think to do so—and had chosen to include a small, anonymous gift he knew would cheer her.

"Indeed, it would be terribly rude to snub them after *such* a gift," her mother said, still in ecstasy over the smallness of the stitches and the intricacy of the embroidery.

"You are right, Mama," answered Elizabeth, then turning to her sister, "but I shall only go if Jane agrees to go as well."

"Oh, Lizzy, I do not wish to. But, if it means I shall get to see you in this gown with these willows in your hair, captivating every person in attendance, then I will."

She hugged her sister tightly, knowing that Jane's presence would help her get through the daunting evening with some composure.

"It will be such felicity to see all the Bennet females in their best looks, though how such natural beauty can be surpassed, I could not say," Mr Collins put forth. "Indeed, I entertain the hope of dancing with all my fair cousins during the course of the evening. And may I take this opportunity of securing yours," he said as he turned to the middle daughter, "for the first set, Miss Mary?"

Mary pinked and accepted prettily, and Elizabeth exchanged a knowing smile with Jane.

"La, I shall have no time to dance with Mr Collins," Lydia exclaimed as if the man were not in the room. "And neither shall Kitty. We shall be too busy dancing with all the officers."

"All the officers," Kitty echoed dreamily.

"I shall dance the first with Mr Wickham," Lydia proclaimed.

"I would not get my hopes up, Lydia," Jane cautioned.

"Why should I not hope to dance with the most handsome man in the room?"

"What Jane means is that he may not be there to dance with," Elizabeth interjected.

"It is because of that nasty Mr Darcy. After everything he has done to poor Wickham, must he rob him of the enjoyment of a ball, as well?" Lydia whined, stamping her foot.

"Hush, girl. I know for a fact that Mr Wickham's accusations are completely false. Why, Mrs Philips heard from Lady Lucas, who heard from Sir William, that Mr Darcy has documented proof that he had compensated Lieutenant Wickham for his inheritance, and that Mr Wickham, in point of fact, has not even been ordained. He never even went to seminary," Mrs Bennet stated proudly, as if she were informing all in the room of these developments for the first time.

Never having been one to let the facts get in the way of what she believed, Lydia simply turned her eyes heavenward.

CHAPTER THIRTY-EIGHT

S tanding amidst the parishioners and facing the church doors, Darcy was doing his best to ignore the constant low chattering of Caroline Bingley berating their neighbours. "Surely, you are just as ready to escape this tedious place as I, Mr Darcy," she finished.

"Not at all, Miss Bingley," was his only reply. Offering her a curt bow, he removed himself from her side.

As he was walking along the stone wall towards the solace of Wentworth's company, he was arrested by the sight of a dark-haired seraph standing in the entrance, haloed in light from behind, completely unaware of the profusion of peace she was creating in his core. He stood rooted to the ground, his lips parted as if to speak, his hand floating up towards her as if he could somehow touch her from across the length of the ancient building.

Flooding back to his mind came thoughts of their time spent together before she was forced to stay at Netherfield and then their intimate hours hidden away in the library. How deeply important she had become to him, how full his affection for her had grown.

She truly had become his most beloved friend. He had put himself in her power, and she had handled him with utmost care.

Darcy had needed it. It only occurred to him at this moment how dazed he had been when he first joined his friend in Hertfordshire. His mind had been a constant abyss of dark and dangerous thoughts, having just recovered—not even fully recovered—from Wickham's bullet and his treachery.

He had been standing aloof at that assembly, gnawing on his rancour, determined—as Elizabeth had once so aptly accused him—to hate everyone, and she walked into his life and refused to allow it. She brought so much light to his days that he eventually forgot to be bitter and resentful. His appreciation for her excellence welled up as he continued to gaze at her, his saviour, standing framed in that doorway.

He was shaken from this hypnosis by the sound of a man very intentionally clearing his throat.

"I say, old man, you are going to have to get a hold of yourself if you do not desire the townsfolk to talk," Wentworth said with a quiet chuckle, gently lowering Darcy's arm. "I take it all is forgiven, then?"

Darcy had not realised how evident his ire towards Elizabeth had been, but at these words, he understood that all truly was forgiven. More than that, he had no wish to get a hold of himself. If he could catch her outside the church and compromise her into marriage as Wentworth had tried so many years before, he would without hesitation.

Alas, it was not to be. The whole village was now shuffling in, and she was lost in the crowd as bells signalled the start of services. Afterwards, as it had begun to rain during the sermon and continued through the hymns and closing benediction, Elizabeth rushed out with her mother and sisters, their large umbrellas shielding her from sight as they climbed into the family's coach.

As he was lamenting her hasty departure, Darcy was faced yet again with the barbs and slurs of Miss Bingley. "What a strange creature is Miss Eliza. She just handed me a note, thanking me for my generous gift," she said, holding up a small piece of paper. "Not that I could even read half of it—her handwriting is so blotchy."

Darcy snatched it out of her hand without a thought to invading her privacy and read it to himself.

To my gracious Benefactor,

How overwhelmed I was to receive the package you sent yesterday. Do not demur, for though it appeared anonymously, I am certain it was you. Words cannot express my appreciation for the thoughtfulness, the effort, and the expense that went into your beautiful and unsparing gift. Of course, given the way you love your family and even your servants, I should have expected such liberality. These gifts shall forever stay a soothing reminder that I have not lost your friendship. I shall think of you whenever I wear them, of your affection and kindness, and I shall pray that God keep you wherever you are. The hole in my heart created by your departure, I shall fill with warm memories of our time together, and I shall force myself to be content. May God bless your generosity. I thank you again and remain,

Your truest friend,

E Bennet

"What can she mean? My truest friend, indeed," Miss Bingley sniffed haughtily.

"I know exactly what she means," Darcy replied under his breath.

Can she know? Yes, she must. And she must have known the first thing Miss Bingley would do was use this missive as a weapon against her. My clever Elizabeth.

When Wentworth approached the pair, Darcy folded the letter and slipped it into his pocket, knowing Miss Bingley would never dare ask for it back—nor, he thought, even recall its existence within the hour. He mustered as disinterested an air as he could and asked him, "Is everything set for tomorrow?"

"All set," Wentworth replied with a wink.

As Bingley sat down across from his friend in the warm glow of the firelight, Italics left his accustomed place on Darcy's lap to greet the newcomer. "Good evening, old man," he said to the friendly feline.

"Careful, Bingley, you are starting to sound like Wentworth," Darcy joked.

The pair chuckled, and Bingley gave the cat the attention he demanded for a few minutes before Darcy asked, "What brings you into the library this evening? Surely, you are not here simply to commune with Italics."

"No, Italics is just a bonus. I have come to speak to you." The worried look on his face smarted, and Darcy was again ashamed that, in his arrogance, he had managed to alienate his most devoted friend.

Bingley, he thought, *must never fear speaking openly with me.*

With this resolution, he closed his book and turned his full attention to the young man before him.

"I am at your disposal," Darcy assured him.

"You see, Darcy," he began, then faltered. He stopped and started several times, clearly hesitant to broach the subject.

Rather than allowing Bingley to continue in his discomfort, Darcy decided to put him out of his misery.

"You wish to marry Jane Bennet, and you would like me to either give you my blessing or keep my blasted opinions to myself."

Bingley shook his head in astonishment at Darcy's frank surmise, then he let his shoulders fall as he nodded, saying, "Yes, that is it exactly."

"Bingley, I have been too high-handed with you. I should never have tried to convince you to go against your own inclinations. Miss Bennet is a lovely woman, as anyone with sense can see, and if you believe she can make you happy, and you her, then you have my full blessing and support."

The expression of relief on his friend's face soon became one of anxious excitement. The last hurdle was crossed. Bingley could now pursue his heart's earnest desire without impediment. Darcy could see how eager he was to get on with the task and so excused him graciously.

Not long after one Bingley had left the room, the other entered, holding a handkerchief over her nose.

"Darcy," she half-screeched. "We must do something. Charles is intent on marrying that girl, and if you do not act, he is going to declare himself to her in the morning."

"Are you suggesting that I attempt to separate your brother from Miss Bennet?" Darcy asked nonchalantly.

"We are to be saddled with that woman and all her loathsome, tedious sisters for life if you do not." Again, she was putting words to her persistent dream of a union between them. Darcy could not restrain the cringe creeping up his spine.

"Bingley is to be happily married to a virtuous and beautiful woman from an old and respectable family, and *you* shall indeed gain five sisters. While I do not know them well enough to loathe any of them, I should not call them tedious —there is never a lack of activity in the Bennets' home."

"How can you say that? You have seen how silly the youngest ones are. And Miss Eliza—the abominable impertinence! As for Miss Bennet, I do not know if she even has a heart. I have never seen such a vapid, grasping woman in my life."

Darcy wondered how she was always so well-turned-out when her dressing table had clearly been without a mirror all these years.

"Caroline Antigone Frances Bingley!" Her brother's voice from the doorway projected a rage Darcy had never heard, and it made him proud. "You will desist in your vicious, ill-mannered attacks on my future wife. As you cannot find it in your heart to accept my decision and rejoice with me, you will be joining Louisa and Hurst when they depart for London. Tomorrow."

"But, *the ball.* After all I have done to prepare. Surely you cannot send me away before the ball," she cried, manifestly horrified at the thought of being banished from her own home.

"You shall leave as soon as your trunks are packed, ball or no." The look on Bingley's face forestalled any argument from his sister on the matter. While he had her silent, he added, "And if you cannot learn to hold your venomous tongue, you will not be welcomed to Netherfield again."

"Nor Pemberley," Darcy added, standing up alongside his friend. "I cannot have the feminine ears of my household accosted by such offences and indignities."

"Mr Darcy, surely you know I would never slight dear Georgiana," she cried, further panicked at the prospect of never seeing Pemberley again.

"I was not speaking of Georgiana," he said as he turned to look her straight in the eyes, "I refer to my abominably impertinent beloved, the future Mrs Darcy."

CHAPTER THIRTY-NINE

"Lieutenant Wickham, thank you for being so punctual." Colonel Forster stood and shook the junior officer's hand.

"Not at all, sir. I am at your service," Wickham replied, oozing charm even at this early hour. If he wondered at being invited by his commanding officer to meet him at an empty public house before eight on a Monday morning, his cool demeanour betrayed none of it.

"May I introduce my new friend, Captain Frederick Wentworth of His Majesty's Navy?" Wentworth sketched him a quick bow, which was returned with a smile.

After asking the men to have a seat with him, Colonel Forster opened a folio containing a dozen or so papers, some filled front and back with names and numbers. Wickham gave a curious glance towards the stack of lists and shifted in his chair.

"Mr Wickham, I have here in front of me documents

detailing the extent of the credit you have drawn with the local shops, taverns, and inn, all of which have been paid in full," Colonel Forster began. Wickham blinked, but otherwise betrayed none of the shock he must have felt.

"I also have written attestations as to debts of honour among your fellow officers. These, too, have been paid in full."

"I try to be a good sport, never leave my fellow man in the lurch," he said, his voice a touch higher than it had been. Wentworth took note as the lieutenant uncrossed and crossed his legs.

"There have also appeared before me receipts for debts paid from London, Kent, and as far off as Derbyshire." At this, the colonel's brows lifted as he finally looked Wickham in the eye.

"What can I say, sir?" His crossed knee was bouncing a bit now and a sheen of sweat appeared at his temples. It was clear that he was all at sea as to the direction of this conversation, which, ironically, was exactly where Captain Wentworth wanted him to be.

"I do not require you to say anything. I do, however, wish to advise you," the colonel began gravely, "that it would be in everyone's best interest for you to give up your lieutenancy and join this fine gentleman when he leaves Hertfordshire Wednesday morning."

"Now, why would I wish to do that? I am quite enjoying Hertfordshire, and as you say, my debts are paid." His legs uncrossed and crossed again. "I see no reason to vacate my position."

"I am sorry; did I say your debts were paid? I suppose it would be better to say that your *debtors* have been paid. The debts themselves were *bought*. You, sir, are still fully answerable for every shilling that has been credited to you, which I was shocked to discover amounts to a number in the thousands."

"What is this? What are you about?" Wickham shouted, his chair flying out from under him as he shot to his feet. The semblance of the repose he had been working to manifest vanished. Before them now stood a frenzied beast, a feral cat cornered into a cage and ready to claw his way past his captors.

"Simply this, Mr Wickham," Wentworth answered him, "if you wish to remain a free man, you will sell your commission and join me on Wednesday. We set sail on the first of December, and I intend for you to be on my ship when we heave off. You will find me a fair captain, and my men are as fine as any you will meet in the army."

"What if I have no wish to join the Navy?" he asked, his eyes darting from the colonel to the captain and back.

"That is your choice. However," Wentworth paused, revelling in the delicious tension he was creating, then gradually finished, "if you refuse my generous offer, your debts shall be called in *en totale*, and you will be sent forthwith to debtor's prison, there to languish possibly for decades. Say, Colonel, are they still using skullcaps at Marshalsea?"

"Undoubtedly, but they favour thumbscrews and simple starvation, I believe," answered Colonel Forster with the slightest of grins.

"Why would you do this, go to all this trouble and expense, just to have me on your crew?" he finally thought to ask Wentworth.

"I wish to protect the respectability of the ladies of our fine country, and I know your reputation. So, to sea you shall

SUCH PERSUASIONS AS THESE

go, and the only ladies you will meet will be those whose virtue is already so sullied that you will be loath to touch them. However, I must inform you, you are labouring under a false assumption; I did not go to any expense. I simply offer an alternative to imprisonment."

"If you did not buy my debts, then who did?"

A QUARTER OF AN HOUR PUT PAID TO THE BUSINESS, and Wickham was anxious to make his exit. He had only been so furious one other time in his life—when Darcy had appeared in Ramsgate the day before he was to make his hard-earned fortune.

But *today*—today was so much worse.

To be muscled onto a sailing vessel, bedevilled by a spiteful sea captain, and carried off in the course of forty-eight hours—

This is too much to be borne.

And just when he was about to convince that pretty little Bennet girl to—

Darcy. Again!

This was all his doing. The vindictive swine had hunted down every debtor he had ever had and bought his liabilities just so he could hang them over his head, like the crossbar holding the strings of a marionette, making Wickham his begrudging puppet.

Just as the humiliation of the truth of this analogy began to sink in, Wickham caught sight of a horse in the early morning avenue. There, sitting atop his steed, not ten yards away, was the man himself, Fitzwilliam Darcy.

He watched in angry silence as Darcy lifted his hand to tip

his shining black beaver, a satisfied smirk suffusing his features. Unable to do aught but sneer, Wickham stood in front of the inn, hands balled into fists, as his eyes watched the man who now all but owned him saunter smugly out of town.

CHAPTER FORTY

E lizabeth retired early on Monday evening, leaving her family to their shoe-roses and speculations. Alongside her usual excitement to be dancing under the lights of an elegantly appointed ballroom, she felt something cold warring with that thrill. It was the constant voice telling her that the last time she spoke to the only man she truly wished to dance with, he was accusing her of double-hearted trickery. The set of her shoulders, which she had worked to maintain as this battle had raged inside her throughout the day, finally gave way as she stared unseeing into the flames of her bedroom hearth.

Had he not sent the dress? She was sure he had; Caroline Bingley would never have shown such generosity. Even with her abundant pin money, this gown would have cost her dearly. Miss Bingley was not Elizabeth's gracious benefactor. But then, a gown so elegant would have taken many days to complete; he must have commissioned it before he found her out.

No, she could not take this gift as evidence of his forgiveness or his good opinion.

At least it had given her an excuse to tell him how she felt. Elizabeth knew that such claims of friendship would bring forth vile insults from Miss Bingley, which she would be unable to keep to herself. Even if he did not actually see the letter, she was sure Miss Bingley would quote it, for no other reason than to prove Elizabeth the impertinent chit she had always thought her. He would hear it or he would see it, and he would know that she treasured his friendship—that she treasured him.

A tear escaped her eye at this thought—adding to the many that had fallen whilst penning her missive. After everything, after every condemnation, even after his testing her integrity in such a humiliating way, she loved him.

'For ten thousand a year...'

Her mind flew back to the deserted road near the market. She had hated him for accusing her, for thinking so meanly of her. He had been cold, his air distant and his words bitter. Then, in the midst of their interview, something had shifted. Their conversation had turned, and he had become fervent, his voice low and breathy.

'Sparkling and charming and handsome,' he had called her. *'Standing there so brazenly...your lips parted...inviting me to... And to think, I was about to go against my family, society, everyone. You must have seen how close I was...'*

She was still blushing at the intensity of her longing when a thought struck her: Fitzwilliam Darcy, Master of Pemberley, a man of unimaginable wealth and rank, had been about to give it all to her with a kiss. His passion had been so strong that he was willing to accept her with all her supposed avarice, believing that she did not love him, believing her to be playing a part to him the whole while. Simply because they were out of earshot of the crowds departing Meryton did not mean they were beyond their sight. He had been a breath away from sealing his fate and engaging himself to her with an open and ardent display of affection.

Why?

Could it be that he truly did feel something for her? That he was willing to marry her with unequal affections simply because his own attachment was so strong? Could he be so enamoured that he was prepared to consign himself to a life with someone whom he would always believe had deceived and rooked him into the union?

Or maybe, Elizabeth hoped against all hope, maybe some part of him knew that she was no deceiver. He knew she was not false. And maybe—could it be—

Could Mr Darcy feel for me what I feel for him?

Was that why he had sent the gown? A man in love, unable to openly undo the spiteful actions of another, sought to provide solace, the comfort only a husband could give, by what means he was able. The thought brought her hands to her face, which she rubbed briskly before shifting her gaze from the fireplace to the mirror across from her. Her eyes peeked through her fingers at her own reflection, sliding down over her mouth, and stayed there for many minutes. Her mind kept playing those words in a loop, in an argument, in a logical breakdown, in a drumbeat that thrummed them into her heart.

Why else would he behave so irrationally? Why else would he have felt so betrayed? Why else would he have been so hurt?

He must be in love with me too.

As was to be expected, Longbourn on the day of a ball was a flurry of disordered activity. Stockings were matched, hair jewels fought over, and stays tightened to an unnatural degree. The giggling from the room of the youngest sisters wafted down the stairs, and it imbued the entire house with a spirit of giddiness.

Jane and Elizabeth were cloistered in front of their dressing table to prepare for the party together. Though there was much to say between them, neither sister volunteered any questions or thoughts. They simply assisted one another with their stays and petticoats and styled their hair, each one the other's. Jane's blonde locks were rolled down the side over her ears and pulled back into a soft, low chignon beset with pale pink glass beads throughout. Elizabeth's chestnut curls were piled atop her head in loose braids pinned about one another and interwoven with apricot and ivory ribbon. Instead of jewels, Jane artistically placed the six willow pins criss-crossed over one another in what became a vine trailing up one side of Elizabeth's head and ending in a tuft over her right ear. In the mirror, each sister smiled at how lovely the other was before espying herself and becoming rather wistful.

Mary, in an effort to make a show of how little importance she placed on such occasions, did not join in the merriment of her sisters, but stayed below stairs to read and walk with Mr Collins until late in the afternoon. It was only when Bessie, the upstairs maid, interrupted them to inform her that she was wanted by Jane and Elizabeth that she finally bid him adieu and left him to ready herself. Awaiting her, her two eldest sisters were fully made up and coiffed, lacking only their gowns to make their preparation complete. They sat Mary in front of their dressing table mirror, and Bessie went to work pulling out her low, practical—although softer than usual—bun and brushing her long curls. Jane reached into a velvet pouch and produced four shining silver and pearl hairpins, while Elizabeth clasped about her neck a silver chain with a large pearl pendant.

Before long, all five sisters were downstairs and ready to be handed into the carriages. Mr and Mrs Bennet would be carried to the ball in a borrowed coach, which now waited behind their own. Mr Collins claimed the honour of handing his cousins into the larger equipage, carrying out this sacred duty with alacrity and voicing no little elation at being surrounded by such a bevy of outstanding beauties. When Mary, last in line, reached out to be helped into the coach, his amorous gaze bespoke how utterly taken he was with her. As his hand grasped hers, he bowed deeply over it and bestowed upon it a kiss that left both parties unable to move for a moment. Soon, however, the group was happily settled in and bobbing along to their destination.

Once inside the park, they sat in the queue while the parties ahead of them were received from their conveyances. Before they knew it, however, the family were reunited and entering through the grand double doors of Netherfield and into a wonderland of candlelight and lace. The whole county, it seemed, had turned out for Mr Bingley's inaugural ball, every one of them in their finest. A melange of fragrances— boughs of fir, melting wax, and hothouse roses—permeated the air, mingling together into a unique sensation which added to the transformation of Netherfield House into a grand ballroom.

The receiving line was surprisingly short—only Mr Bingley. Mr Bennet did not waste time congratulating the gentleman overmuch, whilst Mrs Bennet kept her own compliments to a minimum so that Jane might step forwards just those few seconds sooner. Their host's eyes lit up upon seeing his cherished one, and hers flicked between his gaze and the floor.

"Miss Bennet, how lovely you look. You are very welcome," Bingley said cheerfully, taking and holding her proffered hand.

"You are very kind, sir," Jane replied, evidently unsure whether to believe Mr Bingley's display of favour. After looking about her, she added, "Is Miss Bingley unwell? I do not see her."

"Ah, no, my sisters have removed to town, to the comfort of my brother's home."

"Oh," she said, her brows knit in confusion. "I was under the impression that you would all travel to London together after the ball."

"No, Miss Bennet. I have no plans to leave Netherfield," he assured her, his voice low and his gaze warm, "for nothing gives me as much pleasure as my *present company*."

Elizabeth smiled brightly at this exchange, having been pushed closer than she would have chosen by the crush entering behind her. Holding out her hand in an effort to force the couple into propriety, she interrupted, "We are very glad to hear it, Mr Bingley. Thank you for your gracious invitation—on behalf of all my sisters." This was fitting, as it obliged Bingley to release Jane's hand, and it relieved him of having to suffer the three younger Bennets and their cousin. With that, the whole group passed into the great hall, each one dazzled by a thousand glittering flames.

Elizabeth, who had been oscillating between excitement and anxiety over the expectations of this day, now felt an unexpected peace come over her. She was among friends, she was well-liked and respected by all about her, she was in her best looks, and she truly *had* said her piece to the keeper of her heart.

And maybe, just maybe, he longed for her as she did him.

CHAPTER FORTY-ONE

From the corner of the room, Darcy espied Charlotte Lucas, whom he knew to be Elizabeth's particular friend, and determined to keep an eye on her position, as it must be expected that the two would seek one another directly. Continuing to scan the crowd, he smiled when he saw Wentworth in congress with a small group of redcoats, their tails wagging as they attended his friend's recital, no doubt tales of prowess and prize money. She might seek the captain, so he also made a mental note of his place. Darcy would not miss the chance to dance with Elizabeth, to gain again her good graces, and to repair the breach his barbarous pride had created between them.

Permanently.

"Mr Denny," he heard a familiar feminine voice shout from the middle of the room. When he looked, he saw the youngest Bennet girls, hands in the air, waving their closed fans towards another group of young officers. Behind them, the pretty middle daughter was standing with his aunt's parson. In a blink, the three Bennet sisters drew off in different directions, and there, standing alone in the middle of what would eventually be the dance floor, aglow in apricot and ivory silk, was his Elizabeth.

At some point, it seemed, she had lost the loop attaching her train to her wrist, for it lay splayed behind her as if she were in a portrait. That was what she was to him—a portrait of perfection, a marble statue to which no da Vinci or Michelangelo could aspire. Her hair was pulled up off her neck and styled with the ribbons he had chosen, while a vine of goat willows framed one side of her lovely face. The creamy fabric of her lace matched the milky glow of her skin, and the pink in her cheeks from the warmth of the room—or from her youngest sister's uncouth behaviour—brought out the sparkle in her brown eyes. Her blushes soon turned into that cunning smile—the one he knew bespoke amusement with the follies and whims of those about her—and he was a lost man.

Into the crowd he dove, heading for his Helen of Troy. Alas, his was not the only ship her face had launched, for Wentworth was approaching at the same moment and made his bow just seconds before Darcy. Not to be deterred, Darcy turned to the captain with an outstretched hand.

"Wentworth, old man, how do you do?" Darcy regarded him with intensity.

"Darcy. I confess the hour since we last spoke has been trying," he replied. Noting the amplifying pressure Darcy was exerting on his hand, he added, "I was just hoping to tell Miss Elizabeth how lovely she looks before toddling off to run an errand for Colonel Forster." He squeezed back, inflicting no little pain, before letting go of Darcy's hand and turning to bow his leave to Elizabeth with a wink.

"Miss Elizabeth, might I add my compliments. You are indeed in looks this evening," Darcy began as her eyes moved from a retreating Wentworth to meet his own. "Ravishing," he added not quite under his breath as he bowed over her hand.

She gave him a halting smile and then a look of some confusion. "I— I thank you, Mr Darcy," said she with some hesitation, adding after herself, "How do you do? We have not spoken this age."

"Six days is not so long, Miss Elizabeth," he responded before realising how he was giving himself away.

"Six days—I suppose you are correct." Yes, he had given himself away, and she had caught it.

"Though I would give the world," he said gravely, leaning in close as he made his earnest plea, "if we could go back in time and forget the unpleasantness that has passed between us."

"That is quite the request, Mr Darcy. I confess, it may not be so easy to forget," she offered slowly, putting him in acute torture before continuing gently, "but might we both choose to forgive?"

"I know now *I* have nothing to forgive," he confessed, his hand on his heart. "On the contrary, it is you who bear the burden of bestowing clemency."

She was silent for a moment, her gaze intent on the position of his hand upon his breast. Then she coloured, blinking before answering his entreaty with a bow of her head.

They were interrupted by Charlotte Lucas, who insisted she must speak to his Elizabeth privately. He made his bow to Miss Lucas, acknowledging the necessity of turning her over to her friend, but he could not leave before gaining his object. As impudent as he might be reckoned, he pulled himself close to her ear and asked in almost a whisper, "May I have your first, Miss Elizabeth?"

Still unwilling or unable to speak, she curtseyed her consent before being spirited away, her elegant train following her before Miss Lucas, ever faithful, bent to pick it up and return the end to its place on her wrist. To what would become his everlasting bliss, Elizabeth then turned back to look at him, an expectant smile playing upon her glorious features.

"ELIZABETH BENNET, TELL ME THIS INSTANT, ARE YOU engaged to him?" Charlotte cried in a heated whisper as soon as they were out of his hearing.

"Why should you ask such a thing?" Elizabeth answered, feigning surprise that her perceptive friend would come to such a conclusion.

"I am no fool," she retorted in all seriousness. "Did you not see his lapel pin? Do not try to convince me that the goat willows are a coincidence."

Elizabeth coloured. She could not deny this, as his boutonniere—a cluster of golden willow twigs in the exact style of her hair ornaments—was plain for all to see. She had espied them as he lifted his hand to cover his heart, and her own heart had leapt into her throat, rendering her speechless.

"I know what it must look like, but I am as surprised as you are." This was not a lie. While she had suspected Mr Darcy to have gifted her the golden sprigs, she had never expected he would have made a posy of them for himself. "I received these pins as an anonymous gift. Perhaps he did as well," Elizabeth asserted, sounding less and less convinced with each word. "Some sharp wit playing a joke, I dare say."

"Yes, I *dare say* you are correct," her friend replied drily, her lips pursed. Then, touching the gleaming hairpins, she added, "A very *expensive* joke..."

Charlotte's next words, Elizabeth did not attend. Her thoughts were too occupied with the import of her interview with Mr Darcy—all that was said and all that was seen.

He *was* her gracious Benefactor.

What had he expected people to think? she wondered.

He had admitted he was wrong; he knew she was no mercenary. He wished to revive their friendship, to be granted forgiveness for his beastly behaviour. And he wished to dance. He had asked for her first set.

He loves you, Lizzy, she thought to herself. *Why else would he go to all this planning and expense?*

Elizabeth was now sure of Darcy's affection, and nothing in the world could ruin this night.

OUTSIDE THE LAVISHLY DECORATED BALLROOM STOOD a cold and very bitter George Wickham, intent on having one last bit of diversion before quitting the county.

He watched as his unwitting accomplice made her way up the stairs that led into Netherfield House before disappearing inside. Behind the double doors, the band paused to prepare for the first dance. Yes, it would now be just a matter of minutes.

Darcy could not sweep him out of sight like so much rubbish. Wickham would have the last laugh, and it would be at Darcy's expense.

CHAPTER FORTY-TWO

"Have you seen Lydia?" Kitty asked in a huff just as the musicians were signalling the start of their first piece. The ballroom of Netherfield was teeming, and the excitement of the starting set had caused the throng to stir in every direction as dancers lined up, and those who did not dance made their way to the fringes of the room.

"She is probably standing up with one of the officers," Elizabeth answered hurriedly, her eyes and thoughts on the man walking towards her. Before Kitty could protest, Mr Darcy took Elizabeth's hand and led her to their place on the floor.

Looking down the line, Elizabeth was gratified to see Jane and Bingley opening the dance together and Mary accompanied by Mr Collins as well. Beholding Mr Darcy across from her, she became overcome with joy. Rather than dissolving into tears, however, Elizabeth was seized by an impulse to tease her beloved, to shower him with impertinence and watch as he drank it in.

She began by casting him an investigative eye.

"What is it that fixates you so?" he enquired, apparently delighted at being the target of her perusal.

"Oh," she began as if she did not realise she was looking at him so intently. "I suppose I was just attempting to sketch your character."

"And how do you get on?"

"I do not get on at all," she answered with a feigned sigh. "I must confess, I was rather surprised to have you request my first set. It is quite the distinction, you know."

"Why should you be surprised?" he teased her back. "Should one wonder that I wish to dance with the handsomest woman in the room?"

The dance separated the two smiling partners, then brought them together again directly. She parried, "I seem to remember getting the impression that you were not so interested in my company last time we spoke. How very mercurial of you, Mr Darcy."

He answered this accusation with a momentary wince of pain, but her continued playful demeanour assured him that she was not truly holding this against him.

"Mercurial, Miss Bennet?" he finally said, awaiting her explanation with complaisance.

"Why, yes. I was under the impression that your good opinion once lost was lost forever. Yet, here we are," she paused as they passed about another couple. Arching an eyebrow, she added, "I did not think you so... *inconstant*." She attempted to purse her lips severely, but the merry dimple peeking out from her cheek betrayed her.

"I hate to disappoint you, Miss Elizabeth," he began, mirroring her jovial manner. She had hoped he would play along in her verbal swordplay, and this was just what she could have wished. "I am afraid you have misread the situation entirely, and it has led you to erroneous conclusions."

"Is that so? Pray, enlighten me," she glittered.

"You assume that I have lost my good opinion of you. Though it may have seemed so, that could not be further from the truth. I, myself, was labouring under a misguided presumption, and it had the unfortunate effect of creating an obstacle to our friendship. For this, I sincerely apologise."

"Apology accepted," she said and in such good timing that her words were uttered just as the dance called for a gracious curtsey on her part. As the second song began, she added, "So, you are not inconstant as a rule, then?"

"I am not," he answered earnestly. "My friendship, my regard, my affections, once I give them, I hope I can be counted on to be constant in them." At this claim, he peered into her face with a sincerity that caused her to miss a step in the choreography.

A moment later saw them at the end of the line, and he escorted her to the side of the dancers, bringing his body closer to hers than the dance had allowed before continuing, "I have chosen to make very few promises in my life, Miss Elizabeth, but when I do, I strive to live up to them." She could not speak. He added, "My heart is constant, and I must confess to you now, it has long been—"

"Darcy." The sound of Frederick's voice caused Mr Darcy's face to fly up, halting his speech. Her old friend grabbed her partner by the arm and whispered fervently into his ear, causing the gentleman's eyebrows to rise in shock and then furrow in obvious dismay. He cast Elizabeth a look of regret before excusing himself in haste.

At that moment, Mr Collins and Mary took themselves from among the dancers, the exercise apparently overtaxing the parson. Mary, the one whom this frailty should be expected to affect the most, was unperturbed, preferring, as she always had, to play for dancers rather than join them. The fact that he was a fumbling oaf of a partner, constantly missing steps and apologising to all about him, thus missing further steps, did not seem to bother her. Mary had simply tapped him on the shoulder to remind him where he was and what he was expected to do, and he had fallen in line.

A very agreeable situation for both of them, Elizabeth thought.

"I say, was not that Mr Darcy I saw dancing with you?" Mr Collins asked after catching his breath.

"Ah, yes, he was called away. It seems there was an emergency of some kind, and only he could assist," she answered, attempting to conceal her resentment.

"Oh yes, I can believe it. Why, Lady Catherine relies on him for simply everything. I understand he visits her every spring to care for the household matters at Rosings. And why should he not look after her interests? For indeed, they shall become his own soon enough."

"Does Mr Darcy look forward to inheriting Rosings? Has Lady Catherine not an heir? I understood you to say she had a daughter to whom it would be left," Elizabeth enquired, uncomfortable with the direction of this conversation.

"Yes, Miss Anne de Bourgh, heiress of Rosings and very extensive property. She is a jewel, the brightest ornament, whose true beauty is far superior to the handsomest of her sex, because there is that in her features which marks a young woman of distinguished birth. Which, of course, makes Mr Darcy a very fortunate man indeed."

"I suppose he is fortunate," Elizabeth offered, unsure, "to have such an exceptional cousin."

"As am I," the parson said with a besotted grin as he took Mary's hand once again and bowed over it. Then, in an exultant aside, he added, "I only hope I shall have such felicity with my own cousin as Mr Darcy shall have with his. Just think what a match that will be. Two glorious persons and two glorious fortunes." Then, with a titter, he turned back to his fair partner and entreated her to rejoin the dance.

Elizabeth stared after them, blinking. *Do I understand correctly? Mr Darcy is to marry Miss Anne de Bourgh?*

The room began to spin. The twinkling of the candles, the melange of odours, the movement of the dance, and the warmth of the crowd began to play on her senses. Elizabeth felt suddenly faint. Grabbing the arm of the nearest person, she asked that he might assist her to a chair.

The music went silent in her ears as she heard Darcy's words again, *'My heart is constant, and I must confess, it has long been—It has long been engaged elsewhere. It has long been the property of my superior cousin. It has long been attached to one of distinguished birth and excelling worth, whose great fortune I very much wish to add to my own.*

Looking up, she saw that the concerned and ever-amiable Sir William Lucas was her willing crutch, and he carried out her request with utmost care. After the set ended, Jane and Bingley noted her absence and made their way to her. They found Sir William looming, a glass of wine in hand, ready to bring to her lips. They relieved him of this duty, for he was presently being hailed by a young officer.

Elizabeth was mortified. She could feel her cheeks aflame and only hoped Darcy would not walk in just at this moment to see her in such a state. As the minutes went by, she regained a measure of equanimity and was able to tell Jane she was well, to go back to the dance, and that she only needed a bit of quiet away from the crowd. Jane reluctantly acceded, and Elizabeth made her way out of the grand ballroom.

CHAPTER FORTY-THREE

S ome time earlier, Kitty had approached Wentworth's party in search of her youngest sister. Elizabeth had dismissed her offhand, and so had Jane, as they were both expected to join in the dance. Having searched through the throng of dancers, however, Kitty was sure Lydia was not among them.

Wentworth had been having what he might call an interesting conversation with Colonel Forster and his inexcusably young wife when Kitty appeared. To Kitty's distressed plea, Harriet Forster shot her a look of panic and placed a finger over her mouth, urging her to silence. That finger soon turned into a hand covering a shrill giggle.

"What is it, Harriet?" her husband demanded.

"I cannot tell. I promised," she answered, attempting to stifle a grin.

"*Harriet...*" he warned, his age and demeanour making him appear rather fatherly.

"Oh, pooh," she pouted. "You never let me have any fun. And it was going to be such a good joke too."

"Where is Miss Lydia, Mrs Forster?" Wentworth demanded, a knot of dread forming in his chest.

"But I promised poor Wickham. You shall see soon, anyhow. She was to meet him outside and sneak him in amongst the dancers as soon as the first set started. What a fine joke it will be—to see that nasty Mr Darcy go apoplectic upon sight of poor Wickham. They are probably dancing now."

But Kitty had been right; Lydia was not among those standing up, and it was well into the second dance. Wentworth, knowing what the blackguard was capable of, left them posthaste in search of Darcy, calling behind him to the colonel, "Find Sir William."

"La, Wickham, why should I wish to go into the family rooms when there is dancing to be had?" Lydia Bennet cried. Wickham was trying to convince her that he needed to warm up by a good fire before he could be prevailed upon to join the ball in earnest. They stood near the corner of the great house, shrouded in the shadow of the tall hedgerow that stood between them and the torches of the driveway. The cold November air was proving an opponent with which neither wished to contend much longer.

"I cannot dance; I am frozen to the bone from standing out here all evening waiting for you. Come, now, the least you can do is join me for a few moments' conversation while I regain feeling in my fingers." Wickham had learnt the way to the private rooms from Mrs Forster, who had been a guest at Netherfield with her husband. He took Lydia's hand and led her, not to the front steps, but towards the side of the building, where he knew stood a door which led up to the main floor.

"Where are we going? I thought your whole purpose in coming tonight was to confound that awful Mr Darcy; we cannot do that unless we are *in the ballroom*. And besides, you shall be plenty warm whilst we are dancing. *Come.*" Lydia tugged him the other way, towards the door through which the guests had entered that evening.

He pulled her hard and, with a spin, she was in his arms, her body pressed against his. She let out a yelp, which he silenced with a fervid kiss upon her open mouth. Rather than melting into his embrace as he had presumed she would, however, he found himself having to hold her tighter so as to keep her in his grasp at all.

Oh, she is a fighter, this little vixen! He was equal to it. As Lydia's hands pushed and scratched, he kept his mouth firmly on hers to muffle her screams.

Wickham released her lips only to say, "Come, kitten, retract your claws. This is what you came out here for, is it not? I leave tomorrow, so let us stop all this pretending. You have made your show of maidenly outrage; now let us get on."

That moment of freedom was all she needed to produce a scream that would carry throughout the grounds of Netherfield. Wickham quickly turned her in his arms to cover her curst mouth with his hand, then dragged her kicking into the hedges. He had to decide at that moment whether to carry his point with the flighty little flirt or cut his losses and pretend he had never been there. The cut of her gown revealed to him the glistening sweat beading on her heaving bosom; he made his decision.

It was unseasonably cold, but the biting wind had been far more pleasant than the scratching spikes of holly leaves now attacking him. The accursed shrubbery snagged his jacket and the fabric of Lydia's gown, slowing his progress away from the stone face of the manor house. Not that the wriggling bit of baggage in his arms was any help, either. He had half a mind to leave her go.

In for a penny, in for a pound, he thought as he felt her soft body against his.

Before Wickham could make it through the thicket and find a suitable place to carry out his intention, however, a wrenching pain tore through his injured shoulder. A large hand clutched him from behind, pulled him through to the other side of the hedge, and none too gently threw him to the frozen ground.

Wickham lost hold of his captive, and his lip curled into a sneer of pure contempt as he watched Lydia Bennet fly into the arms of none other than Fitzwilliam Darcy.

DARCY HELD LYDIA BENNET'S HEAD CLOSE TO HIS chest, much as he had when comforting his own sister after her encounter with the same man. Unlike his mild and calm Georgiana, however, Miss Lydia was sobbing, weeping into the lapels of his wool frock coat in utter distress. Georgiana had been a willing participant in Wickham's schemes; it was clear that Lydia Bennet had not. At least, not in the schemes he had put upon her after their agreement to meet outside the ball.

When Sir William and Colonel Forster arrived, alerted to their location by Miss Lydia's wails of fear and grief, the girl threw herself into the more familiar embrace of her neighbour, who stroked her hair and asked her in fatherly tones, "What has happened, dear one?"

"He tried to get me to go with him to the family rooms, to be alone with him, and when I would not, he grabbed me. I tried to scream, but he kissed me and covered my mouth. Oh God, what would he have done to me?"

"He seized you and intended to take you somewhere, away from here? Is that right, Miss Lydia?" Colonel Forster asked seriously.

She nodded furiously and burst into a fresh flush of tears. "I tried to fight him off, but he was too strong."

"That would explain the scratches on his face," Forster said.

"This man must be placed under arrest immediately," Sir William commanded.

"Oh no, this is a military matter. And we take kidnapping and the attempted assault of a gentleman's daughter very seriously," the colonel stated firmly.

"Kidnapping is a capital offence, is it not?" Wentworth asked, still holding the villain by the neck, one hand digging into his shoulder.

"I believe so," Forster replied, casting a repugnant glare upon the man who had charmed them all so heartlessly. "I shall see that he is dealt with, one way or the other."

CHAPTER FORTY-FOUR

U pon the assurance that Wickham was no longer on the premises, Darcy turned to Wentworth and patted the fine captain on the back.

"That was well done, old man," Darcy commended him.

"No," Wentworth replied shaking his head. "I should have known he would try something like this; they always do when their backs are against the wall."

"Something tells me you did know. You read the situation expertly and saved a young lady from ruin. Your quick thinking ruled the day, Wentworth. I am honoured to call you friend."

"Likewise." Wentworth shook Darcy's hand, urging him to run back to the bewitching partner from whom he had been so abruptly separated.

"Heigh up there, Wentworth," Darcy called as the captain began making his way back inside. "You cannot know everything, but I believe you have single-handedly changed the course of my life. Even tonight, you rescued me again from a lifetime of dealing with that haggard thorn in my side, George Wickham. That, in itself, is worth a king's ransom. What I am trying to say is, I wish to relieve your suffering in some way, as you have done for me."

With that, he reached into his coat pocket and pulled out an envelope. He had asked for it to be included when he sent to London for the documents he needed to clear his name against Wickham's calumny. As soon as he had heard that Wentworth had ties to Somersetshire, it occurred to him that having these papers on hand might prove useful.

Passing the envelope to his friend, he explained, "I wish to offer you a seven-year lease on a property I hold in Somersetshire. It has several tenants and a capable steward, so one person should be able to run it on their own most of the time with no trouble. You will find the rent quite reasonable."

Wentworth blinked, completely taken aback, doubtless wondering whether he should be offended at such presumption.

"This should give you a perfectly respectable place to *keep a wife* while you are at sea and a pleasant situation to enjoy with her when you are not."

Captain Frederick Wentworth stared at the packet in Darcy's hand, unwilling to take it, but evidently afraid to lose what he was offering him. Finally, he held his hands up and shook his head. "I appreciate what you are trying to do, but I cannot take charity, not even from Croesus himself."

"Do you know what you have done for me, Wentworth? You have given me back the woman I love. You have made me see myself for who I truly am, and helped me to become a man who might one day deserve her. I shall benefit from your friendship till my last breath. I owe you more than I could ever possibly give. Please, accept this as the small token of my great appreciation that it is," Darcy said earnestly, pressing the document into his hand. "Besides, you shall be a paying lessee; it is not charity."

Wentworth took the document and, without opening it, secreted it into his jacket's inner pocket. "This is not a yes."

"Of course not," Darcy acquiesced with a smile.

"Good luck tonight, old man. Miss Elizabeth is a gem; I have no doubt you will cherish her as she deserves."

"I intend to," he promised.

Upon re-entering the ball, the gentlemen found that their absence had been of little note. Couples were moving through the dance, matrons were talking about their children, and old men were hidden in the card room.

Wentworth headed to his guest quarters to undo the effects of his scuffle, while Darcy simply patted his lapels down to smooth them after the fierceness of Miss Lydia's grip, eager to seek out Elizabeth.

Darcy espied Bingley and his angel, as well as the cler-gyman courting Miss Mary. Mrs Bennet was coddling a still-shaken Lydia, who was also being lovingly attended by Miss Kitty.

Scanning the length and breadth of the ballroom, however, he noted that there was one Bennet female who was nowhere to be found. Darcy's heart started pounding as his eyes moved from corner to corner of the grand room, taking in every dark pile of curls, searching for his goat willows.

Could she have left? Where could she be? How can I finish making amends?

He had been determined to repair all that was broken between them this night, indeed he thought he had made rather a good start. He had listened with forbearance as she called him out for his changefulness and for not living up to his own ideals. He had taken the opportunity to assure her that his heart was not so inconstant. He was about to tell her just where his heart lay when he was so abruptly interrupted by Wentworth—by Wickham, really.

Wickham.

When had that knave not tainted everything Darcy had worked hard to protect? And tonight, he had almost made Elizabeth's family a subject of infamy. Thank Heaven for Wentworth and his quick thinking—they had descended the stairs outside just in time to hear Miss Lydia's terrified scream, and it was Wentworth who had noted the rustling in the bushes. He had then suggested they split up—one following them into the hedgerow and the other sneaking upon him from behind. And it had worked beautifully.

How happy Darcy had been to offer the captain the chance of a situation that might answer his immediate needs. The land had been in his family for decades but without a master or a mistress since the distant cousin who had kept the house had died. Darcy had not thought about it for years, except to check that the groundskeepers were being paid and the steward was running things as he ought. If he could make it available to Captain and Mrs Wentworth, it would be as much a blessing to himself as it would be to them.

Truth be told, he had expected another blessing tonight. He looked down at the clutch of goat willow pins on his lapel. Pulling out one golden twig, he sighed as he twisted it between his fingers and thumb, thinking of how lovely Elizabeth had looked adorned with them in her hair. Perhaps he had been too forward, too overt. Was this yet another case of him being high-handed with those he loved? His cursed pride!

When would he recognise it for what it was and finally have it in hand?

Under good regulation, indeed, he berated himself. *Coxcomb.*

He was sure now he had gone too far—he might as well have told the whole county they were engaged. Of course she would be mortified by such gossip-fodder. His grand romantic gesture—had it been the death-knell of his hopes? Had she run home as soon as the townsfolk started talking? Elizabeth would not have gone back alone, would she?

Where is she?

Just then, he saw Miss Bennet approaching Mrs Bennet and her youngest daughters. Surely she would know where her sister had disappeared to.

"Did I not see her speaking with Wentworth?" Bingley volunteered.

"Did you? I am sorry, Mr Darcy, I do not know," Jane said, obviously troubled that she had to disappoint him. "She simply told me she needed some time alone." Looking down at Miss Lydia, she added, "Perhaps a quiet refuge would be of benefit to you, as well, darling."

Refuge. A quiet refuge.

Darcy knew exactly where she was.

It took him two breaths to reach the library door. At the sight of the heavy, ornately carved hardwood planks before him, something made him halt, his hand on the knob. Should he go in? Should he knock? Would she wish to see him? What if she was seeking refuge from him?

On the other hand, he finally reasoned, *what if she has been waiting there for me these three quarters of an hour, and I have disappointed her long enough?*

Certainly, she knew what his intentions were. His

thoughtlessness had made that plain to all. *Is that why she went into hiding rather than continuing to dance?* She no doubt had a line of beaux awaiting the chance to escort her for a set; anyone who had eyes would wish to be seen with such a divine creature. Why was she not in the ballroom, rejoicing in her triumph?

Perhaps she was awaiting him after all. He tightened his grip on the knob and turned it slowly, allowing the weight of the door to pull him into the room. He did not wish to startle her, and so gave a gentle greeting by way of, "Miss Elizabeth?"

There was no answer. He pushed the door the rest of the way open, a vision appearing in his mind of his sweet conqueror standing before him, arms wrapped anxiously about her torso, the light of the hearth revealing to him her shapely legs in silhouette through thin white muslin. His breath caught in his throat, and he stumbled towards the mirage, only to have it disappear as he stepped onto the thick floral rug.

It was not she. Elizabeth was not there.

He turned about to inspect every corner. Alas, he was indeed alone. His blood was coursing in his ears, and the realisation that his careful designs were frustrated quite unmanned him. Robbed of strength, he fell into his accustomed chair, and, setting his elbows upon his knees, held his head in his hands.

He was surprised—though he should not have been, he knew—to hear a roaring purr at his feet, then to feel Italics's soft body as the cat snaked through and about his legs in a figure-eight. Finally, the feline lifted himself up with his front paws on his knee to rub his face against Darcy's, causing the man to change his position and allow the mongrel onto his lap.

"I have done it this time, old man," Darcy told him, his voice dripping with regret. Italics, ever the comforter, put his heart into giving him the solace he needed by way of allowing him to stroke his back, his chin, and even his belly, all whilst emitting a voluble purr of delight, which could not help but soothe Darcy's inner ache. Soon they were forehead to forehead again, Italics nuzzling Darcy's face as the forlorn lover whispered his sorrows to his feline friend.

It was whilst in this attitude that Darcy heard light footsteps behind him, followed by a feminine voice.

"Oh, to be a cat," Elizabeth said. "Kisses and sweet nothings from the worthiest of creatures..."

CHAPTER FORTY-FIVE

E lizabeth kissed the cheek of her dear friend Frederick and made her way to the ballroom directly. How could she have doubted Mr Darcy? *The ball gown? The goat willows?* Sending her these things at all was far beyond the office of a friend, so why should she believe that he had a previous understanding that would bar their attachment?

No, he loved her, she knew—a fact confirmed by her precious Frederick.

I must have more faith in him.

"Elizabeth," Jane exclaimed as she saw her wandering through the crowd. Enquiring of Jane whether she had seen Mr Darcy, her sister told her of their conversation, and as soon as Elizabeth had heard the words 'a quiet refuge', she knew just where to look for him.

"I have done it this time, old man," she heard Darcy say from inside the library. Tiptoeing past the open door, she watched in adoration as the tall, strong Master of Pemberley kissed, cooed, and whispered to the Master of the Netherfield

Library, nuzzling his face against the furry monster's fore-head. The sight brought back to her mind her beloved's words of those interminable days ago when she first saw him in the same posture.

"Oh, to be a cat," she finally spoke, "to be nuzzled and kissed by the worthiest of creatures..."

"Elizabeth," he uttered as he rose, the cat falling uncere-moniously onto the carpet below.

She walked over and stood before him, the gold flecks in his eyes glittering in the firelight. "Mr Darcy," she curtseyed before giving him a stern look. "This is twice in one evening you have attempted to evade my company."

"I assure you, nothing could be further from the truth, Miss Elizabeth." A silence overtook the couple for several moments before Darcy stepped nearer and reached out his hands to take hers. "In point of fact, there is no one whose company I desire more." He lifted her hands and pressed them to his lips, his eyes closing as if revelling in her close-ness. "And if I had my way, I should be blessed to have you near me every moment of every day."

Elizabeth responded to this earnest declaration, not with impertinence or wit, but with a single tear falling from a shining eye.

"Elizabeth, my truest friend," he implored, lowering her hands to clutch them over his heart, "how I have longed for you. It was deplorable of me to accuse you, to impute such ignoble motives to your pure heart. You have given and sacri-ficed and suffered for my ease, and I vow to you now that, if you will have me, I shall spend the rest of my life doing the same for you. You shall have every comfort, every luxury; indeed, I could never give you enough to demonstrate how dear you are to me."

"I do not want them," she finally found her voice, "I do not want the jewels and fine carriages. You must know that."

"I do know, my darling, I do know. Then, may I offer you," he asked in quiet tones as he lifted one hand to her face, his fingers slipping into the hair behind her ear while his thumb caressed her blushing cheek, "the constant and unalloyed affection of a most devoted husband?"

It was everything Elizabeth had expected, everything she had wished for, and yet, being here in this moment, it was so much more than she could have imagined. He loved her. He loved her and treasured her and wished to have her at his side forever. She did not feel a fluttering in her stomach, nor a lump in her throat, which thoughts of him had up till now conjured in her psyche; rather, she was overcome with a calm contentment.

This was simply so right.

She had vowed that nothing but the very deepest love would induce her into matrimony. At one time, she had feared she would never find it, nor recognise it if it came. As his mouth found her own and they shared their first expressions of affection in that dimly lit book-room, however, she wondered why she had ever worried. It had found her—*he* had found her—and she determined at that moment that they should always be perfectly happy.

When the pair re-entered the party, they discovered that the throng of guests was heading towards the dining room. *Could all of this have happened before supper?*

As soon as his company was seated, their host stood and clinked his glass with a silver knife. "My esteemed guests, I thank you for joining me for our little gathering this evening," he began.

"Crush, more like," came Frederick's laughing voice, followed by snickers from about the room.

Bingley good-naturedly chuckled along with the crowd before continuing, "You, the kind people of Hertford-shire, have made this incomer feel very welcome, like a genuine part of the neighbourhood. Your fine hospitality has been very appreciated. In my short time here, I have made many new friends; ones I hope to keep through the years. But, there is *one* person," he said, his eyes falling upon Jane, sitting serenely to his right, "who has made me see my *future* in Meryton."

Jane blushed and demurred before accepting his proffered hand and standing up to join him before the party.

"And this evening, Miss Jane Bennet has given me the singular honour of accepting my proposal and has agreed to become my wife."

Gasps and applause filled the room as Mr Bingley kissed the hand of his betrothed before them all. None was more vociferous than Mrs Bennet, whose cry of joy and relief cut through the utterances of all those about her as she rushed towards her eldest daughter. Falling upon her neck with kisses and an eager embrace, she declared, "I knew you could not be so beautiful for nothing."

DARCY, NOW STANDING AT AN APPROPRIATE DISTANCE from his unacknowledged affianced bride, exchanged a look of sheer delight with Elizabeth before striding towards his friend with an outstretched hand of congratulations. Bingley shook it heartily as Darcy gave him a firm pat on the shoulder. "Well done, my friend," Darcy told him, "I know you two will be very happy together. And I could not be more pleased for you."

"Thank you, Darcy. That means more than you know," he told him seriously before turning his attention back to his blooming betrothed and the crowd's many wishes of felicity.

Elizabeth, who had been standing in the doorway searching out her seat, made her way over to Miss Bennet, and the two squeezed one another with such warmth that no words were needed. They regarded one another at length while the revellers again began to reclaim their seats.

The cheerful commotion had not subsided before another knife was heard being tapped against another glass. The elegant guests of Mr Bingley's ball turned their attention towards the Bennets' austerely attired cousin, who was standing halfway down the dining table. Elizabeth and Jane both gasped, evidently horrified at what might come out of the pompous parson's mouth, but there was no stopping him now.

"Ladies and gentlemen," Mr Collins began in a nasally projection. "First of all, as a near relation to Miss Jane Bennet, I should like to offer my sincere compliments to herself and her betrothed on behalf of all her family, and, if I may be so bold, on behalf of my noble patroness, Lady Catherine de Bourgh. I am sure she would approve of your choice, Cousin Jane, as Mr Bingley is perfectly well set-up without being too far above your station, a situation a lady of rank such as Lady Catherine cannot countenance. And so I feel free to wish you every felicity in your marriage."

Darcy's eyes drifted heavenward as the man went on about his patroness, as if that woman had, or indeed desired to have, anything at all to do with the couple at the head of the table.

At the clergyman's deep bow, Bingley rose to thank him,

but Mr Collins put his hand to his lips in a silent command to hush his host before continuing, "Many of you have no doubt noticed *my* marked attentions towards *another* young lady by the name of Bennet, and I should like to take this opportunity to declare before you all the violence of my affections and to beg my fair cousin, Mary," he said, dropping to his knees before his rosy-cheeked maiden, "to make me the happiest of men and consent to be my helpmeet and life's companion."

This passionate proclamation was met mostly with silence as Mary appropriately nodded and covered her mouth in surprise. As the couple looked over their audience, obviously expecting similar applause to the previous announcement, the friends and neighbours of the young lady slowly began to clap and call out kind congratulations. Mary, ever one to accept the smallest of encouragement as the greatest compliment, could not have been more satisfied with this reception of her happy news. And her partner, looking upon his answer to Lady Catherine's clear directives, could not remove the smile from his face.

At this, both Miss Bennet and Elizabeth approached their younger sister and embraced her tenderly. Mr Collins bowed low in acceptance of their good wishes, and they curtseyed before returning to the head of the table where Elizabeth and Darcy were assigned for supper alongside Miss Bennet and Bingley.

Darcy and Elizabeth shared many conspiratorial glances and smiles as the meal wore on, but neither would speak their joyful news. Though they had not discussed it, it seemed they both felt the need to allow Elizabeth's elder sister to have her moment as the star of the evening. She would stand up with Bingley for the closing set, and she would accept the handshakes and embraces of all who knew her and wished her well. His beloved's elder sister would float through the room the happiest of creatures—closely followed by Bingley in both bliss and proximity—and Darcy and Elizabeth would keep their secret and earnestly rejoice with them.

If anyone took note of the gentleman from Derbyshire sharing two more sets that evening with the second Bennet daughter, no one seemed willing to comment on it.

EPILOGUE

"What is it, love?" Elizabeth asked her husband as he finished reading the letter he had just received. The weeks since their wedding, which they had shared with her sister and his closest friend, had taught her that Darcy's eyebrow tended to twitch whilst reading correspondence that gave him joy, whether a grin accompanied it or no.

"Wentworth has moved into Snow Hill and finds it very agreeable," he answered simply.

"I have never been to Somersetshire; does it snow there?"

"I believe not," he told her. "And before you ask, it is not that hilly, either. But that is beyond the point. Captain Wentworth and his bride find that it suits their tastes and more than meets their needs." At this bit of news, a broad smile overspread his face, and Elizabeth snatched the paper out of his hand, eager to read of her old friend's good fortune.

Apparently, Frederick had taken her urgings to heart and, upon his return to Somersetshire, did all he could to rescue his beloved from her deplorable family. "Write to her. Tell her you shall come for her. If her love for you is in any measure comparable to my affection for Mr Darcy," she had implored him in that corridor on the night of the ball, "she will wait for you. Tell her to do so. *Beg* her to do so."

And he had. As soon as it was known that he was the leaseholder of a seven-hundred-acre parcel of land with five tenant farmers, a great house to rival Upper Cross Manor—wherever that was—and an income of several hundred pounds a year, it was decided that Anne Elliot's attaching herself to a sea captain was not such a bad thing after all. In short order, Sir Walter began to confess he had always had a fondness for young Wentworth and only hoped his eldest daughter might find half such a man. Furthermore, as the captain was to head back to sea so soon, it was deemed most proper to forgo a long engage-ment. The Elliot family, and indeed his nemesis, Lady Russell, it seemed, could not dispose of Miss Anne quickly enough.

"Well, good for him. And good riddance to the rest of them," Elizabeth crowed as she set the letter down on her husband's heavy walnut desk. Walking about it to stand over him, she added, "And well done you, Mr Darcy." He caught her about the waist and pulled her onto his lap, placing kisses on her cheek, her jaw, and her neck before she protested, "Georgiana might walk in at any moment."

"Mm. Let her," he mumbled against the sensitive skin of her throat. "She must get used to seeing these expressions of affection. One cannot have a wife as tempting as you and be expected to keep his hands—or his lips—to himself."

"Tempting? Me? I did not believe you thought so," she informed him in as serious a tone as she could muster under the onslaught of his ardour.

"How on earth could you have missed the fact that I find you tempting?"

"She is tolerable, I suppose, but not handsome enough to tempt me," she said in a mocking, manly voice.

He started, then looked into her eyes with knitted brows before asking, "What kind of unmitigated fool would ever say such a thing about a woman as charming," another kiss, "handsome," another kiss, "alluring," another kiss, "and *devastatingly tempting* as you?"

"I confess, I wondered the same thing," she answered as she bent her head back to accept his further ministrations. "I suppose I must have imagined it."

"Mm," he smiled, his lips whispering kisses along her collarbone. "Must have."

As WENTWORTH MADE HIS WAY UP THE LONG, TREE-lined drive towards the grand double staircase that would bring him home to Snow Hill House, he pondered his blessings. Already, he was taking prizes; he had just been offered a frigate; and now he had four weeks leave to spend with his Anne.

It had taken every vestige of his humility to write to her, but he had done it. He knew it was proper to send a letter of acknowledgment in response to her rejection, to return any correspondence or gifts she may have given him, but he could not. How could he acknowledge sentiments so patently false? As if he could ever return her letters! Instead, he took the only opportunity he might ever have again to put to paper everything he felt for her. Elizabeth had begged him to lay his heart open to his beloved, to beg her to believe in him, to assure her of his constancy and his belief that, despite her family's protestations, he and Anne *would* be successful. After telling Anne of Darcy's offer—and that only the assurance of her happiness and security could induce him to accept a proposal that smacked so much of charity—he concluded:

I am half agony, half hope.

Your letter pierced my soul with grief. Weak and resentful, I momentarily became, but never could my affection be so easily extinguished. I shall love none but you. For you alone, I think and plan. Have you not seen this?

I leave for Somersetshire on the morrow, uncertain of my fate. A word from you, a look, will be enough to decide whether I importune you for your hand once again that very moment—or never.

Perhaps your family have claimed that I shall forget you, cease to love you, as if your worth or the strength of our attachment could be diminished by time or distance. Pray know that there does exist true devotion and constancy among men. Believe it to be most fervent, most undeviating, in—

FW

His missive had reached Kellynch Hall only a day before he himself did. Wentworth had not even thanked the stable boy for taking his horse before Anne Elliot was out the door, down the steps, and in his arms.

Her joy made his own complete.

Staring at the façade of the fine house they shared, he caught sight of her standing before the parlour window. She smiled brightly when her gaze met his, and his steps quickened. To think, if it were not for Darcy and Elizabeth, he would not be here today, knowing that the love of his life was awaiting him beyond those ornate doors.

He sent up a short prayer to thank Heaven that Anne Elliot had not been his *first* love.

"SHALL THEY BE HERE TODAY, LIZZY?" GEORGIANA asked with understated eagerness.

"The note I received from Jane sets their arrival for just before tea, and your brother foresees no delays based on the weather. So, yes, with any luck they shall." Elizabeth could not have been happier that her new little sister looked so forward to meeting her eldest. Having heard much of Jane, Georgiana no doubt wished to see the glowing paragon of loveliness with her own eyes.

As charming as Mrs Bingley was to look upon, however, Elizabeth had always been careful to extol to Miss Darcy the beauty of her character, her innate good nature, how she always sought and found the very best in everyone.

It had taken many weeks for Elizabeth to become 'Lizzy' to the young woman, and that only with careful prodding and personal interest. Georgiana was still so unsure of herself after her summer's escapade with George Wickham that she did not feel there was anything of value Elizabeth might find in her. News of that man's having been cashiered and eventually transported to Australia for his crimes had not helped matters. Eventually, though, as she and Darcy shared their every joy with the girl, she began to speak more freely, and soon they were a family, the three of them.

Elizabeth only hoped that Jane's sweet and loving temperament would encourage Georgiana to be her delightful self with their guests.

278

It turned out her worry had been for naught. Jane and Bingley were so easy that the whole party was able to relax and enjoy themselves as if they had never parted, not a stranger among them.

Georgiana was indeed awestruck with Jane's beauty, as had been expected, but so was Elizabeth, for added to her natural magnificence was the glow that only expectant motherhood brings to a woman. Her eyes were brighter, her skin was creamier, and her hair was shinier. There truly was not another woman in the land who could compare to Mrs Charles Bingley.

"And how do your sisters do?" Elizabeth asked as they were settling in after tea.

"Ah, Louisa and Hurst are the same as always—ever on the lookout to invade our home and empty our larder. And Caroline—this is news—she has married," Bingley said, evidently having taken lessons in gossip-mongering from Mrs Philips, so eager was he to impart the intelligence.

"Married? To whom? How did this come about?" Darcy asked.

"Well, shortly after your wedding, Caroline suffered a...a bit of a turn," began Jane sweetly.

"*A bit of a turn*? She pulled the Rembrandt off the wall and broke it over Hurst's head!"

"It was, as we now understand, an acute brain fever. Naturally, Charles and I wished to assist her through this distress, so we made discreet enquiries throughout London and found the finest mental physiologist—" Jane continued before being interrupted again by her boisterous bridegroom.

"A bloodletter for lunatics is what he is."

"—the *finest mental physiologist,* a man by the name of Herr Doctor Maximilian Schweitzenheim-Bluchenhauser, who worked with her individually for many weeks and finally helped her to understand that her worth lies in her charac-ter..." Jane shot her husband a disapproving look at the snort he let out in response to this explanation before adding, "and not in her standing in society. And he has helped her to... *improve*...her character so as to...*find* that worth."

Darcy and Elizabeth were both awaiting the love story that must follow, whom she might have met and how, but an awkward silence fell over the party. "And?" they enquired in unison.

"And in improving *her* worth, he greatly improved his own —by twenty thousand pounds!" Bingley crowed.

"She married him?" exclaimed Darcy, having expected to hear that her improved character had attracted some fitting suitor or other. Bingley nodded in great motions, still finding humour in the delicious ridiculousness of it all.

"So, Miss Bingley is now Mrs Caroline Schweitzenheim-Bluchenhauser? Does she reside in London?" Georgiana asked sweetly, as if the lady had married a Shaw or a Brooke.

"Yes, and Darcy, this is the best part," Bingley turned to his friend. "His house is not three blocks from Cheapside—right in front of Edward Gardiner's warehouses!"

The party laughed heartily at the irony of it whilst Jane chided them for triumphing over a person whom she said no longer existed. Her new sister, Mrs Schweitzenheim-Bluchen-hauser, was now quite modest and accommodating, and "just think of how nice it will be to see her whilst visiting Aunt and Uncle Gardiner."

When the rest of the party had retired to repose and dress for supper, Darcy whispered to his wife that he wished to show her something before making their way upstairs. He held her hand, his expression almost giddy, and tugged her down a great corridor and into the library. It had been rearranged, she was told, before she moved in, so that two new plush reading chairs were sitting atop an ornate floral rug, facing one another. The great hearth cast its glow in just the same manner as the one in front of which they had spent so many hours at Netherfield. Darcy led her to her chair and lowered her into the seat, then disappeared behind his own.

The next thing she knew, a guttural and familiar roar began emanating from Darcy's position. Her eyebrows flew up in thrilled surprise as she watched the long-haired feline she knew so well snake between her husband's legs and then, noting Elizabeth's presence, bound towards her and onto her lap.

"Italics!" she cried, laughing as the cat eagerly rubbed his face against her own. "But, how?"

"Mrs Nicholls is leaving Hertfordshire, and it turns out your sister gets a bit of a tickle in her throat when he is near, so Bingley offered to bring him up when they came," Darcy answered, kneeling before her to stroke Italics's ears and back. "Look at him—how could I refuse?"

"Thank you," she told him with a long kiss of gratitude. "This is a lovely surprise,"

"You are happy, Mrs Darcy?" he asked when the enthusiastic nuzzling of the animal forced them apart.

"Yes, Mr Darcy," Elizabeth said, reaching up from the sweet bundle before her and caressing her husband's face. "You have made me perfectly happy."

ABOUT THE AUTHOR

Emilia Stratford is a lifelong Jane Austen enthusiast and has been crafting Austenesque variations for several years. Her works reflect her passion for all things England and classic literature. When not writing, she enjoys traveling, learning languages, and experiencing diverse cultures. She lives bodily in North Carolina, but her heart resides in Regency England. A career volunteer, Montessori mom, knitter, and avid reader, she loves connecting with people through stories and experiences.

a BB f

ALSO BY EMILIA STRATFORD

Some Particular Evil

There is, I believe, in every disposition a tendency to some particular evil.

FITZWILLIAM DARCY WOULD HAVE NEVER IMAGINED the depravity dwelling in the hearts of those he thought he knew best. On the run from hired killers, he is forced into hiding in the mean streets of London with the only person he can trust being Elizabeth Bennet.

LEFT BEHIND IN KENT, Elizabeth Bennet is still reeling from Darcy's presumptuous marriage proposal when she discovers the plot to kill him. Leaping to the gentleman's aid, she helps him go into hiding and then sets about trying to learn what she can of the plot against him—all of which reveals, gradually, new insights into Darcy's true character.

FALLING INTO A CLANDESTINE CORRESPONDENCE, she and Darcy share pieces of their hearts and together discover family secrets that could shake the very foundations of Darcy's being—and put Elizabeth in mortal danger. Afforded a second chance at the sweetness of love amid the foulness of evil, will their romance prevail?

Made in United States
North Haven, CT
19 July 2025

70635174R00173